C000129745

JONATHAN JANZ

DUST DEVILS

This is a **FLAME TREE PRESS** book

FLAME TREE PRESS
6 Melbray Mews, London, SW6 3NS, UK
flametreepress.com

Distribution and warehouse:
Marston Book Services Ltd
160 Eastern Avenue, Milton Park, Abingdon, Oxon, OX14 4SB
www.marston.co.uk

Thanks to the Flame Tree Press team, including:
Taylor Bentley, Frances Bodiam, Federica Ciaravella, Don D'Auria,
Chris Herbert, Matteo Middlemiss, Josie Mitchell, Mike Spender,
Cat Taylor, Maria Tissot, Nick Wells, Gillian Whitaker.

The cover is created by Flame Tree Studio with
thanks to Nik Keevil and Shutterstock.com.
The font families in this book are Avenir and Bembo.

Flame Tree Press is an imprint of Flame Tree Publishing Ltd
flametreepublishing.com

A copy of the CIP data for this book is available from the British Library.

HB ISBN: 978-1-78758-236-1
PB ISBN: 978-1-78758-235-4
ebook ISBN: 978-1-78758-237-8
Also available in FLAME TREE AUDIO

Printed in the UK at Clays, Suffolk

JONATHAN JANZ

DUST DEVILS

FLAME TREE PRESS
London & New York

Those familiar with New Mexico's geography might notice that I have taken several liberties with the locations of towns, mountain ranges and other landmarks. The vampires, however, are real.

'It is the nature of vampires to increase and multiply, but according to an ascertained and ghostly law.'
Joseph Sheridan Le Fanu

'For all have sinned, and fall short of the glory of God.'
Romans 3:23

This one is for you, Jack. You're the best son a dad could ever ask for, and you've filled the past thirteen years of my life with joy and wonder. I'm thankful beyond words for you, I'm proud of you for being the amazing person you are, and I'll love you and cherish you forever.

PART ONE
SOMEWHERE
OUTSIDE LAS CRUCES

CHAPTER ONE

New Mexico, 1885

Cody peered over the rim of the cliff and felt his throat tighten. *Jesus Christ*, he thought. *Jesus Christ Almighty.*

There, cupped in the rocky basin far below, were the devils. Stripped of their acting garb, the five powerful men capered about the fire like cackling demons. Blood slicked their chests, their rugged chins glinting like sloppy jewels. Over the broad, seething fire revolved the corpse of an old man, spitted from anus to mouth on a cottonwood pike. Price, their leader, was thrashing something on the basin floor, pounding it as though in the thrall of some childish tantrum. And though Cody's mind revolted at the very thought, he realised the object Price wielded was a human leg. As the scene wavered out of focus, the fire heat shimmering the naked men, Cody saw the ragged bone stub jutting out of the severed leg. It was all he could do to keep his gorge down.

He was so transfixed by the grotesqueness of the scene that he hardly noticed the boy on the ledge below him. Small, frail-looking, aglow with moonlight, the boy resembled some creature of the desert, a lizard or a scorpion washed pale by the sun. The boy crawled forward, toward the lip of the outcropping, and Cody realised how skinny the kid was. A slender cage of ribs stood out under a shirt that might once have been white. The wool pants didn't come close to touching the ratty shoes. Cody figured the pants for hand-me-downs.

Below, one of the men – Horton, Cody now saw, the youngest of the devils – kept time on a metal wash drum, dust puffing from his strong hands as he slapped out his arrhythmic tattoo. It was a damn good thing the men below were occupied, for the boy on the ledge was sitting straight up and peering openly at them now, making no attempt at all to conceal himself.

Cody thought, *What're you doing, kid? Get down before they see you.*

But the kid didn't, only continued taking in the scene, his legs dangling over the ledge as if he were watching a carnival sideshow. Jesus, if the boy didn't watch out, he'd lose his balance and plummet straight down at them, and if the impact didn't kill him – which was nearly a sure thing; the drop was a hundred feet easy – the devils sure as hell would. They'd enjoy it, too. Cody had seen them slaughter ones almost as young.

The distance between Cody and the boy was only fifteen feet or so, yet it was a sheer drop down bald sandstone. He could no more make it to the boy unobserved and unhurt than he could bring Angela back from the dead.

The thought of his wife blurred his vision, made his nose run. He ran a savage wrist along his upper lip and choked back the tears. No, by God. Now wasn't the time for that. He'd come all this way to study them, to learn their tendencies. Not to shed more tears over the woman who'd betrayed him.

The little boy below – the stupid son of a bitch – had rolled over onto his stomach, head toward Cody now, clearly intending to slide down the verge on his belly. *And then what?* Cody's mind demanded. *Become their next meal? Serve yourself up on a platter?* If they spotted the kid, they might well spot Cody too, and he knew once they saw you, there was no escaping.

Not knowing why he was doing it but knowing he had to do it just the same, Cody mimicked the boy's movements, lay flat on the stone ledge and lowered himself down, hoping to God the drop wasn't as sheer as it looked, hoping he'd slide down and land gracefully instead of free-falling toward a broken leg or much, much worse.

As Cody's hips grated over the scabrous edge, he did his best to cling to the rock wall, but the perpendicular drop eluded his reaching legs. *Damn it all*, he thought. *Here I go.*

CHAPTER TWO

A vertiginous drop through black space, then a fearsome pain in his back. Cody lay still a moment, staring up at the pinprick stars in the inky night sky. He'd landed decently enough – his legs were numb but unbroken – but his lower back felt like it had been flayed open. He reached down and fingered the area just above his tailbone. His hand came away wet. He reached down again and touched the warm gash. A superficial wound, but painful all the same. He listened for the washbasin drum, the hellish voices howling their terrible dirge, but there was nothing now. The valley had fallen silent.

Please, Cody thought. *Please let them resume without seeing me. I'll turn back and leave them to their hunting. I won't chase the devils anymore.*

Then he remembered: *the boy.*

Cody rolled over and beheld the frightened face, the tiny hands pawing at the gritty ledge for purchase. The child was about to fall but knew any noise would alert them, draw them up the verge like a pack of ravenous wolves.

The plea in the boy's eyes broke Cody's trance. He leaped forward and seized the chicken-bone wrists. Rearing back, he hauled the child toward him. Without thinking, he embraced the boy – more to calm himself than the kid – but the boy's hands lashed out, furrowed Cody's cheeks just under the eyes.

Cody shoved the boy away. "Jesus, kid," he hissed. "I risk my tail for you and you try to claw my eyes out?"

Cody froze, remembering the devils below. He scrambled toward the edge to see if they were coming.

They weren't. Ranged in an undulating half circle, they feasted before the fire, most of the old man's corpse still steaming on the spit. Idly, Cody noted that both the old man's legs were intact, which meant the leg Price had been swinging belonged to someone else. Was it Angela's?

Cody heard a whimpering and, looking up, saw the child's small eyes shining out of a dirt-grimed face. The kid was fighting the tears but losing. Some of Cody's asperity faded.

"You know that man down there?" he whispered.

The kid looked at him but didn't reply.

"The one they're roasting," Cody said. "The old man."

For a moment the kid seemed to look through him, beyond him, to the terrible chapter that had just concluded in his young life. Then he nodded. Moments later he joined Cody at the edge of the cliff.

The smell of seared flesh drifted up to them. Though Cody tried hard to breathe through his mouth, its acrid stench insinuated itself anyway. Growing up, one of their hogs had gotten caught on barbed wire once, and the wound had turned gangrenous. The smell of the old man's flesh reminded him of the hog's, though this odour was somehow worse, the wrongness of the cannibalism somehow communicating itself in its scent.

Price placed the leg on the ground beside him like a gory walking stick and sank his white teeth into a bit of shoulder meat he'd ripped off the steaming corpse.

In response, the boy whimpered louder.

"Shut the hell up," Cody said, but the kid only shook his head and moaned.

He seized the kid by the collar. "You want them to hear you?"

When the kid didn't answer, Cody grabbed him by the scruff of the neck, shook him. The boy glared at him as though about to strike again, but Cody stayed the child's hand with his fiercest stare.

He brought his face close to the boy's. "You shut up now or I'll toss you over this cliff."

The boy's eyes widened.

Cody nodded. "That's better."

They watched as the biggest devil, the one called Penders, rose and lumbered over to the edge of the flickering firelight. Grasping his penis with an immense paw, Penders voided his bladder into the dust.

Cody remembered the huge man, his black-stubbled face grinning as he fondled Angela in front of a roomful of men.

As if reading his thoughts, the boy asked, "They kill your kin too?"

The thickness in Cody's throat prohibited speech. In answer he turned and spat.

"Bastards," the boy said, a break in his voice. Suddenly, Cody was desperate to get away from the smell of scorched flesh, the monosyllabic chatter from below. How different these men were from the characters they portrayed. How different they were now than they'd seemed upon entering Tonuco that afternoon three days ago.

Cody remembered the premonition he'd had, that sense of fatedness that caused him to stop in midspeech, Angela staring up at him curiously. Try as he would, Cody could not look away from the six black quarter horses – their blinders as dark as their hair – towing a black carriage car with red-curtained windows. It seemed a rolling piece of hell, an emissary of darkness come to shatter the uneasy truce he and his wife had negotiated. And when Angela, too, beheld the dark carriage with the gilded cursive letters spelling *Adam Price and His Travelling Players*, Cody knew something catastrophic had been set into motion.

Almost as though it had been waiting for Angela's attention as its cue, the carriage stopped, the black horses obeying a half-obscured driver, in front of the Crooked Tree Saloon. For several moments nothing happened. The carriage remained as motionless as the mares that powered it. Cody took a hesitant step in the direction of the general store – the intended destination of their visit to town that afternoon – but Angela was transfixed.

Then Adam Price stepped out of the carriage, and Cody felt his wife slip away.

Price had smiled winningly and beckoned them over. The tall man was hatless but wore a long black cape. Eyeing his tailored clothes, Angela asked him if he was really an actor. Price had indicated the wooden sets stored beneath the coach as proof of his thespian profession.

"I've always wanted to act," Angela had said.

Price's grin broadened. "It happens that we're in need of a female lead for our two weekend performances." Smiling grandly, Price had proffered a hand.

"Angela," Cody said.

"It's just for fun, darling," she answered. "Don't be so solemn all the time."

"*Angela.*"

"Two little shows," she said. She slid her hand into Price's.

And without a backward glance, Angela had followed the tall actor into the Crooked Tree Bar.

Remembering it now, Cody's chest went as hard as stone. Though the night air up here on the ledge was cool and crisp, he found it nearly impossible to breathe.

On the ledge beside him, the kid whispered, "You keep your mouth open that wide, a bird'll come along and shit in it."

Cody jerked back to the present, fixed the kid with an annoyed look. But the kid just grinned and said, "My grandpa always used to tell me that."

The feast continued below. The twins – Dragomir and Dmitri Seneslav, they were called, though Cody had no idea how you could tell them apart – were grappling a few feet from the fire, some dispute having broken out between them.

"What are they doing?" Cody asked.

"Fightin' over the tongue," the kid said in a sick voice, the glimmer of good humour having quickly evaporated.

"The old man's?" Cody asked and immediately regretted the stupid question.

He regretted it even more when the boy answered, "Grandpa's."

Cody couldn't even look at the kid as he broke down into quiet sobs. What the hell could he say? *I'm sorry about them eating your grandfather?*

Horton finally ceased drumming on the basin. He stood and stretched, his body roped with muscles. He looked like a wrestler or a runner – not a cannibal percussionist. Horton bent and came up with a fillet knife and, unmindful of the intensity of the fire, reached out and proceeded to excise a bit of rib meat from the kid's grandpa. Cody had to look away. He was thankful to see that the kid hadn't witnessed the latest atrocity. The boy was lying on his stomach, his small face buried in the crook of his arm.

"Come on, kid," Cody said and dragged the boy away from the lip of the ledge. Out of sight from the devils, Cody already felt better. Though he could still hear the men laughing and snorting, not seeing them was a relief.

The kid slumped against the sheer rock wall down which Cody had, moments before, descended. The boy looked very vulnerable, very pathetic like that. His small, freckled face was difficult to discern tucked away in the shadows, but the moonlight shone on his tattered pants, his worn-out shoes.

Cody sat next to him, asked in a low voice, "What's your name, kid?"

The boy mumbled something.

"Come again?"

"Willet Black," the boy repeated.

"Where'd you get a name like that?"

As if by rote, the boy said, "My daddy taught me my letters early. His name was Theodore, so my middle name's Theodore. My handwriting's not very good, so when I wrote my name at school – Will T. Black – the teacher thought the first two names were connected. 'Willet?' she asked me, and all the students thought that was hilarious. 'Specially my brother. He was in the same class as me even though he was older, but he got killed last night too."

A chill coursed down Cody's spine. At length, he said, "Pleased to meet you, Willet. My name's Cody Wilson."

Willet didn't answer, only continued staring at nothing in particular. As the silence drew out, Cody surveyed their surroundings, realised at once their only chance of escaping was a meagre outcropping on the western corner of the ledge. If they could make it onto that and avoid falling – it extended no more than a foot from the sheer rock face – they might be able to follow it gradually up until they reached the top of the wall. Then they could get on Sally, Cody's old mare, and get the hell gone.

Willet was sniffling.

"Soon as you collect yourself, we'll get moving," Cody said.

"I ain't going nowhere."

"You aim to sleep up here tonight?"

"I aim to get my daddy's leg back."

Cody searched the kid's face for signs of insanity, but other than appearing really tired, Willet seemed in his right mind.

"You got some sort of plan?" Cody asked.

The kid spoke in a tight, controlled voice. "I don't have a plan. I'm going down there and get my daddy's leg."

The child's audacity rankled him. Misplaced as it was, it was still a stark contrast to his own paralysing terror. Cody said with more heat than he intended, "And I suppose you're going to do that by reasoning with them. I suspect they'll respond pretty well to that sort of thing."

Willet's brow creased. "You don't need to make fun of me."

Cody sighed, an enervating weariness seizing hold of him.

Willet glanced at him, defiant. "You wanna run so bad, why'd you follow them?"

Cody looked away. "I've got my reasons."

"They got something of yours too?"

If you only knew, Cody thought. *My life, my manhood. What goodness I thought there was in this world.*

He said, "What they took I can't get back."

"So get out of here," Willet said. "I can deal with this myself." The tinny sound of his voice, the curl of his upper lip, the boy sounded fifty years old. Fifty and full of bitterness.

The kid's petulance awakened something in him, a ghost of his former pride maybe. "What are you gonna do to them, Willet? Hit 'em with rocks?"

The boy reached down, drew up the front of his shirt. Protruding from the baggy waistband of the boy's wool pants was the pearl handle of a gun.

"It's a thirty-eight," Willet said. "Daddy kept it hidden in the hayloft."

Eyeing it, Cody felt a chill. "I suppose you're gonna kill all five with that."

Willet held it up so the starlight played over its smooth silver barrel. "It's a hammerless," the boy said, sounding even older. "I can hit damn near anything with it."

"Let me see it."

Willet appraised him with baleful eyes.

Cody held out his hand. "Jesus Christ, if I was gonna kill you I'd have already shoved you over the edge so those bastards could eat you for dessert."

"I wouldn'ta let you push me," Willet replied, but he handed the gun over. Cody scooted forward enough so the shadows weren't in the way but not far enough for the men below to see him. The Smith & Wesson was a double-action automatic, far nicer than Cody's own .32. He wondered fleetingly if Willet's family had money, a gun like that stashed away for emergencies. Then again, the kid's clothes were so old, so shabby…

"Give it back," Willet said.

Cody regarded him. "How old are you, kid?"

"That don't matter," Willet said. "Give me my gun."

Cody watched him with raised eyebrows.

"Twelve," Willet answered. "Now gimme my goddamn gun back."

Cody handed it to him and felt a pang of sadness at how clumsily the boy handled the .38. The kid no more knew guns than he knew how to fuck. If Willet tried anything on the devils, they'd take the gun and have him spitted within seconds.

Willet stood up straight. Cody sucked in surprised breath. Even though they were seven or eight feet from the edge, the boy might well be visible from below. He grabbed the boy's wrist, but Willet jerked away, said through gritted teeth, "I'm *sick* of talking. I'm doing what I came to do." Willet crammed the gun down the front of his trousers.

Cody controlled his voice with an effort. "You go down there now, you might get lucky and shoot one of them. Two at most." He glanced at the .38, then back up at the kid. "Then what? The remaining ones'll get you before you can blink."

"*Then they'll get me*," Willet shouted.

Cody held up an imploring hand. "You need to keep—"

"And I'll say what I want," Willet went on angrily. "I'm tired of hidin' up here like a rabbit…"

Voices below them, a commotion.

"...while they feast on my granddaddy..."

Price's voice, commanding.

"...the murdering bastards, I'm gonna show—"

Cody leaped forward, clapped a hand over the kid's mouth and slammed him to the floor of the ledge. "You stupid son of a bitch," he hissed, but his voice was tremulous, plaintive. The fear paralysis was seeping back in. Willet was struggling beneath him, the small hands grabbing for the gun stuffed in his waistband. Cody remembered his own .32, left above on the ridge with his old horse. If only they could clamber up the rock wall, mount Sally and ride away...

Price's voice, echoing up the canyon and dangerously pleasant: "Hello, Misters Wilson and Black! Mr. Penders is on the way up to pay you a visit!"

CHAPTER THREE

"*Lemme go*," Willet said. The boy whimpered and bucked, but Cody held him down, too terrified to do otherwise. The idea of Penders, stark naked, with his immense barrel chest and tree-trunk thighs scaling the rock wall and discovering them, was enough to turn Cody's legs to water.

"Come on," he said. The kid shouted something at him, but Cody was on his feet and breaking for the western edge of the plateau, where the outcropping ledge began snaking its way up the valley wall.

"Up there," a voice called out from below. "Up there, Horton. No, to the left!"

Cody stepped onto the narrow ledge and began sidling his way up. He sensed Willet behind him, though he dared not glance back for fear of losing precious seconds. The rock exploded a couple feet in front of him and he knew they'd been spotted, the bastards taking target practice from the basin below. He could make out the devils' glimmering forms as they swam in the firelight.

Cody climbed toward the shadows of the cliffside, through them. He chanced a look back and saw that Willet was right behind him. Popping sounds from below, more dust and rock shattered around them. If it weren't so damned dark up here, they'd be dead already.

Cody glanced up. Halfway there, he saw. With a dull *ping*, the craggy rock wall splintered a foot to his right, and he felt something bite his forearm. He hoped it was a fragment of rock and not a bullet. Out here in the wilds an infection could kill a man, and though he knew it was folly to worry about such matters now, he could not help remembering that hog with the gangrenous wound, the rancid-cheese smell it put out.

Willet moaned and Cody turned to see him windmilling his arms, his balance going. Worried he'd fall himself, Cody shot out a hand and clutched the boy by the shoulder. For a moment Cody felt weightless and was sure they'd both plummet to the valley floor, save the devils the trouble of killing them. Then Willet leaned forward, hugging the rock wall. Cody did the same. He heard laughter and looked down. Two of them were taking aim, Price and one of the Seneslav twins. Above the gunmen, Penders was climbing slowly upward, his mouth fixed in a grim line. Cody glimpsed the other Seneslav disappearing around the corner of a rock formation. That left Horton, the youngest, the one who had screwed Angela right in her and Cody's marriage bed. It was the memory of Horton's arrogant face that got Cody moving.

A couple more shots sounded as they neared the place where the ledge curved and – Cody hoped – the outcropping delivered them to safety. Penders had narrowed the distance between them, but if they kept moving, they would beat him easily. The idea of Horton lurking somewhere in the shadows troubled him, but there was nothing he could do about it now. They had to keep moving.

Another shot sounded and Willet cried out. Cody's stomach sank. He looked back and saw the kid's face frozen in a rictus of agony. He had no idea where Willet had been hit, but if they remained here frozen, they'd surely die.

"Come *on*," he said and tapped the kid on the head. Willet blinked and looked at him like they'd never met before. Then, wincing, he did as he was told.

Cody was turning away – he saw the ledge did indeed lead to the crest of the wall; God, almost there – when the kid cried out again. This time it was fear rather than pain in Willet's voice. Cody glanced down and beheld what had caused the fear.

Penders was nearly even with them. The huge man's agility was astonishing. With his close-cropped black beard and his powerful naked body, Penders resembled some great warrior from Greek myth. Or some monster. Somehow he'd threaded his way up the rock wall, and now it looked as though he'd meet them at the crest. And then what?

Cody glanced back at Willet. "Give me the gun."

The kid's face was a dazed mixture of bewilderment and anguish, and dammit, they didn't have time for either. Cody reached down, yanked the .38 out of Willet's pants.

He barely heard the kid's protests as he levelled the gun at Penders, who was climbing toward them at a delirious angle, a knife clamped in his teeth. Another moment or two and the huge man would have them. Cody aimed. Penders plucked the knife from his teeth and slashed at Cody's legs. Simultaneously pain flared in his calf and he pulled the trigger. He had no idea where he hit Penders, but the huge man bellowed and fell away from the rock wall. Baring his teeth through the sting in his leg, Cody watched the man's ox-like body tumble end over end into darkness.

As Cody's eyes came into focus, so did the pain. He imagined a sinister gnome down there, flaying his calf like the walleyes he and his daddy used to catch. The muscle would be pink, the denuded bone a glistening ivory. A nauseating haze of dizziness greyed his vision, nearly drove him to his knees, though he knew there wasn't enough room to kneel.

A hand on his shoulder. Shaking, entreating.

Cody knew they were still in peril, perhaps more than ever. Willet was hollering at him in his high, insistent voice, *Get moving, get moving.* Cody's eyes happened on the valley below, and he saw that the other twin was gone.

But Price remained.

The tall man stood there gazing up at him, unaccountably meeting his eyes through the murk and the distance. Adam Price stared at Cody and through him. Cody stared back, hating Price with every fibre of his being. The firelight flickered over the man's penetrating dark eyes, the wavy brown hair spilling in thick locks over the man's shoulders, the chiselled torso speckled with drying blood, the rippled belly – full of Willet's family – rising and falling in agitation. Beside Price lay Penders's huge, unmoving body.

Cody hugged the valley wall. They were close to escaping, terribly close, but the sizzling pain in his calf made movement impossible, sucked his will.

Then he remembered Angela, her stomach shovelled out and her pale ribs pointing heavenward. He jolted forward.

They made the crest and stumbled onto level ground. He expected any moment to be dragged down by Horton, by one of the Seneslav twins, but so far no one appeared to be pursuing them.

"Where's your horse?" Willet asked. Rather than answering him, Cody set off in the direction he hoped was correct. Who could tell out here in the wilderness where everything looked the same? He'd gone a good twenty paces before he remembered how much his calf hurt, but once aware of it there was no forgetting it. He limped on as best he could, but that side of his body felt weighted down, moored to the ground like a trout line affixed to a sludgy river bottom.

A strident cry broke the silence and Cody realised it was Sally, dear old Sally. Something had spooked her. He'd chosen the right direction after all – the cry came from straight ahead – but what if Horton or the twins were already there? What if they were torturing the old girl, feasting on her?

They busted through a willowy tangle of deer grass and into the clearing where he'd left Sally. The gaunt old horse was still there, tied to a bigtooth maple, but she was not alone.

Horton leaned back in the saddle, the cigarette between his lips sending up a ghostly ribbon of smoke. He looked as though he was just passing the time, his unlined face eerily serene. The man should have been absurd atop the horse, naked as the day he was born, but instead Horton seemed perfectly at home that way, as if he were a centaur who'd just paused to have a smoke and appreciate the beauty of the night. Horton held the reins with one hand and carried a pistol in the other. Cody noted without surprise the gun Horton held was Cody's own.

Horton looked beyond Cody as though he weren't even there. To Willet, he said, "You with that Black clan?"

Willet looked as though he was about to cry. Cody glanced at the bulging gun butt in the front of the boy's shirt and wondered if he could grab it and get off a shot before Horton cut him down. Either way it had to happen quick. The Seneslav twins would be here soon.

"You favour your mother, boy," Horton said, his sardonic face grinning wickedly. "I doubt you got a pussy like hers though." Horton took a long drag on the cigarette and let the smoke release slowly from his nostrils. "That snatch was so sweet, I felt like I was fuckin' some high-dollar whore."

"Don't say that," the boy warned. Cody noted with surprise that Willet had drawn his Smith & Wesson.

Horton noticed it too, yet his face remained dangerously serene. He nudged the brim of his porkpie hat higher as if to be sure he was seeing the boy clearly. "You have that thing last night, kid? You did, you should be ashamed." Horton chuckled. "What'd you do, watch us slaughter your family?"

The way Willet's face crumpled, that was exactly what he'd done. Cody wanted to hug the boy. At least Cody wasn't the only one to turn to stone when faced with unfathomable horror. At least he wasn't the only—

A blast sounded behind Cody, and as he dropped to his knees he saw Horton's face disappear in a messy crimson spray. The man described a half-turn, and as Sally reared up, Horton tumbled off. Already dead, the naked man landed in a puff of dust.

Sally was frantic, her eyes impossibly white, her lean neck muscles straining against the rope that bound her. Cody hurried forward and spoke as soothingly as he could, but the mare seemed unaware of all save the dead man lying underfoot. She trampled Horton's motionless body, punched holes in his flesh, and try as Cody might to seize the reins, Sally remained perpetually beyond his grasp. Desperately, he leaped forward and looped an arm over Sally's neck, and though she still flailed about, she seemed to notice him for the first time. "Calm down," he told her. "Shhhh... Calm down, girl." Her neighs quieted down, her trembling body reassured by Cody's touch.

He grasped the reins and called for Willet to hop on. When no response came, he glanced over his shoulder and saw that the boy was still standing where he'd been, the gun dangling limply at his side. Willet gaped at Horton's ruined body like it was a vase he'd accidentally shattered. Cody knew he should say something to buoy the kid's spirits, but they didn't have time for such counsel.

"*Get your ass over here*," was what he did say, and it proved enough. Willet was beside him in seconds.

The reins still in his right hand – Cody didn't trust the animal not to bolt – he used his left to untie Sally from the maple. Mounting her, he made the mistake of leading with his good leg, for when he pushed off with his injured calf he nearly swooned from the pain. Head spinning, he leaned against Sally until the nausea passed. Then he moved around Sally, heaved his useless right leg onto the horse and shoved with his good one. Without pause he offered Willet a hand, and the boy used it to clamber up behind him.

Sally didn't need goading. She set off at a pace too brisk, and only providence kept Cody from tumbling off and taking Willet with him. He felt the boy's arms slide around his waist and fought off a memory of Angela doing the same. She was dead, goddammit, and there was nothing anyone could do about it, least of all him.

Behind him the boy tensed, and before Cody could tell the kid to calm down, a pale figure emerged from the darkness. It was one of the twins, his wraithlike body appearing from the left and dashing toward the trail ahead of them. He clearly meant to head them off.

Cody shouted at Sally to go faster, faster. She seemed to absorb his fever, but he compelled the old mare forward with merciless vigor. Her aged hooves pounded the trail harder and harder, and just when Cody thought they'd bested the twin, the pale body leaped at them, and then Willet was screaming, his arms having slipped away from Cody's waist. Cody made a desperate grab behind him, but it was too late.

Willet was gone.

CHAPTER FOUR

Cody threw a backward glance and glimpsed the struggling pair, Willet looking very much like a field mouse in a hawk's clutches. Cody's first impulse was to gallop on, a dreadful place deep within him glad it was Willet and not him back there being mauled. Then a wave of self-loathing stronger than any he had yet experienced washed over him. He knew he couldn't leave the kid. With a sense of fatalistic doom, Cody reared back, and heedless of Sally's protests, they pounded back the way they'd come.

For the first time he remembered leaving his .32 on the ground beside Horton's corpse. Why hadn't he retrieved it?

Because you were scared shitless. What the hell does it matter now?

It didn't. In the moonglow he saw Seneslav raise a huge knife, and though a thick stand of sage stood between him and the struggling pair, Cody rode straight for them. One of the mare's forelegs got snagged in the scrub brush. Sally half stumbled and nearly pitched him off. As the twin looked up, Cody launched himself off the horse and for a moment feared he'd overshot his mark. Then he slammed the naked man square, Cody's shoulder snapping Seneslav's neck back. The knife skittered into the brush.

Cody was dazed, but he could tell by the way Seneslav was groaning he'd done some damage. Cody scrabbled about for some weapon, preferably the knife, but when his hand happened on a jagged shard of slate, he seized it and swung. The point embedded in the man's side, but the rest crumbled upon impact. Worse, the stabbing seemed to rouse the twin, rally his senses. The man's face curled into a feral grin, his square jaw flexing. Seneslav swung a haymaker that narrowly missed Cody's face. Where was Willet? By Christ, the boy had a gun, and now was the time to use it.

Seneslav swung again and this time grazed Cody's shoulder. The blow knocked him off-balance, but before he went down

Seneslav punched him in the small of the back. Pain spiralled through his midsection. Cody endeavoured to put some space between them but was dealt the indignity of Seneslav grabbing the rear of his pants and hauling him back by the belt.

The stronger man whipped him to the ground. In the moment just after Cody hit, a desperate idea materialised. As the twin approached, his hands extended like some mindless ghoul, Cody undid his belt, yanked it off and swung it at Seneslav's leering face. The solid steel buckle opened the man's cheek. Seneslav uttered a cry of disbelief as a torrent of blood spilled down his neck. But quicker than Cody would've thought possible, Seneslav's bare foot shot out, caught Cody under the jaw. Cody stumbled back, landed in a nasty tangle of brush. He turned his face, intending to extricate himself from the branches holding him captive, and as he did he perceived the little blue flowers all around him, the kind his dad used to place on his mother's grave. Dazed, Cody looked up and saw Seneslav advancing. Cody balled a fist, prepared to strike, but when the twin's eyes lighted on Cody's cocked arm – then something beyond it – he retreated.

As the twin backpedalled, his eyes rolled in unreasoning panic. Cody pushed to his feet and kicked the man as hard as he could in the belly. Seneslav's head whipped forward, the blood from his flayed cheek spattering over Cody's arm.

The warm feel of it incited him. Cody kicked again, this time thumping the man in the groin. As Seneslav doubled over, Cody swung a knee into his throat. Coughing, the pale twin landed on all fours.

Cody was about to wrap the belt around the twin's neck when something glinted to Cody's left.

Seneslav's knife.

Cody went for the knife, got hold of it, but Seneslav was already groping for him. With a cry Cody lashed out with the knife and watched it slice through Seneslav's larynx.

The twin clasped his wound, but the knife had been so sharp and the force of the stroke so great that the blood spurted around Seneslav's fingers, the man's life force spraying out in all directions.

Cody expected the twin to finally fall then, and for a moment it looked as if he would. The gurgling noises issuing from

Seneslav's gaping mouth, coupled with the dead glaze that was seeping into his eyes, gave Cody a grim satisfaction. The son of a bitch was tougher than hell, tougher than any man Cody had ever seen, but he was still—

Seneslav lunged for him.

He knocked Cody backward, both men tumbling into the dust. The flow of blood pumping out of Seneslav's gaping neck wound covered them both, drove Cody into a state formed half of terror, half of bleak determination. As Seneslav groped for him again, Cody rolled away and noted as he gained his feet how sluggish the twin had grown. He didn't allow himself to linger on this thought. He'd underestimated Seneslav once, but he wouldn't do it again. Grimly, deliberately, Cody circled his bloodied adversary until he was directly behind him. Then he looped the belt under Seneslav's chin and reared back. The belt caught in the slick notch of Seneslav's wound, and when Cody redoubled the pressure on it, the tough leather belt ripped deeper into the meat of the man's throat.

Perhaps realising the extremity of his situation, the strong man began to struggle, his iron jaw working, his blunt fingers slapping at Cody's forearms. But though smaller, Cody had leverage. The twin fell forward, Cody grafted to him like a shadow. He sat on Seneslav's back and strained against him. There was a cracking noise. Dimly, he heard the man break wind. Seneslav's struggles dwindled. A weird mewling sound issued from his throat, but Cody refused to take anything for granted. He wound the belt around his wrists and hauled back again, placed a foot in the middle of Seneslav's back, and soon Seneslav's arms hung limp. Cody stayed that way, pulling with all he had, until he could no longer pull. He knew not what he was waiting for – the man to bust in half? But still he pulled. And pulled. Then he slumped forward and lay on the ground beside the dead man, utterly spent.

Cody glanced over at Seneslav and was greeted with the sight of the man's nearly severed head gaping at him in permanent disbelief.

Cody closed his eyes and breathed deeply of the night air. By degrees the fragrant sage usurped the faecal smell of death emanating from Seneslav. The air had cooled considerably, but the sweat was still warm all over Cody's body.

He remembered Willet and opened his eyes.

How long had Seneslav had the kid down before Cody intervened? Twenty seconds? Thirty? There was an ugly roiling in his gut. A kid that small and a sinewy powder keg like Seneslav, Willet wouldn't have stood a chance. The boy was surely dead.

Cody got up and scanned the darkness for Willet, but there was no movement at all save Sally, who was tossing mad, twitchy looks all over creation.

"Easy," Cody told her, though he knew it would have no effect. As he whispered, he gathered a handful of reins. She seemed not to hear him, slowly but surely towing him away from Seneslav's corpse. It was just as well, Cody thought. He too wanted distance from the body. He couldn't yet think of the murder as having anything to do with him. He wasn't a killer. Men like Price and Penders were the killers.

Cody was nearly upon Willet when he heard a groan. Cody whirled and beheld the little body lying there half-hidden by the scraggly sage. Worried Sally would bolt at any moment, Cody snagged the boy by one trouser leg and hauled him back toward the horse. If Willet's wounds were fatal, well, getting dragged wouldn't make any difference. If they weren't fatal, so much the better. Cody was banking on the latter, for despite Willet's barely conscious state, the boy's body seemed intact. There was one cut a few inches to the left of where his belly button would be, but other than that and the gunshot wound to the leg, it looked like Will T. Black was in decent shape.

Careful not to touch the glistening gash in the child's stomach or the injured calf – it didn't appear to be bleeding too badly – Cody lifted him up into the saddle, leaned him forward onto the animal's neck and climbed on behind him.

He urged Sally into a trot as quietly as he could, but it was an awkward struggle managing Sally's skittish nerves and preventing the kid's limp body from lolling right off the saddle. They couldn't dally though, for at any moment one of the remaining two devils might come charging out of the darkness to tear Cody and Willet apart.

A sinking feeling in his gut, Cody whipped his head around, sure Price or the other Seneslav would be right behind them. But the barren hardpan was devoid of life. Just where the hell had they gone?

They'd ridden for less than a minute when a bloodcurdling wail arose behind them. It perplexed Cody nearly as much as it frightened him until he understood who was wailing and why the heartbreak was so profound. Then, thinking of the other Seneslav twin back there discovering his dead brother, fear usurped all of Cody's other emotions. If they weren't in trouble before for what happened to Penders; if Price somehow managed to forgive them Horton's murder; even if those two unlikely events took place, Cody knew that the slaying of one twin would never be brooked by another. It seemed entirely natural that Dmitri or Dragomir Seneslav – whichever one was still alive – would harbour a death vow toward his brother's executioner.

Cody spurred Sally faster, and even though Willet was only half-conscious, the boy held tighter to her without complaint.

CHAPTER FIVE

An hour's ride brought them to the edge of an imposing run of badlands. Cody had meant to head back the way they'd come, thinking to find the boy medical attention in Las Cruces, but he must have veered the wrong way at some point.

His calf a screaming agony, Cody slid off Sally, whose breathing had grown harsh and uneven. If he didn't water the old girl soon, she'd be a goner.

He tugged on the boy and caught him in a rough embrace. Willet was conscious, but he was mumbling gibberish about bloodsuckers, about monsters in the woods. Cody tried not to think about the boy's words as he rested him on the hard earth. Then, his own calf throbbing from the knife wound, he flopped down beside Willet. He wanted to find water for them and Sally, but at the moment all he could do was rest. Cody closed his eyes and forced himself to think.

That the devils would follow them he had no doubt. This was the true reason he'd hoped to reach Las Cruces. There, he might find someone who'd believe his story. Back in Tonuco, Cody had been ridiculed as a fool when he rode into town claiming Angela had been butchered and eaten. Every man there already knew what had transpired with Angela and the actors at the inn.

Against his will, Cody recollected that first awful night, the night he'd lost his wife to the devils. He'd ventured into the Crooked Tree a short while after she'd gone inside with Price. Under his breath he'd told her it was time to head back to their ranch. Angela had made a scene. Red-faced, with those bastards Horton and Penders smirking at him, Cody had stormed out of the bar.

But after a walk through town in the deepening twilight, he'd decided that maybe he'd overreacted. It was true that Angela had always talked of becoming an actress. He'd invariably reacted to this aspiration with indulgent politeness. After all, what were the chances of Angela actually making good on her wish? But now that it was here, he figured he might as well keep an open mind about it.

He returned to the Crooked Tree and took a seat in the back of the house. A placard outside the saloon read THE RETURN OF THE MAIDEN CARMILLA. Damn near everyone in Tonuco had packed the Crooked Tree for the performance. Cody did his best to blend in with the jostling, shiny-eyed men, but there were snickers and contemptuous grins directed at him nonetheless.

Soon, though, they forgot about Cody and focused on Angela. She first appeared as a maiden walking through the forest. Her blond hair lustrous in the manufactured stage moonlight, she had never looked so beautiful. The white gown they'd given her was slit high – nearly to the waist. As she glided through the forest, Cody caught glimpses of her milky thigh that made his throat constrict. Several male voices hooted and catcalled, but she seemed not to notice. Then a dark figure appeared from behind a tree and everything grew silent. The figure was tall, elegant but wholly evil.

The first time Adam Price approached Angela, Cody nearly leaped onto the stage to intervene. The malice radiating out of his face and his black flowing cape made Angela seem utterly vulnerable. Cody even took a step in the direction of the stage, thinking to rescue her from Price's clutches. To make matters worse, two more figures had joined Price, a pair of square-jawed twins with short, dark hair and fair skin. Like trained panthers they prowled on all fours on either side of Price, starting and halting at his sibilant commands.

Then Horton appeared.

Looking virile in his open-throated flannel work shirt, Horton stepped between Angela and her pursuers and demanded that Price recede into the shadows. For the first time Cody realised that Price and the twins were supposed to represent vampires. Their white teeth gleamed sharp and hungry in the flickering stage light as they stalked their prey. Horton produced a gun but Price kept coming. The gun fired – a sound absolutely realistic in the confined space of the Crooked Tree – and Price staggered. But the vampire strode on. Horton fired another shot, and when this one did even less to impede the vampire's progress, the young man shouldered Angela and hurried offstage.

In the next scene Horton was placing Angela on Penders's bed and explaining to his stage father what had happened. Penders listened sympathetically and told his son to go stand watch at the front door.

Angela proceeded to explain that in another life she'd been transformed into a vampire and had become a slave to her own insatiable thirst. She had preyed on young women and had therefore deserved her ultimate fate.

Because Cody's father was such a prodigious reader, Cody was familiar with the story, having read *Carmilla* only a month or two before meeting Angela. Of course, he'd never mentioned the tale to her, which was why he found it uncanny that she could essay the role so effectively. Granted, it was obvious she was improvising her lines, often pausing or stumbling to keep up with the other actors. Yet despite this, she was convincing in the role. Like Le Fanu's eponymous temptress, Angela's Carmilla was at turns vulnerable and beguiling, naïve and infinitely wise. She explained to Penders's character that she'd been given a second chance on earth by the most merciful God, but that her redemption had been marred by the unceasing attempts of other vampires to reindoctrinate her into the life of a bloodsucking predator. Price and the twins, of course, were three of these vampiric fiends.

Angela begged Penders to please protect her from the monsters. Penders said he'd do his best. Angela declared her willingness to do whatever it took to show Penders her gratitude. Penders asked what she had in mind.

Then the pain began.

Sitting on the bed next to Angela, who lay in a half swoon, Penders began to stroke first her pale arms, then her shoulders. When his big hands graduated to her breasts, Cody thought he would die of grief and humiliation.

Yet he couldn't look away.

It wasn't arousal he felt – not as Penders drew down Angela's top and began lapping at her pink nipples – it was something akin to death. The woman he married was not the woman allowing herself to be defiled onstage in front of fifty men. The Angela up there was something else entirely, an accursed creature of the night. Even though she hadn't yet taken her belongings from the ranch, she was already lost to Cody.

As Penders's hand slipped under the hem of Angela's dress, the house lights were snuffed.

Wild applause and a few frustrated groans accompanied the changing of the scene. When the guy they'd hired to orchestrate the lighting finally got enough kerosene lamps going to illuminate the stage again, the set had changed to the suggestion of a horse barn. Horton was alone onstage with a pitchfork in his hands; shirtless, he was miming the work of tossing hay. He paused to wipe the sweat from his brow, and as he did, his father poked his head in the door of the stall and announced he'd be heading into town to buy supplies for their visitor.

"How's the girl?" Horton asked.

"Still resting," Penders said with the merest hint of lasciviousness.

Horton watched after his dad and soon went back to work. Barely any time passed before Angela appeared in the doorway of the barn, a glass of water in her hand. Her hair was tousled, her dress boldly open to reveal a wide swath of cleavage.

Cody leaned against the wall, numb to it now.

Angela handed Horton the glass. As he drank from it, her frank gaze travelled down his bare chest, his ridged stomach. When he finished the glass at a gulp, he wiped his mouth and regarded her hungrily. She asked him something – Cody couldn't make out what – and he stepped toward her and chucked the glass against the wall. It shattered. Horton enfolded her and kissed her. Angela yielded herself up. He tore the straps of her dress and began to lick her bare shoulders. Then the rest of the gown slipped down her body, and Cody saw without surprise that she was naked beneath. The men in the audience whooped and hollered as Horton's hands kneaded her bare buttocks.

That's my wife, Cody thought. *That's my goddamned wife.*

The scene ended before Horton could rut with her in front of God and everyone, and when the house lights came on for intermission, the men around Cody began to slap him on the back and offer to buy him drinks.

"That's some woman you got there, son," one old man crowed, his voice rank with something like curdled cheese. Cody longed to stick his .32 in the man's leering face, but he knew if he did that, his life would be over tonight, and then he could never kill the men he was truly angry with.

After what seemed an eternity, the house lights dimmed.

Angela had her feet kicked up on a table. She wore a revealing, dark-green dress now, one that suited her character much better. She was filing her nails and watching Horton pace around the kitchen.

"He should be back by now," Horton was saying. Penders was several hours past due, and Horton was about to strike off into the woods in search of him when the huge man lurched onstage, his bedraggled body a horror of cuts and bruises. Price and his men, Penders said, had gotten him. They were furious at Penders for harbouring the girl. Horton had to avenge him, Penders said. Then the huge man died in his son's arms.

Good riddance, Cody thought.

But Penders wasn't dead after all.

In the penultimate scene, when Horton found himself backed into a corner by the Seneslav twins with all his ammo spent and nothing but the pitchfork with which to defend himself, his burly father stumbled onstage with what looked like a long wooden spear. One of the twins whirled just as Penders plunged the spear through his chest. It was obvious that the sharp tip had merely slipped between the twin's arm and his side, but from Cody's angle, it really did appear as though it pierced the man's heart. The still-living twin gaped at his brother, who fell lifelessly onto the stage. Horton, seeing his advantage, impaled the remaining Seneslav with the pitchfork. Horton and Penders watched the twin fall beside his brother on the stage; then father and son grinned at each other.

Their grins vanished when demonic laughter sounded from offstage.

In the next and final scene, Penders and Horton rushed onstage to find Price bent over Angela, whom he'd carried into the bedroom, his long white fangs inches from her exposed throat. Penders reached into the bedside table, brought out a wooden cross and brandished it before Price's aghast face. Demanding the creature leave the lovely maiden alone, Penders drove Price into a corner, where the hissing vampire cast frantic glances about the bedroom. But before Price could find some means of escape, Horton stepped grimly forward with the same stake that had been used on one of the twins. Horton thrust the spear into Price's heart, defeating the vampire and manumitting the maiden Carmilla from her dread fate.

The play ended with father, son and Angela locked in a triumphant embrace.

The stage darkened, and Cody escaped before the kerosene lamps were twisted on again.

CHAPTER SIX

They rode on in the darkness. It was at least half an hour before Cody felt safe to ease up on Sally a little. The bone-weary mare let loose with a grateful sigh that showed plainly how hard she'd been toiling. He didn't know whether it was loyalty to him or sheer terror of the devils that had endowed Sally with such prolonged stamina, but regardless, he was overcome with an urge to lean forward and embrace her mottled neck. Of course, had he done that, Willet might have slipped sideways off his perch in front of Cody, and Cody doubted he had the energy to pick the boy up should he fall.

From his right came the plaintive call of an owl. Cody started at the sound, which always reminded him of a little dog yapping to be let inside.

He blew out a tremulous breath. Lord, but he was thirsty. Poor Sally had to be parched too. As he'd invariably found out here in the wilderness, water was never present when you needed it. The wettest thing they'd encountered since escaping the devils was his leaking calf muscle. He knew he had to tend to it soon, yet an atavistic dread of Adam Price kept him moving.

Got three of them, he thought and gazed up at the lucent sliver of moon. *At least, I think we did.*

Cody had a clear image of Penders tumbling down the stark rock face of the valley, heard the brittle thump the big man made when he hit bottom. Like the crunch of a heavy cudgel on the base of a heifer's skull.

Cody shivered recalling it, yet it went a long way toward reassuring him. Next to Price, Penders was the devil he'd most feared. He'd been the muscle of the group, though all five were twice as strong as the average man. Almost like the supernatural creatures they played...

Knock that crap off, a voice scolded. It was Jack Wilson's voice – his father's voice – and as often happened, it was accompanied with a hollowing gust of guilt. Cody tried to shake that off too, but the old regret lingered, stronger now than ever because every damned day he seemed to realise more and more just how unfair to his dad he'd been.

Focus on now, he reminded himself, but the voice was weak, as if whispered through gauze.

It was the blood loss, he knew. It was past time to stop riding poor Sally toward her grave and time to see what he could do about his and Willet's wounds.

Yet he made no move to halt the mare. Idly, he thought about this and realised he was still afraid the devils were following.

Just how in the hell they gonna follow you, Cody? his dad asked. *By smell? They're men, not bloodhounds. They could no more scent you in the darkness than they could guess you'd have ridden for miles on end through the sage, risking a broken neck for yourself or the boy, not to mention inviting a snapped foreleg for your mare, and then where would you have been?*

We made it though, didn't we? Cody thought, and raised his chin at the black dome of sky looming over the ghostly skim of hardpan. Granted, riding blindly into the wilderness might have been a foolhardy move, but it worked.

He jumped at the death cry of some animal, then realised it was Willet. The small body slithered sideways, and Cody shot an arm out to seize a handful of the boy's shirt.

"*Canna...*" the boy moaned.

Cody drew the pitiful little body against him and scanned the area for a place to tether Sally. It was too much, he knew, to hope for water, but if they could find a strand of hackberries or willows, he might be able to dig down, find a little moisture. He'd do like his dad had once shown him, use the fabric of his shirt to soak up what he could find and then wring the water into Willet's parched throat. He doubted he'd find enough to slake both his and Willet's thirst, but at least it would take the edge off, make their throats feel as though they weren't lined with nettles.

"*Cannafeel...*" Willet moaned, and again his body shifted.

One reed-thin arm slapped at Sally's neck. Cody tightened. He recognised the onset of panic. The kid was at his extremity, had no idea where he was. Who knew how much blood he'd lost, how much worse the pounding of the trail had made his leg wound?

"Take it easy," Cody said, mouth rigid with indecision. Had he been smart, he would've stopped a half hour ago to examine Willet's leg, but visions of the devils crawling on all fours, sniffing the ground, following their leaking bodies through the wilds, had compelled him on.

"Can't feel my leg," Willet said, and though the boy sounded lucid now, the meaning of his words chilled Cody worse than the disorientation had.

Sally's breathing reminded him of a wobbly wagon wheel, and the feeling grew in him that he'd delivered them all from one kind of death to guarantee one that was infinitely slower and just as terrible. He had no idea where they were. Somewhere west of Las Cruces, but how far there was no telling.

So stop; it doesn't matter where. Stop and fix Willet up.

Cody didn't trust this voice, knew it was born of panic, yet it carried a seductive persuasiveness. He was about to halt Sally when he distinguished, far off and to their left, the gentle stir of a willow, its drooping leaves a mound of incandescence in the brilliant wash of moonlight.

"Oh thank God," he said and drew Willet closer to his sheltering chest. With his other hand he guided Sally toward the willow, the weakening mare staggering forward, no longer bothering to skirt the winterfat and paintbrush, her cracking hooves trampling the staring ghost flowers like a mean child squashing bugs.

Careful not to let the boy slip, Cody leaned forward, urged Sally on, "Almost there, girl. Almost there."

They ascended a small rise, and Cody realised with almost transcendent joy that the willow stood atop a plateau, beyond which he could already see a dozen other treetops, a veritable Eden in this godforsaken country. Another minute brought them even with the willow, and when Cody spotted the narrow black shimmer wending its way through the sparse forest, he had to choke back a cry of gratitude. Though her head hung despondently between her forelegs, Sally too seemed to scent the water, and without any prodding from Cody, she began to trot toward the grassy bank. Cody waited until she reached the water's edge, the old girl nearly lunging toward the lazy trickle, and then he slid off, doing his best to make sure he didn't jostle Willet too much, or worse, allow the boy to slip off the other side of the mare and break his neck.

Though his throat burned for the cool kiss of the water, Cody forced himself to concentrate on the boy. The small, dirty head lolled in a way Cody didn't like as he slid Willet off the mare and toted him the few steps to the creek bank. Willet's eyes were open, but there was a stolid glaze on them that again reminded Cody of slaughtered livestock, their life force dwindling but their eyes still seeing. As if they were memorising the last moments of their lives.

Laying the boy flat on the soft grass, Cody dipped his hand in the creek and patted Willet's crusty cheeks, his cool forehead. Though the water and dust formed muddy whorls on the boy's skin, the moisture did seem to revive him a little. The eyes blinked, the cracked lips opening and closing like a hooked perch. Cody endeavoured to cup the boy's head so Willet could sip creek water from his palm. The boy drank, choked on it, the racking coughs croupy and raw; then his skinny arms began to spasm. Cody thought at first of fits, of the weird convulsions he'd seen a classmate pitch on the playground back in grade school. Then he realised Willet was grabbing for his gun-shot calf, the pain of it finally taking hold.

Feeling like a fool, Cody gently laid the grimy head on the bank and crawled forward to take a look at the injured leg.

The wool covering it was tattered and black, the wasted fabric a discouraging curtain of sodden ribbons. He pushed the pant leg up, but a small hand clawed at his arm, indicating plainly that Cody should swear off the examination.

Cody glanced down and saw the scared eyes, the abject twist of the mouth. Unaccountably, he remembered a time when he'd eaten some delicious-looking red-capped mushrooms as a very young child and had been tortured with stomach cramps for the better part of two days. His dad had sat with him the whole time, leaving only to empty the bedpan and bring him fresh water and food that wouldn't aggravate his system. God, his father had been patient...loving...better than any nurse could've been. Could Cody do as well by this boy as his father had done by him?

The boy watched him with large eyes.

"Hurts a lot," Cody said, nodding. "Wish I could tell you the pain will go away quickly, but you're smarter than that."

Willet shuddered, but he was listening.

"I gotta take off your trousers to see what I'm dealing with, and either way I do that, it's gonna hurt like a bastard."

Willet whimpered. From downstream came the harsh soprano trill of a plover.

"You rather I cut 'em off? They're ruined anyway."

Willet frowned and shook his head.

Cody sighed. When he reached over, unbuttoned the boy's fly, Willet's eyes narrowed, something other than physical pain seeping in.

"I'm not going to mess with you," Cody said. "You don't need to worry about that."

"It isn't that," Willet said, his voice miserable. "What am I gonna wear if you throw my pants away?"

Cody tried not to smile, but lost. He shrugged, peered up at the overhanging boughs. "We need to, we can fashion some new pants out of those willow leaves."

Willet's brow furrowed momentarily. Then he chuckled softly. "You're fulla shit."

It felt good to laugh. He unzipped the boy's fly and slowly lowered the trousers, noting as he did how grubby the boy's underpants were. It reminded him how long Willet had likely gone since his last change of clothes, and because that brought back memories of the devils, Cody shook his head to scatter the thoughts.

"What?" Willet said.

Cody set his mouth in a firm line. "Hold still. This is gonna sting something fierce."

Though he did his best to keep the wool from scraping the wound, it did anyway, and to make things worse, he remembered too late what his dad had told him about dressing a wound: put the new bandages over the old, but don't remove the old unless they're really filthy.

Willet screamed as the wool ripped the clotted blood off his calf.

"Dammit," Cody muttered as the boy's bare feet drummed on the grass. "I'm sorry about that, but I couldn't see the—" He cut off as the boy kicked him in the ribs.

"Stupid sonofabitch," Willet was moaning. "Aw, it hurts."

"Hey," Cody said, his ribs throbbing. "Take it—" The foot lashed out again, but Cody deflected it. The sight of the boy's grungy face writhing from side to side restored some of Cody's pity. "Okay," he said, moving up to cradle the boy's head. "Okay, Willet. Shhh…"

Willet was crying, but some of his anger seemed to dissipate. Cody pushed the filthy hair off the kid's forehead, spoke what soothing words he could summon. After a time, Willet drew in a deep, shuddering breath and returned his gaze.

"I gotta wash out the wound," Cody said.

Willet's eyes narrowed. "How?"

Cody glanced about, chewed on his lower lip. "I guess we scoot you forward till you can dangle your legs in the creek."

"Then what?"

Cody shrugged. "Then I guess I splash water on it till it's clean."

Willet eyed him doubtfully. "You don't know what the hell you're doin'."

"My dad knew something about this kind of thing," he said. "He learned about it in the war, and he treated me plenty of times."

Willet's eyes were defiant. "You never got shot."

"I got stabbed tonight."

Willet's gaze swept Cody's torso, his stomach.

Cody shook his head. "Mine's in the leg, too." He brought his right leg closer, but it cost an effort. "See?"

Willet's eyes settled on the dark blotch behind Cody's knee.

"But mine isn't as deep," Cody said, lowering the leg. "That's why we're dealing with yours first. The bullet went clean through your calf." When the boy's eyes widened and darted to his own leg, Cody added, "Lucky for you, the bullet did exit your body. Woulda been worse had it stayed inside."

The fear and mistrust seemed to drain from the boy's eyes. He peered up at Cody, his dirty face like an ink smudge surrounded with old hay. "Will it hurt much?"

Cody held his gaze. "It'll be painful, yes." When Willet's face began to crumple, Cody squeezed the boy's arm. "But it's gotta be done. Get the pain over now so the leg doesn't get worse." Cody stared meaningfully at the boy. "We don't want that to happen, do we?"

Willet swallowed, his expression sobering. Cody could see him thinking it over, chewing on the possibility of losing the leg. Then Willet clenched his jaw, sat up a little. Together, they scooted him forward until his legs dangled over the grassy bank into the slow-moving creek. The water didn't smell like manure, which gave Cody hope it would cleanse the wound the way he wanted it to. He was dying to bury his face in the creek and gulp from it the way Sally was gulping a few feet downstream, but he knew he had to put all his energy into the boy now. Willet would be watching him, and he had to give the boy courage.

"All right," Cody said, standing and unbuckling his pants.

"What're you doing?"

"I'm getting in," he said. "Someone's gotta hold you still so the water can do its work."

Praying some flathead catfish or water snake wouldn't swim along and bite him in the penis, Cody stripped naked and eased into the creek. It was deeper than he'd suspected, nearly up to his chest, but after the brutal ride through the wilderness, the water felt exhilarating. The creek bed was comprised of sand and pebbles – another good sign – and the gritty feel of the creek bottom on his bare feet almost took his mind off the sting behind his knee. Goddamn, but it hurt. And if Cody's wound ached this badly, how much worse would Willet's be?

He placed his hands on the boy's knees as gently as he could. "Now, I want you to think of your family."

Willet blanched as if Cody had struck him. His voice thick, the boy said, "Why the hell would I wanna do that?"

"Because it hurts," Cody said, hating himself, "and remembering that hurt's gonna remind you of what you gotta do."

A tear spilled down the boy's sooty cheek. "And that is?"

"Make sure you have two good legs to finish this on."

CHAPTER SEVEN

Willet sniffed, but Cody could tell he'd gotten his attention.

Cody said, "You didn't ride all this way to kill three of them, did you?"

Willet's eyes widened.

"'Cause that's what we did, right? We know for certain that bastard Horton's dead. You got him in the face, remember? Hit him square? That was a hell of a shot, kiddo."

The boy nodded, something other than fear and grief coming into his eyes. A hesitant species of pride perhaps.

"Penders is dead too, unless he knew how to fall more than a hundred feet without dying." Cody cocked an eyebrow. "The son of a bitch weighed so much I swear I felt the earth shake when he hit."

Willet's mouth threatened a grin.

"And I can guarantee you that Seneslav twin, whatever the hell his name was – Dmitri, Dragomir, Dragon Dick – he ain't walking away from what I did to him. His head was damn near off."

For the first time in a while, Cody saw Willet smile, heard the boy's sweet, silly laugh and thought, *Do it now. Cleanse the wound before he has time to worry about it.*

But something held him back. He didn't want the kid to feel betrayed. Willet had experienced enough heartache for twenty lifetimes already; Cody didn't need to add any more, even if he was doing it for the boy's own good.

He said, "So here's the plan, Will T. Black. I'm gonna wash out this wound, and I ain't gonna lie – it's gonna be awful. I gotta do it quick, and I gotta do it thorough. It's the only way to make sure the flesh doesn't turn sour." He studied the boy's eyes. "You know what I mean by that?"

Willet nodded.

"Then I'm gonna wrap it as well as I can. That'll have to do until we get to Mesquite."

The boy's brow furrowed.

"It's where they're going next," Cody explained. "They've stuck to the main road for the last several nights, and even though their party's busted up, I suspect they'll keep doing what they've been doing."

The mettle Cody had seen in the boy's eyes back at the valley was slowly returning, and as before, it made Cody rue his own lack of courage.

Willet asked, "How'll they do their play with only two men?"

"I don't know about that, but I know the kind of men they are. They're not going to stop killing just because of a setback."

Willet's voice was barely audible. "They enjoy it."

Cody nodded. "They'll be in Mesquite by tomorrow night, which means we gotta be there too."

In that same soft voice, Willet asked, "We gonna kill 'em?"

"Right after we find someone to tend to this leg." Cody cleared his throat, tapped Willet on his good knee. "You ready now?"

The boy stared down at his wounded leg, nodded several times. Steeling himself, Cody could see. *You're a brave kid*, he thought.

He submerged Willet's leg in the water.

The boy hissed, sat forward and nearly toppled into the water onto Cody. But Cody braced the boy with a shoulder, one hand grasping Willet by the thigh, the other massaging the wounded calf underwater to work as much of the dirt and lead residue free as he could. Willet howled, batted at Cody's face, but Cody kept at it, kneading the meat of the boy's calf in the cool dark water.

"Son of a biiiiiitch," Willet groaned, but the words sounded like sobs.

"Almost done," Cody said and swished the leg around in the water. The boy's body was a tense, shivering plank, and without thinking Cody heard himself whispering words his father had whispered long ago, whenever Cody had torn himself on a nail or sprained an ankle horsing around: "I know, honey. I know."

The words seemed to have an effect on Willet, whose body relaxed just a little, so Cody repeated them, a trifle louder this time. Willet still sobbed, but it sounded like the tail end of a cry now, the worst having spent itself in the crisp night air. "I know, honey..." Cody whispered. He swished the leg slowly, the small, bare foot making tiny eddies in the water. "I know."

Carefully, he eased Willet backward onto the creek bank. He bent the boy's knees, placed the wet feet on the soft grass. Then he hauled himself out of the water, plucked the leather saddlebag off of Sally's flank and fished out the cleanest thing he had, a once-white handkerchief Angela had bought for him a couple years before. Funny, but as he swaddled Willet's leg with the cloth and tied it, he didn't feel anything at all at the thought of his dead wife. He doubted the emotional numbness was permanent, but it was a welcome change from the mixture of shame and rage that had been afflicting him since that night outside Tonuco.

The night he'd watched them murder Angela.

"You called me honey," Willet said.

Cody gave a little start and glanced down at the boy, who was eyeing him from the bed of grass. Getting to his feet and fetching their clothes, Cody answered, "Sorry about that."

"It's okay," Willet said, his voice subdued. "My mama used to call me that."

"Yeah?" Cody said. He sat down on the moist grass beside the boy. Careful to use the present tense, he asked, "What's she like?"

"Pretty," Willet said. "She's big for a woman, but she's pretty. Light hair. Nice smile. She's got a pig tail on her lip."

Cody frowned, worried the boy was slipping into incoherence. "What do you mean she had — she has a pig tail on her lip?"

"It's a scar," Willet said, smiling a little. "She got it when she was a kid. Her brother — my uncle Matthew — was whippin' around a rock he'd tied up with a piece of string."

"Hit his sister, did he?"

"The rock did. When it came loose of the string."

"Bet that hurt."

"They dragged her outa the house," Willet said, his voice suddenly thick with grief. "They made her go inside that goddamned coach of theirs. The black one." Willet shivered, stared up at the night sky with brimming eyes. "I heard her screamin'. I heard those bastards laughin' at her. She kept screamin' and—"

Willet broke off with a convulsive sob. Cody lay next to him and held his hand. They stayed that way several minutes, Cody telling the boy it was all right to cry, that he didn't blame Willet for feeling the way he did. After a time the tears subsided, and Willet lay there in a morose silence.

When he thought the boy was relatively calm, Cody ventured into the dale through which the creek serpentined, forded the water, and climbed a rise. He peered into the darkness and felt his breath catch in his throat. At first his reason discredited what his eyes told him; it was too close to good luck to be true. When he returned to Willet, he hunkered down beside the boy, who still lay with his knees bent and his eyes shuttered wide, the wan moonlight turning the boy's eyes doll-like and glassy.

Cody reached out, touched the boy's arm and for the briefest of moments feared the worst, that the young skin would be cold to the touch. But Willet's eyes shifted to his, the expression as alert as Cody hoped it would be.

"When are we goin'?" Willet asked.

Cody studied the boy a moment. "There's an old road just over that hill. I expect it leads to Mesquite."

Willet started to sit up, but Cody put a hand on his shoulder. "You sure you don't want to rest some more?"

"I don't wanna be out here any longer," Willet said, and Cody could see the naked terror lurking behind the boy's tight expression.

Cody nodded. "We better get goin' then."

They dressed and untethered Sally. Cody hoisted Willet onto one shoulder, gripped the reins and trudged along the bank. They found a shallow spot a couple hundred feet downstream, and though Sally protested and whined, Cody managed to bully her across. It was hard work sloshing through the creek with his dual burdens and his injured leg, but Cody managed. When they'd climbed the bank, Cody patted Sally on the withers and told her what a good job she'd done. Then, awkwardly, Cody and Willet sat on the horse and ambled across a stretch of smooth prairie. A few minutes later they were on the road to Mesquite, the ghostly rind of moon attending them like a newly sharpened sickle.

CHAPTER EIGHT

Cody passed the time and filled up the eerie silence by telling Willet all about his father, all about Jack Wilson.

"With a name like that, he sounds like an outlaw or something," Willet remarked. "Like Sam Bass or Billy the Kid."

Cody chuckled softly. "Dad's about as far away from those fellas as a man can get." He sobered, remembering Jack Wilson as he'd last seen him: broad-shouldered and reddened by the sun, his fair hair, brilliant blue eyes and open good nature marking him as something very different from the other ranchers in southern New Mexico. Cody imagined Jack Wilson as he'd been three years ago, standing at the front gate of his ranch in Escondido. Jack Wilson smiling and beckoning them forward, doing his best to pretend there wasn't a bad history there. Doing his best to pretend it wasn't all a futile charade...

It had been only a few months since Cody had married Angela, so the tension between him and his dad was already stretched taut enough to be uncomfortable for everyone. Cody remembered his stepmother Gladys taking him aside and pleading with him to show more respect. *The hell with that*, had been Cody's muttered response. *The moment Dad starts treating my wife with more respect is the moment I'll show him some too.*

He could still recall Gladys's disapproving silence, her thin-lipped exasperation. At the time he attributed it to her clannishness and to her unreasoning loyalty to Jack Wilson.

Only later did Cody realise that his father was worthy of that veneration, that it was Cody who was behaving like an ass.

Of course, it was too late to do anything about that now.

"So what'd y'all fight about?" Willet asked.

The boy's voice had lost much of the strain it had held only a few minutes prior. Cody suspected it was because he was distracted by their discussion, so despite the fact that it was painful for Cody to recount – despite the fact that he'd never shared it with anyone – he figured he ought to continue.

"My ex-wife...dead wife...whatever the hell you want to call her, she thought my dad was a jerk." Cody laughed humourlessly. "Hell, I thought he was too. Only later did I understand he was just trying to help me. He wasn't as diplomatic about it as he might've been, but his intentions were good." Cody sighed. "Dad's intentions were always good."

They rode in silence a few moments until Willet said, "You gonna leave it at that, or am I gonna hear about the fight?"

"It wasn't a fight necessarily. At least not a physical one. Had it been, my dad would've kicked my butt. It's been three years since then, and I'm older and stronger...and he's three years older too. So now I don't know who'd win. But then at least I knew he'd embarrass me in front of Angela if I challenged him. So I acted cold toward him instead."

"Cold how?"

Cody shrugged, his gaze sweeping the black horizon for signs of the devils. Somewhere in the distance Cody heard a grouse thumping its wings, but other than that, the wilderness seemed deserted. "I refused to do aught but shake his hand when we arrived at the ranch, and even that I did quickly, like it was just business. Dad, he was always the type for a hug, or even a kiss on the cheek, so I could tell it hurt him that I kept my distance."

"You hurt him on purpose," Willet put in.

Cody nodded. "If I couldn't beat him with my fists, I knew I could hurt him in other ways. By withholding."

Willet glanced back at Cody. "You and your wife stayed at your dad's ranch?"

"Just for a night. Less than twenty-four hours. Took longer to get there than the time we stayed." Cody hawked, spat into the scrub brush. At the sound a startled owl took flight from a nearby cottonwood in a frantic flurry of wings. "Angela didn't even want to stay that long. She hated Dad."

"He treat her mean?"

Cody shook his head. "Not then. He was very gracious to her once we were married...tried to treat her like his daughter.

I suppose he and Gladys always wanted one to go along with their son."

"Then why was she so against him?"

"Angela hated him because when we were first courting, my dad warned me off of her. He'd heard about her from some of the guys he traded with in Escondido. Heard she wasn't..." Cody cleared his throat, heaved a sigh. "He heard her ways were a trifle loose."

Willet didn't say anything straight away, but Cody could tell by the boy's posture that he was thinking hard.

Choosing his words carefully, Cody went on. "Angela had a restless soul. She was always wanting more. In a way you'd probably call her hungrier than those bastards we fought back there. She had to have everybody looking at her all the time. Had to have all the nicest, newest things."

"You give 'em to her?"

"When I could," Cody said. "Course, that wasn't often. Despite his objections, Dad gave us some money to make a go of it when we first got married. Dad wanted me to set up shop near Escondido, where he'd moved us when he got remarried, but I insisted on starting a new life somewhere else. So I bought a homestead not far from where we'd lived back in Tonuco. Back where my dad and mom had me. Where my mom died of tuberculosis a month before my fourth birthday. Where Dad raised me till he met Gladys."

"What's your stepmom like?"

"She's a mestiza."

"Huh?"

"Part Spanish, part Apache. My dad met her in Mexico."

"You get along with her?"

"Gladys?" Cody grunted. "We never saw eye to eye. But I guess that was my fault too."

Willet looked back at him. "You withhold from her?"

"I suppose I did. Plus there was always that stupid part of me that had to lash out at Dad. I guess I used my coldness toward Gladys as a way of striking at him."

"So you two never got along? You'n your stepmom?"

Something cracked in the brush behind them. Cody whirled

and peered into the gloom, but nothing there stirred. The trail was as barren as it had been before, the scrub as lifeless as a graveyard.

The thought made Cody shudder.

Willet's voice was stitched with nascent panic. "Somethin' wrong?"

"Uh-uh," Cody said, patting Willet's shoulder. "I was just gonna say my stepmother and I were fine until the grogger."

Willet squinted back at him. "What the hell's a grogger?"

"Watch your mouth."

"Why can you say it but I can't?"

"A grogger is a wooden noisemaker. They're annoying as hell. Kids love 'em though. They're a novelty."

"I never heard of one."

"Well, that doesn't matter, does it? The point is, my stepmom got one for me when we went to the Gulf of Mexico one time."

"That was nice of her."

"I guess it was," Cody said, his voice resigned. "But I didn't think so at the time. I thought it was patronising, getting me something you'd get for a little kid."

"How old were you?"

"Fourteen."

"That's still a kid, ain't it?"

Cody shook his head, probed the darkness for signs of life. The only thing he saw was what looked like a good-sized jackrabbit taking refuge behind a rock. "Not to me," he said. "Not back then."

"So what happened?"

"I told her to take her grogger and shove it."

"Bet that went over good."

"About like you'd expect. Dad smacked me in the butt. Hard. It was right there at the beach in front of all those people. Dad was strong too. Hurt like hell, but I guess my pride hurt worse."

Willet shrugged. "So what's the big deal? You was disrespectful and you got whupped."

"The big deal," Cody said, hating the whiney sound of his own voice, "was him choosing her over me."

"So'd she take it back?"

"Take what back?"

"The noisemaker."

"Hell if I know. Dad probably threw it in the ocean."

Willet frowned over his shoulder at him. "I don't understand what the problem was."

Of course you don't, Cody wanted to say. *You're a little boy with no idea of how the world works.* But he held his tongue, not only because Willet had been through a lot and was badly injured, but because Cody knew deep down he'd been an insolent little kid himself who'd deserved the punishment he got.

They rode on in uneasy silence for a good while. Beyond a scraggly thicket of olive trees to their left, a broad mesa loomed like a hunched sentinel. Willet leaned forward a bit, as if dozing off, but Cody suspected the boy was just weary and was shifting his position on Sally's back to alleviate the aches in his young body.

Cody said, "I wish I could go back and reason with my fourteen-year-old self, but I don't suppose that's possible, is it?"

Willet didn't respond. Maybe he really was asleep.

Cody went on. "Just as much – maybe even more so – I want to go back and talk some sense into the Cody who was barely into his twenties. I want to tell him to listen to his father. To not marry the first girl he screwed just because of her long legs and her pretty face."

Cody stiffened, realising the inappropriateness of his comment. He hurried on. "I guess it has to play itself out, doesn't it? We act like assholes to our dads, and then we become dads and have our own sons act like assholes to us."

Cody cringed, realising what he'd just said was infinitely worse. *Jesus, Cody,* he chided himself, *could you be any less sensitive to Willet's situation? Why don't you come right out and remind him his dad just got butchered?*

"Listen, Willet," Cody began. "I'm sorry for what I said about dads and sons and—"

With a violent lurch in his stomach, Cody realised Willet wasn't moving at all. Heart thudding, he craned his head around Willet's shoulder to look at the boy. If the kid had somehow died, if the blood loss had been worse than Cody'd suspected, he'd never forgive himself.

Willet's eyes were closed, his body motionless. He put a hand to Willet's back.

Cody blew out quavering breath. Through the kid's shirt, he could feel a steady heartbeat. *Thank God*, Cody thought. Willet was sleeping peacefully, his respiration smooth and deep.

Cody let out a long, trembling exhalation. He guessed it meant he'd begun to care about Willet Black. With a pang of surprise, he realised he'd been enjoying telling the boy of his own childhood. He'd never unburdened himself much with Angela. What was the point? Sharing his soul with her wouldn't have helped him heal; it would have given her further ammunition for an attack. Angela hated Jack Wilson because she knew the man never approved of her. But that wouldn't have stopped her from taunting Cody with the knowledge that he'd broken his father's heart.

So, with Willet dozing comfortably in front of him in the saddle, with Sally meandering along at a gradual but even pace, Cody slipped back into the snarl of his past again.

Back to the time when Angela gave herself to the devils.

★ ★ ★

The night of the Crooked Tree betrayal, Cody waited for Angela in their kitchen until well past dawn. By the time the pallid blue ghost of moonlight was seared away by the yellow-white blaze of the New Mexico sun, Cody's belly was aching and his anger was giving way to a suffocating shame. He attempted to fry an egg, but he couldn't keep his mind to it and burned all but the top of the yolk. The two or three bites he did manage to choke down only made him feel worse, and to rid himself of the foul aftertaste, he swallowed a shot of Irish whiskey. The alcohol didn't help, but it didn't worsen things. So he carried the dark brown bottle to the front porch and sipped absently from it and waited for Angela some more.

By noon there was still no sign of her. A black worm of fear squirmed in his empty belly, and Cody damned himself for still caring. Goddamn the woman, he couldn't imagine what base instinct had compelled her to leave him for those bastards. Had they promised her jewelry, a life of leisure? God knew she complained enough about the hardships she had to endure out here on the ranch.

He'd always attributed her carping to her soft upbringing. Hell, her father never even required her to use a broom in the mercantile store he owned. Yet the horrors of last night's show had spawned in him a new perspective on a childhood he'd merely regarded as insular before. Had she been allowed to indulge her every whim? Had she, like some capricious princess, spent her days and nights in a hedonistic carnival that alternated between feverish flirtation and languid acquiescence? Just what in the hell had he married? He'd never heard of a person swapping out one character for an entirely new one, and the humiliating truth with which he was now faced indicated that Angela had been this way all along, that her three years with Cody here at the ranch had been the anomaly, that last night was merely a return to the life she had always known.

That his father had been right about her whoring.

At one or so in the afternoon, judging from the blazing sun, Cody hopped off the covered porch and was surprised to find himself quite drunk. He leaned over, palms on his knees, to stem the dizziness and to level the slowly canting horizon before it toppled him into the dusty yard. He managed to remain standing, but the puking came anyway, a painful retching that deprived him of breath and caused him to fart like an old mule. He was sure for a moment that Angela would arrive and find him like this, but when the dry heaves finally ended and he could breathe again, the lane leading to the ranch was still vacant and he was still without his wife.

Cody staggered toward the house, meaning to escape the unceasing assault of the sun, but had to stop and steady himself several times before wriggling lizard-like onto the covered porch. He lay on his side for a time in the hope that the shelter of the shaded porch would restore some of his energy, but the continued heat and total lack of breeze only conspired to weaken him further. He had no idea what time it was – midafternoon maybe – when he managed to crawl through the front door and into the bedroom. His parched throat shrieked for water, but he could do nothing but claw his way onto the bed and collapse, his consciousness evaporating even quicker than his marriage had.

As occasionally happened, Cody awoke but found himself unable to move or speak. He was aware of everything around him: the lace of the white bedcover chafing his neck, the inside of his mouth painted with bile and whiskey, the comforting sound of the cows snorting in the pasture out back. And something else.

Cody listened, the fog of sleep searing away. He paused his breathing, for holding his breath was the only action of which his body seemed capable, and concentrated on the sound coming from his left. He tried his neck but it wouldn't turn, nor would his limbs cooperate. Directing all his energy, he found he could make his eyelids respond, and when he attempted to focus on the ceiling, he was surprised to find the bedroom gloomy with dusk. The sound continued, and though Cody now recognised what it was, he hadn't the faintest notion of how to respond to it even if his body were to escape its paralysis.

With a herculean effort he was finally able to turn his head and look at the person in the bedroom with him.

Angela, taking her possessions out of the bureau and placing them inside a giant leather suitcase lying on the foot of the bed, its smooth brown edge actually shoved up against his leg.

She hadn't noticed he was awake yet, only went on with her packing, methodically tossing aside the garments she no longer wanted and laying the ones she fancied carefully inside the suitcase. She wore a white dress, different than the one from the play last night, but no less elegant. The only real difference Cody could pinpoint at a glance was that the neckline of this one rose nearly to her chin and covered a good deal more than she'd displayed to the townsfolk.

Cody opened his mouth to speak but found his throat completely bereft of moisture. When she turned in his direction, cradling a stack of dresses, he tried to reach for her, but his hand scarcely twitched from its resting place. He thought of the play, of Adam Price draining his victims of blood, and for a moment Cody was almost sure he too had fallen victim to the king vampire.

"*Angela,*" Cody muttered.

He was sure she hadn't heard him, but a few seconds later he noticed her mouth tighten to a grim line. Still riffling through her bureau drawers, she said, "Don't bother saying anything. I'm leaving after tonight's performance."

She went on with her separating. Cody was stunned to find tears blurring his eyes. Of all the emotions he wanted to feel right now, sadness was the one he desired least, but the pain deepened, the lump in his throat so large and painful he'd soon gag on it.

"They don't love you," he said to her, but if she heard him she made no sign. He watched her heft a handful of jewelry from the top drawer and place it atop the dresser. He was surprised at the amount of it and only recognised one piece – the cameo brooch given to her by his grandmother this past Christmas. His grandma had died in March, and to his knowledge this was the only remnant of the woman in the house despite how close Cody had been to her.

Cody was finally able to sit up. He propped onto his elbows and said the first thing that popped into his mind. "Grandma wouldn't have given you that brooch had she known what kind of person you are."

"And just what kind of person is that?" a voice asked from the doorway.

Cody whirled, his heart instantly thudding.

Billy Horton leaned against the doorjamb, his brown porkpie hat tipped back arrogantly.

Cody sensed Angela's eyes on him and told himself to keep steady, to damn well show this asshole what happened when a man wronged Cody Wilson.

"The kind of person Angela is," Cody said in a voice that shook, "is gullible. The type of person who'll forsake her vows and run off with the likes of you in the hope she can have an easier life."

Horton glanced at Angela with innocent surprise, then returned his gaze to Cody. "We ain't promised her anything, Wilson. She *wants* to take up with us. And as far as vows go, I'd say you're the one hasn't lived up to your end. You been married how long?"

"Three years," Cody said, though his throat had gone so dry his voice came out in a croak.

Horton whistled softly. "Three years and you ain't got her with child? Sounds to me like you've got problems performing your marital duties."

Buried under the avalanche of self-loathing and outrage, Cody's reason pleaded with him to not climb out of bed, pleaded with him not to stride over to where Horton stood to take a swing at the man.

That's exactly what Cody did. Ignoring the tempest of nausea and dizziness that enveloped him, Cody reared back and swung at Horton. So great was Cody's disorientation and so poor was his balance that the blow would have done little damage even had it connected. Horton dodged it easily, but rather than striking back at Cody, the muscular actor gave him an effortless shove in the middle of the back. It was enough to send Cody sprawling on the floor. Furious and close to puking, Cody pushed to his hands and knees, but before he could stand, Horton booted him squarely in the buttocks and sent him skidding forward on his chin. While the kick was humiliating, it was his skinned jaw that stung the worst. But Cody couldn't let on he was hurt, couldn't allow this to be the end of it.

He swayed to his feet and spun, meaning to catch Horton off guard. The man was ready for him. The haymaker Horton struck Cody lifted him a foot off the ground and hurled him backward like a sack of meal.

Dumbfounded and sure now he was going to vomit, Cody rolled onto his back and tried to rise one last time. But Horton's boot came down on his chest, the bastard grinning down at Cody in triumph. "Now I'm goin' on in there to fuck your wife some more. You'll have to wait out here awhile 'cause I don't do my business as quickly as you." Horton shook his head, his grin broadening. "Way Angela squeals when one of us sticks it to her...it musta been a long time since she's been pleasured by a real man."

And with that, Horton had lifted his boot and stomped on Cody's face.

It was some time later that Cody awoke to find Horton still riding his wife.

CHAPTER NINE

Cody first distinguished the buildings in the distance just before dawn and worried they'd get to Mesquite too early to find help. He imagined riding down the main thoroughfare in ghostly silence while Willet's situation grew gradually worse, then shunted the image away.

But the town's closeness proved an illusion, and it was actually well after dawn when they pulled even with the first building, a morose-looking outpost that was simply labelled BROGANS. Cody didn't know if that meant they sold clothing or the owner was named Brogan, but it didn't matter. They had to locate a doctor.

The boy's voice shattered the stillness of the morning. "Where's Rusty?"

Cody started, glanced down at Willet and noticed the boy's eyes were still closed. He'd just about made up his mind to ignore Willet, when the boy repeated, with more insistence this time, "Where's Rusty?"

"You talkin' in your sleep, kid?"

"Goddammit," Willet muttered, his voice slurry. "I ain't sleepin'. Rusty's my daddy's sorrel. I rode him to the valley after those bastards."

Cody suppressed an urge to slap himself in the forehead. Things had been so horribly confused back when he and Willet first met that he hadn't even considered how the boy had arrived at that godforsaken valley.

"Where'd you tether him?" Cody asked.

"'Bout a quarter-mile from that rolling coffin."

It took Cody a few seconds to realise Willet was referring to the coach the devils travelled in. It was large and festooned with gilded letters and black paint and all sorts of fancy scrollwork, but the more Cody thought about it, the more he thought Willet's comparison apt. If the coach wasn't the shape of a coffin, its sensual curves and obsidian exterior did remind Cody somewhat of death.

Cody shook off the thought. "I don't know what happened to your horse, Willet. There wasn't time—"

He cut off abruptly when Willet's body jerked and went rigid, the slender tendons in the kid's neck straining against the pain. Cody put his hands over the kid's shoulders to ensure he wouldn't buck sideways off the mare. Willet's back was as stiff and ungiving as a harrow blade.

"Willet?" he said, trying to keep his voice steady. "Hey, can you tell me what's wrong?"

But before the boy could speak, Willet slumped forward onto the mare's neck, unconscious.

Oh hell, Cody thought. He had no idea what a physical reaction like the one he'd just witnessed might mean, but he knew it couldn't portend anything good. Without ruminating on it further, he spurred Sally forward and rode toward town as hard as he could without spilling Willet out of the saddle. They passed a few scattered dwellings, ramshackle hovels that looked more likely to burn down or blow away than they did to remain standing another six months. These gave way to sturdier structures, ranch-style wooden ones and a couple built of stone. The business district came next. It wasn't much, just a smattering of two-storey buildings spread out over four blocks, but one of them had a sign that simply read PHYSICIAN. Taking care not to jostle Willet too much, Cody guided Sally toward the nearest hitching post, dismounted and did his best to tie the old girl to the post before she could get surly and hurl the boy off.

Cody got under Willet and gathered the boy into his arms. Before he pivoted to cross the street toward the doctor's office, Cody's gaze happened upon a single word carved into the side of the wooden two-storey building looming over the hitching post. The word, painted in a deep wine colour, was MARGUERITE'S. Cody turned toward the road, and seeing that a pair of riders had moved past, he bore Willet toward the doctor's office.

As they neared the door, Cody wondered how he'd knock with both his arms full of Willet. But before he could think about it further, an older man appeared in the doorway. The man certainly looked like a doctor with his snowy mustache and wiry spectacles. The clothes were plain, but the jaunty bowler he wore and the slight paunch in his midsection spoke of a man who'd enjoyed more than his share of monetary success.

"I've got an injured boy here," Cody said.

The doctor stood in the doorway but made no move to allow them in. Even in the ashen early morning light, Cody could see how pale the man's blue eyes were, like memories of younger days.

Willet was growing heavy in Cody's arms. Standing there that way, cradling this twelve-year-old kid the way he was, Cody felt like a groom attempting to carry his wife over the threshold of their new home, only to find he's forgotten the key to the front door.

Cody returned the doctor's inscrutable gaze. "You gotta help us, sir."

The old doctor eyed him impassively.

Cody licked his lips, glanced down at Willet. "He's my brother. He got shot last night, and now he's talking crazy."

The doctor continued appraising him, and Cody pictured himself as this man must be seeing him: dark hollows for eyes due to sleep deprivation, a week's growth of beard, clothes so draggled that he looked like an indigent.

But the old man surprised him by giving a barely perceptible nod and receding into the building. Taking care not to bang Willet's head against the jamb, Cody hurried after the old man and, without being invited, laid Willet on a table in the dim room's centre. The doctor removed his hat and began to study Willet's leg.

"His pants are damp," the doctor said.

Cody steeled himself for a reproach.

The doctor paused, his bushy white mustache hovering over his open mouth like a fresh dump of snow, and fixed Cody with his light blue eyes. "How'd they get wet?"

"I rinsed his leg in the river."

When the doctor only continued watching him with a look that might have been disdain or perhaps disbelief, Cody went on, "My dad always said it was best to wash out wounds. I thought I was helping the boy."

Without comment, the doctor resumed his examination of Willet's leg. The air in the small room felt thick with accusation. Cody longed to be outside, but that would mean leaving Willet in here with this sullen old man.

The doctor produced a large pair of shears and began slicing through the thick wool of Willet's pant leg.

"Should we just take 'em off?" Cody suggested.

"Got to make sure there aren't other wounds to worry about on the leg," the doctor said. "Could be we'll start them leaking again."

"He just got hit in the one place," Cody said, but the doctor ignored him, continued cutting right on up to the boy's upper thigh. Cody had a vague worry about what the kid would wear now that his one pair of pants were ruined, but he pushed away the thought. First things first. He had to make sure Willet's leg was all right before he worried about the kid's wardrobe.

Might not even need pants with two legs, a cruel voice whispered.

Shut the hell up, Cody thought and stared grimly out the window. The view of the sky was obstructed by the buildings across the street, but judging from the number of passersby outside it had to be getting on toward seven o'clock.

That was still a long time before he could get a drink. God, he'd never wanted one so badly in his life.

Cody remembered the two-storey building across the street. "What's Marguerite's?"

The doctor was pinching the skin around Willet's wound, the half-conscious boy groaning at the inspection. "It's a saloon," the doctor said without looking up. The thumbs and index fingers continued their squeezing, one time actually expressing a fresh dribble of blood along the rim of Willet's wound. Cody repressed an urge to jerk the man's wrinkled fingers away, to tell him to take it the hell easy, the kid had been through enough.

Mercifully, the doctor's hands went away. Willet sighed as the ministrations came to an end. Cody relaxed too.

The doctor went over to a bowl of water and plunged his hands inside. As he washed them, Cody became aware of just how thirsty he was, and if *he* was thirsty he couldn't imagine how poor Willet must feel. Without asking, he went over to the wooden water barrel by the door and ladled a bit into a filmy glass. He went to the boy, raised his head as gently as he could and brought the glass to Willet's lips.

"I wouldn't..." the doctor began, but Willet responded the way Cody knew he would, the thin, cracked lips opening and sipping steadily at the glass rim. Out of the corner of his eye, Cody could see the doctor towelling off his hands, watching as Cody set the glass aside and used the sleeve of his shirt to wipe off Willet's mouth. When Cody laid the boy's head again on the folded blanket and glanced up at the doctor, something about the man seemed to soften.

He eyed Cody speculatively. "You two don't look like brothers."

Though Cody had expected this, he still didn't know how to respond. He hesitated a moment, said, "I lied about that. He's just someone I met."

The doctor reached up, brought a bottle of pills off a shelf. "You the one who put that hole in his leg?"

"Do I look like I'd do that?"

"Then maybe you're the reason why it's there. You get him shot?"

Cody chest tightened. "No."

The doctor unscrewed the lid off the bottle, shook out a couple large white pills. "No," he said, coming back to where Cody stood over Willet. "You don't seem the type."

The doctor put a hand under Willet's muddy neck. "Help me get him up," he said.

Cody wrapped an arm around the boy's back and raised him to a sitting position.

"You hear me, son?" the doctor said into Willet's ear.

Willet only moaned.

"I need to give you something for your wound," the doctor said. "If I put a pill in your mouth, can you swallow it?"

The faintest of nods. The doctor glanced at Cody, who held Willet steady. The old man placed a pill inside Willet's barely parted lips. Then the doctor brought the glass up again, waited for Willet to get the pill down. After repeating the process, the doctor nodded at Cody, who eased Willet onto the table.

"One'll help him sleep," the doctor said. "The other will help with infection."

The doctor produced a small amber vial of liquid. He used swabs to dab it onto the wound.

Cody wrinkled his nose. "What is that stuff?"

"Creosote," the doctor said, eyes narrowed in concentration.

"Isn't that what they use to finish wood?"

The doctor chuckled softly. "There are different kinds. This one serves as an antiseptic and prevents necrosis if used early enough."

"Necrosis?" Cody said. "Is that what I—"

"Gangrene," the doctor said. "But you won't have to worry about that. I suspect you got him here in plenty of time."

Cody relaxed a little. Willet's wan face looked like a death mask in the sallow morning light. But the doctor didn't seem worried. And if the doctor wasn't worried, Cody reasoned, he shouldn't be either.

The doc doesn't care about Willet though, the cynical voice reminded him. *You do.*

On the heels of that came another, more unwelcome thought, one that Cody had a hard time shaking. As the doctor unbuckled Willet's trousers, Cody said, "I don't have much money."

The doctor threw a nod down at Willet. "Help me, would you?"

Cody joined the doctor in taking down the boy's ruined pants. Without asking, the doctor balled them up and tossed them into a wicker wastebasket. The dingy underwear the boy wore made Willet seem more pathetic than ever. The old man took a brown woolen blanket off a shelf and covered Willet with it.

"Best if you got some sleep," the doctor said to Cody. "You've been wounded too."

Cody blinked at him. He'd been sure the man hadn't noticed the hole in his own trousers, but apparently the pale blue eyes were sharper than they let on.

"I'm okay," he said, but the doctor was bending and reaching under the examination table. Standing with a slight wince, the doc dragged out a shabby little cot that nonetheless beckoned to Cody like a newly sewn featherbed.

"You can stay with him long as you need to," the doctor said, going toward the door. He paused, nodded at a cabinet. "You need 'em, there're more blankets there."

The doctor went over to the same bottle he'd used earlier, shook out a couple more tablets and handed them to Cody. "You know where the water is," the doctor said. "Speaking of that, I'll water your horse while you rest."

The tears in Cody's eyes surprised him. God, he was cracking up.

"Anything else you need?" the doctor asked, the pale blue eyes not noticing or maybe pretending not to notice the tears in Cody's own.

"No," Cody said, averting his eyes and running a hand through his greasy hair. "I'm indebted."

He sniffed, wiped his nose with the back of a hand. His breath came in short, husky intakes. When he was certain the man had gone, he looked up again, but the doctor was still moored to his spot by the door. The old man's eyes were on a timepiece he'd taken out and stood polishing with a red rag.

"Those men," the doctor said, huffing hot breath onto the watch's glass face. "The ones shot you and the boy."

Cody went cold all over. "What about 'em?"

Another huff of hot air. Even from this distance Cody could see the glass fog, the red rag describing brisk revolutions over the timepiece. "They apt to follow you two?"

Cody thought about it. Horton dead. One of the twins dead too. Penders smashed like an egg someone dropped. That left Price and the remaining Seneslav twin.

"They'll come," Cody said. "But I wouldn't count on 'em until nightfall."

"Any reason for them to wait so long?"

Cody waited a long time before replying. A still inchoate suspicion was forming somewhere deep in the recesses of his mind. At length he said, "They just seem to like the dark better."

The pale blue eyes fastened on his. Then, without another word, the doctor went out.

★   ★   ★

Cody awoke with a start. Despite the thunderbolt of pain in his calf, he managed to sit up and gaze out the window. It didn't appear as though much time had passed. Midmorning at the latest, maybe not even nine o'clock. His stomach clenched angrily. He imagined it in there, a shrivelled, pulsing pink raisin. If he didn't get something in it soon, he'd pass out, and that sure as hell wouldn't do. If he and Willet were both unconscious when the devils rode in...

Cody shivered, pushed to his feet as if to outrun the thought. He shuffled over to the door in the corner, which he assumed led to the doctor's office, or perhaps even to his residence. Without knocking, he opened the door, stepped through and nearly stumbled over the doctor, who sat reading in a red brocade armchair. Cody's vision swam as a wave of lightheadedness rolled through him. He steadied himself by placing a hand on the back of the doctor's chair.

When the room clarified again, he saw the old man looking up at him, not unkindly. "I thought I might be sick," Cody explained.

"The boy still asleep?"

Cody nodded. "I was wondering if there was food somewhere around here."

"I don't typically take lunch until eleven," the doctor said, "but Marguerite might be open by now. Usually is by this time of morning. I tethered your mare out front, by the way."

Cody nodded, tried to make out the title of the book the man was reading, but the words at the top of the page were too small, Cody's eyes too bleary.

"You need help?" the doctor asked.

Cody shook his head. "I can make it."

But the doctor accompanied him anyway, one firm hand on the middle of Cody's back. Together, they made their way back to the table on which Willet lay. The boy's skin was still very pale, but somehow he looked cleaner, as if sleep or the fresh light of morning had washed the trail grime away. And though the frail little body was moveless under the heavy brown blanket, the forehead was unlined, the breathing deep and regular.

"Is the sheriff in yet?" Cody asked.

The doctor chuckled without mirth. "Bittner? Not likely."

"When can I talk to him?"

"I'd be surprised if you see him before noon. He tends to linger at Marguerite's most nights and makes up for it by sleeping in."

Cody nodded. Based on prior experience, he estimated that Price and his men wouldn't arrive in Mesquite until after sundown. Either way, he would have plenty of time to grab a bite to eat, talk to the sheriff and get back to Willet by one. That was six or seven hours until sunset.

Cody eyed Willet's bandaged wound uneasily. Six or seven hours of cushion should have been enough to reassure him, but still he hesitated.

What if they come while you're across the street?

Cody bit his lower lip. He had no answer to that.

You really willing to risk it? For a sandwich and a beer?

Then another voice sounded in his mind, one far less scathing, less remonstrating. *You won't do Willet a bit of good in your current state. Get some food and get back here. Then you'll have all day to figure out just what the hell you'll do when they arrive.*

That sounded better. More reasonable.

He straightened, brushed a bit of hair off of Willet's closed eyelids. *An hour*, he told himself. *Two at most. I'll be back well before noon. Then I'll figure out what to do.*

And in answer the cynical voice whispered, *You better figure it out. If you don't, Adam Price is going to kill you both for what you did.*

But Cody didn't want to think about that. Quickly, he went out.

CHAPTER TEN

Marguerite's saloon was darker than he expected, but the place had class. To the left of where he stood in the foyer, there were several fancy-looking billiard tables tucked into a windowless side room. Straight ahead and to his right, there were multiple dining tables, which gleamed as though newly polished; the chairs were all pushed in neatly, and they too shone with a sleek burgundy glaze. Beyond the tables there was one of the nicest theatre stages Cody had ever seen. It made the Crooked Tree look like the stage in some kid's puppet show. This one was broad, tall, and had a vast red curtain that looked like it might be real velvet. Moving deeper into the foyer for a better look, Cody glanced up and spotted what appeared to be the bottom edge of a catwalk that hung suspended above the stage. He knew nothing about how proper stages worked, but he guessed it had something to do with the lights. In Albuquerque he and his dad once saw a person fly above a stage using some kind of wire and pulley system.

On the left side of the large room, Cody spied a woman behind the bar. She had her back to him, her tanned shoulders half-exposed by the white ruffled blouse she wore. The bar hid most of her lower half, but above the burnished wood Cody could just make out a swath of light blue fabric. Moving closer, he saw it was a skirt. It hugged her hips, showed off her shapely rear end to considerable effect.

Cody caught himself staring, but it was too late. The woman had been watching him in the bar mirror all the time. He felt like turning and leaving, but he'd seen no other establishment that looked remotely like it served food. He just hoped she wouldn't spit in his drink for being so disrespectful.

She turned and smiled at him as he took a seat at the bar. If she was mad at being ogled, she didn't let on. Her dimpled cheeks were really quite lovely, her dark eyes large and long-lashed.

Somehow, the sight of her made Cody miserable.

She seemed to pick up on this. "Rough night?" she asked. Her voice was low, mellifluous.

He grunted, tried to muster a grin, but it hurt too much. He reached into his pants pocket to see what money he had left. As he did, she wetted a small towel, placed it on the bar before him.

He stared at it stupidly a moment before surmising its purpose. Then, giving her a grateful smile – this time it didn't hurt so badly – he used it to swab his face, the back of his neck. Christ, it felt good.

"How far did you ride?" she asked.

He realised with some alarm that she was as tall as he was. It made him glad he was sitting down.

"Yesterday evening I was in Las Cruces."

Her eyebrows rose. "That far?"

"We rode all night," he said.

He exhumed three coins from his hip pocket. It was enough for food and a drink, but then what? *It all comes back to money*, he reflected. Had he been able to support Angela the way she'd wanted, she maybe wouldn't have strayed. If he used up what little he had now, he'd never be able to pay the doctor, or for that matter buy food for Willet.

He stared sourly at the coins in his palm, as if the act of looking at them would make them multiply. "You know of a place where I can trade some things?"

"Connors a couple doors down does that, but he doesn't give fair value."

"You do any trading?"

Something guarded came into her face, and Cody knew she'd mistaken his meaning. He considered explaining himself but found he was simply too exhausted. By way of apology, he asked, "How much for some bacon?"

"What to drink?"

"I don't have enough—"

"You need whiskey?" she asked, and though it reminded him of the night Angela had betrayed him, he found he'd never wanted a whiskey more in his life.

He scratched the stubble on his cheek. "Can I wash dishes or something? I really need to save—"

"The dishes are clean," she said, drawing herself higher.

"I didn't mean that."

"Bacon, cornbread and a whiskey," she said. "You want water too?"

"Yeah, I want it, but—"

She took the white towel, dipped the clean end in the water basin and returned it to him.

He accepted the towel, said, "Look, it's nice of you—"

"Wash your ears," she said, moving toward a door. "There's dirt in them."

Cody watched after her, then did as he was bidden.

★   ★   ★

The sandwiches were juicy and delicious. Cody devoured the first one with ravenous greed, then took his time with the second, savouring the good meat, the salt in the bread, even the metallic kiss of Marguerite's grill. She stood a fair distance off as he ate, glancing over at him from time to time, perhaps to see if he was enjoying her cooking. He complimented her once but was too deep in rapture to bother to do so again. If she was offended by this, she didn't show it. Her full, unpainted lips never smiled while he ate, but her eyes did, a wry humour that communicated itself to him in an arched eyebrow or the occasional shake of the head. Alone with Marguerite in the bar, he experienced a weird sensation. It wasn't sexual desire precisely, though he found her extremely attractive. She didn't seem much older than he was, yet something about her comforted him, made it unnecessary to throw glances into the mirror to make certain the devils weren't coming through the door.

What if they don't cast reflections?

Cody paused in midbite. Now where the hell had that notion come from? In a moment, he had it: the play. Of course it was the play. He'd only heard the word *vampire* in books up until a few nights ago, but after watching the play he knew several more facts about vampires than he had previously. They didn't cast an image, and they didn't like crosses. They could only be killed by a stake through the heart. That's how Horton's character triumphed over Price and the Seneslav twins in the final scene. Perhaps Cody could get ahold of a similar spear and treat them the way Horton had treated them in *The Return of the Maiden Carmilla*.

The hell are you talking about? a truculent voice demanded. *You really wanna get that close to those bastards? Have you forgotten how strong they are, how easily they can kill a man? Almost like…almost like…*

Strike that out of your head, another voice snapped, and Cody was gladdened to hear his father's sandpapery growl, the voice itself gruff and dry but the emotion it conveyed nearly always girded by real regard.

I'm sorry, Dad, Cody thought. *I was just thinking—*

Enough of that, the gravelly voice cut in. *You need to think about the here and now, not the spooky stories your imagination conjures. Price and his men are tough, vicious and amoral, but they aren't characters in a penny dreadful. Now quit cowering and* think, *boy.*

His dad was right, of course. There were no vampires, were no bloodthirsty creatures who—

Who said that? his dad's voice interrupted. *Listen, dammit, I'm not saying anything about what they are or what they aren't. I just want you to think rationally.*

Cody glanced over at Marguerite, who was pretending to polish the gleaming bar top, but was likely waiting for him to speak.

Like a rancher listening for thunder in the distance, Cody stared down at his plate and strained to hear his father's voice.

What do we know about them? Jack Wilson asked.

In his youth a question such as this would have annoyed the hell out of Cody, who always felt like his dad was wasting their time by turning everything into a riddle that needed to be solved. But since moving away from his father's house, Cody had come to realise that what his dad had really been doing was teaching him how to *think*, how to solve problems on his own. If his father's way of preparing him had been tedious and a mite condescending, it was a hell of a lot better than no preparation at all.

Think, Cody!

All right, all right, he told the voice. *I'll think.*

Cody sipped at his water, laid out what he knew.

There were two, maybe three of them still alive. He hadn't seen Penders die, but no one, not even a man as brawny as Penders, could have survived such a fall.

Always plan for the worst, boy. The best will always be a pleasant surprise when it comes, but planning for it is a fool's move.

Three then. Three men against one of him. The odds would've been bad enough had Price and the others been normal men. He couldn't believe they were vampires, but they sure as hell weren't normal either. Cody's gaze drifted along the shelves below the bar-length mirror, taking in the many dark bottles, a few painted figurines, a brightly coloured vase stuffed with miniature blue flowers – the same kind, he now realised, he'd tumbled into during his fight with the Seneslav twin. He recalled the guy's wiry strength, the chest that reminded him of a diagram of the muscle system stripped of skin. He thought of the way Seneslav had recoiled at the sight of Cody's drawn fist, as if for one fleeting moment the man had forgotten who was physically superior. Seneslav's eyes, glassy and black in the gloom, fixing on Cody's fist...something just beyond it...

Stay sharp, boy.

I'm staying sharp, dammit, Cody thought. *At any rate, they're strong as hell, and they'll kill without batting an eyelash. They eat people. They drink their blood first and then they cook them over a campfire until the bitter smoke settles into your nostrils and makes you wish you were dead already too, because what kind of a world is it that lets a kid like Willet Black witness the killing and roasting of his entire family?*

You've got a gun, Cody.

He exhaled shuddering breath. *Yeah,* he thought. *I've got Willet's gun.*

You need more ammunition. See if this woman will help you with that.

Cody's mouth spread in a rueful grin. *She'll probably castrate me when she finds out I don't have enough money to pay for all this food.*

She's not that kind and you know it.

He closed his eyes. He supposed he did know it.

Ammunition, food for Willet. What else do you need?

How about a miracle? Cody thought.

Make your own luck, kid. God gave you a brain, didn't he? Use it and stop making excuses for yourself.

I'm not—

The hell you're not! his dad thundered. *Angela left you because she wasn't made for marriage to begin with, and even if I was wrong to inform you of that the way I did, I told you the truth, didn't I?*

Yes, Cody thought. *You told me several times.*

What's done is done. She chose to leave, and she got herself killed for it. It wasn't your fault, so don't give up now because you think you're cursed.

Cody clenched his fists. *Who's giving up?*

That's more like it. You got a boy to protect and a whole lotta people to avenge. They've murdered seven in three days. How many others you think they've killed?

Hundreds.

But you killed Horton, didn't you?

Yes.

And Seneslav.

And Seneslav.

Maybe even Penders, his dad said.

God, I hope so.

And that means you can get the others too if you play it right. Now finish your damned sandwich and ask this pretty Mexican girl for some help. You can pay her back when it's all done.

What about the doctor?

What about him? You think he's gonna throw the boy out in the street before he's well? C'mon, Cody, think a little. Not everybody in the world's bad. There are more good ones than Adam Prices.

Then why do the Adam Prices win?

They won't if you get your head out of your ass.

"You okay?"

He glanced up sharply and saw Marguerite leaning across the bar. He could see a good deal of cleavage bunched within the frilly white dress, but rather than inciting lust, it made him feel tired and happy. He wanted to press his face into those breasts and inhale the scent of her dark skin. It wouldn't be long before he could fall asleep that way, and Cody couldn't imagine a nicer place to be.

She said, "Are you going to tell me what happened to your leg?"

Cody realised he'd been staring, but when he met Marguerite's gaze he saw neither rage nor humour. If anything, the woman looked slightly bored. He was a man, her expression seemed to say, and men were entranced by breasts.

"My leg's fine," Cody said.

"You always limp that way, I suppose."

"I hurt it riding."

"You've been to Dr. Jackson."

He frowned, was about to ask her how she knew that, but decided it didn't matter.

She nodded toward the window. "I saw you and the boy come in."

"You were up early."

A small shrug. "I don't sleep a lot. Since my father died I run this place alone. There isn't time for sleeping."

"You aren't married?"

She stared appraisingly at him, her eyes perhaps searching his for signs of irony or salaciousness. Apparently finding neither, she said, "I was married once."

"What happened to him?"

"Were you ever married?"

Cody's stomach coiled, his innards suddenly aquiver with shame.

"You were," she said.

Cody set the last of his bacon on the plate.

"What happened to her?" she asked.

He blew out a trembling breath, folded his hands on the bar. "She left me."

"Sad."

"I suppose so."

He was sure she'd ask for money then, but she surprised him by patting the back of his hand. He looked up at her, noticed one of the little blue flowers tucked above her ear. His glance shifted to her eyes, which remained fixed on his a long moment.

"Let's sit together," she said. "I want to hear more about your wife."

* * *

They sat at a table not far from the bar, and though the light was dimmer here away from the bar mirror's reflecting gleam, Cody found himself better able to relax sitting across a table from Marguerite. Here it didn't feel so much like business owner and patron. More like a man passing the time with a nice woman.

"What happened to your husband?" Cody asked.

Marguerite didn't answer for a goodly while, only gazed down at glass of water on the table before her. When she spoke, her voice was toneless, nothing like her ordinarily playful lilt. "Slim was a deceiver. He married me so he could steal my father's business. When my father died, Slim ceased his gentlemanly treatment. He struck me and bedded other women."

Cody let that sink in a moment. He asked, "What did the sheriff do about it?"

"He deputised him."

"Come again?"

"Slim Keeley is one of Bittner's deputies. The other two, Boom Catterson and John Ebright, are no better than my ex-husband."

"Those aren't real names."

A bitterness shone in Marguerite's large, dark eyes. "Whatever sort of trouble you're in, you won't find any help from these men. You're better off taking the boy down to the cellar and hiding until your problems blow over. I keep my father's crossbow there in case there's trouble."

"I'm not gonna hide from anybody."

"The law here is a farce. They'll make whatever's wrong worse. Use the cellar."

Cody took a sip of whiskey, glowered at Marguerite. "I suppose I'm not man enough to take care of them. Is that what you're saying? You think Bittner and your ex and Boom and Bam or whatever the hell their names are could do better?"

Marguerite sounded unperturbed. "I don't even know what your problems are. I know you got hurt last night, I know you brought in a boy who isn't your kin to Doc Jackson and I know you're spooked about something."

"I'm not spooked about—"

"Hush," she said. "Being afraid isn't a bad thing, contrary to what men want to believe. The average man pretends he's afraid of nothing until the danger actually arrives. Then he's full of terror and an absolute coward."

Cody eyed her. "You figure me for a coward?"

"If you'd listen, you'd realise I'm complimenting you. You're afraid and you probably have reason to be. So take precautions. My advice? Relax and get some sleep. It'll be several hours before Bittner comes on."

"You don't think there's a chance the sheriff might help us?"

"He'll only make things worse." Marguerite ran a thumb around the edge of her glass. She looked up at him. "Is this business as bad as it sounds?"

Cody took another drink of whiskey, set the glass on the table with a dull clunk. "Bad as it gets."

"Does this involve your wife?"

"My dead wife," he corrected. "And yes, it does."

She watched him steadily. "Would you like to tell me about it?"

"Not particularly."

Marguerite nodded. "My ex-husband is a craven piece of trash."

Cody couldn't suppress a chuckle. "What makes him so bad?"

"He used to beat me with a wooden mallet."

Cody's good spirits evaporated.

Marguerite went on, her tone conversational. "Slim thought it was funny to use my father's carpentry tools to inflict pain on me. Once he chopped off one of my toes with an adze."

"You're kidding."

She raised her eyebrows. "You want to see?"

"Didn't the sheriff help?"

"I told you. He made my husband deputy."

"They didn't believe you?"

"The sheriff thought it was funny. My father was a great man, so men like Bittner and Slim hated him. My father's ability to earn an honest living through his skill and labour alienated him from those with neither an ounce of skill nor an inclination to work.

You notice all the fine craftsmanship in here?" She gestured at the ornate designs carved on the side of the bar.

Cody said that he had.

"My father's work."

"He must have been a good man."

"He was. Too good for this place. I should never have married Slim Keeley. I should have seen him for what he was. But I was stupid."

Cody grinned wearily. "I can relate to that."

"Can you?"

"The way your ex treated you, I'm surprised you didn't shoot me on sight when I came in."

"You're different from them," she explained. "I can see decency in your eyes."

"You don't know me."

"I know a good man from a bad one. I know my father had honour, and I know he knew fear. He was afraid because he valued life. He never wanted anything to happen to his wife or his daughter."

A lazy, drawling voice spoke up from the entryway of the saloon. "But Daddy's dead, ain't he?"

In the moment before Cody turned, he saw Marguerite's face go tight with surprise and what might have been loathing. When he did turn to see the tall man striding toward them, he knew who it was right away.

Slim Keeley was a tall man with a long, horsey face and a small gold star on his blue shirt. He was slender, but his limbs were imbued with a tensile strength that reminded Cody a little bit of Billy Horton. And like Horton, Slim Keeley wore an arrogant expression that made Cody want to knock his teeth out.

Slim approached, moving with a swagger that suggested he owned the place, despite Marguerite's claims to the contrary. "I suppose Margie here's been bellyaching about how unfit I was for marriage. Claimin' I was cruel to her." Slim neared the table and stood between Cody and Marguerite, one long-fingered hand resting casually on the holstered butt of what looked to Cody like a Colt Peacemaker. With the other hand, Slim reached out, brushed a lock of dark hair off Marguerite's forehead.

With a convulsive swipe, she smacked his hand away, her dark eyes blazing. "Get out of my saloon."

Slim's smile was easy. "Easy, Margie. You keep talkin' that harsh, you might scare this youngster away."

Cody pushed up from the chair, took a step toward the tall deputy.

Without turning Slim said, "You'll wanna sit down, boy. 'Less you're a good deal tougher than you look."

"She asked you to leave," Cody said.

Slim chuckled. "Margie never asks anything. It's why I had to get rough with her so often. I hadn't done that, she would've never stopped trying to act like a man."

Cody took a step nearer, less than a foot away. "What do you know about being a man?"

For the first time, Slim looked at him. The height difference was several inches, but Cody was angry enough it wouldn't matter. Even though this man had likely never been to Tonuco, Slim's face suddenly looked very much like one of the devils. It wasn't hard for Cody to imagine Slim taking a turn on Angela the way Horton had, the way Penders and the others had. Slim was the same kind of snake—

From the corner of his vision, Cody saw Marguerite's expression change. He made the mistake of glancing that way, and by the time he realised that Marguerite was looking at Slim's left hand – the hand hidden from Cody's view – the hand had balled into a fist and crashed into Cody's jaw.

The next thing he knew, he was on his back, the ceiling an impossible distance away. A yawing dizziness spun through his head.

Pain exploded in Cody's side. Doubling up, he saw Slim's receding black boot. Before he could bring up a hand to defend himself, Slim lashed out again, this time kicking Cody squarely in the chest. Cody's breath rushed out in a tight *whoosh*, the pain between his pectoral muscles akin to a puncturing spear point. Vaguely, he heard Marguerite shouting something at Slim, glimpsed a whir of tawny arms and glossy black hair, but Slim only laughed at her, called her a painted cat and a goddamned harlot. Shrieking, Marguerite battered at Slim, tore at his face until, still laughing, he retreated toward the foyer.

Cody heard the door slam shut. He closed his eyes against the dizziness and heard the faint sound of Marguerite's furious weeping.

Failed again, Angela's voice taunted him.

You go to hell, he thought. The dizziness slowly abated. Footsteps approached, then grew muffled as they passed behind the bar.

With an effort, he pushed up to an elbow and watched Marguerite emerge from behind the bar, a key in her hand. Wiping her eyes, she crossed to the front door and locked it.

She returned to kneel over him, one dark calf exposed by the movement of her dress. It was very tan and very smooth. Somehow, the sight of it reduced the agony in Cody's jaw and chest.

"Thank you for standing up to him," Marguerite said.

Cody grunted. "Don't know that I'd call this standing up."

"You trusted to his honour," she said absently. "You thought he would fight you fair."

Cody rubbed his aching chest. "Guy kicks like a damned mule."

"He doesn't know what honour is," she said as if Cody hadn't spoken. "He does what he wants and doesn't care how he hurts people."

"I should've hit him first."

Marguerite looked down at him in silence. Cody felt even worse under her unblinking scrutiny. At length, she said, "What's your name?"

Cody told her.

"Thank you, Cody. I owe you something for trying. Most men would have let it pass without saying anything." Then, to Cody's surprise, her face melted in a radiant grin. She looked as if nothing unpleasant had just taken place. "Follow me," she said.

Without waiting for a response, she rose, started up the staircase and curved around the balustrade above him. As she passed, he caught another glimpse of her tan ankles, her strong calves.

Before he could rise, a door opened and another female voice sounded from the balustrade above. "You need me yet, Marguerite?"

"We're closed until tonight," Marguerite answered brusquely.

"Really?" the other woman asked. "Who's the guy?"

"Shut your door, Eliza."

But rather than doing as she'd been told, the one named Eliza sauntered down the staircase and stood sizing him up from the shadows of the overhanging walkway. Cody got groggily to his feet and gazed back at her, waiting for her to make a crack of some kind. She looked like the type who'd have a wicked tongue. Reddish hair in tight ringlets depending from each side of her face. Her mouth half-open, her painted lips and her tongue both very red. Her light green dress was plain enough, but the neckline was cut so low that Cody could see the twin bulges of her milky white breasts jutting out. She noticed him looking and her grin widened.

"You coming?" Marguerite asked from above.

Cody went over, took one last gulp of whiskey and put it on the table with a shiver.

He bypassed the one called Eliza and followed Marguerite upstairs.

CHAPTER ELEVEN

When he reached the room into which Marguerite had disappeared, her back was to him. She was arranging bottles on a narrow bedside table. The bed itself was a broad, sturdy-looking affair. The headboard carvings reminded him of scorpions, though there was no real design to the swirls and protruding contours. Her room – if indeed this was her room – was sparsely decorated, but what décor there was seemed tasteful. Of course, Cody had never had much of an eye for such things, but to him the room seemed classy enough. It smelled good, too. Like citrus, with an undertone of jasmine. Cody inhaled the fragrance, which was a far cry from the odours of sweat and death radiating from his clothes.

Marguerite drew back her hair and tied it with a light blue ribbon.

"Take off your shirt," she said. "Leave the trousers."

Cody looked around, touched his belt buckle uncertainly. "Leave them where?"

She turned and looked at him with an arched eyebrow. "On. Leave them on."

"Oh."

He stripped off his shirt and folded it neatly on a chair.

"Lie there," she said, nodding toward the ornate red blanket stretched out on the bed. Cody lay on his back, the blanket satiny against his skin.

"On your belly," the woman said.

Cody did as he was told, but he wondered what the hell the woman had in mind. In profile she was even more beautiful, the prominent nose and sensual curve of forehead giving her the aspect of some dream-conjured maiden, not a saloon owner who'd probably known men beyond counting.

He glanced out the window overlooking the street but could

not make out the doctor's office from here. He moved a trifle to the right and to his great relief was able to spot the weathered grey façade, the safe haven in which Willet slumbered.

Safe for how long?

The insinuating voice set his heart to racing. Cody was about to thank Marguerite for her kindness and head back to Willet when she leaned over the bureau to set her rings down and her frilly white shirt breathed open, her lush tan cleavage momentarily and achingly visible. Though the sight of it sent warm currents spinning through his loins, it also brought with it memories of Angela. He thought of his wife's naked breasts, lighter and smaller than this woman's, thought of Angela as she'd been before their lovemaking soured, before the isolation and monogamy bred a resentment in her he never fully understood or acknowledged. That was, until he watched her being pawed all over the stage of the Crooked Tree by Horton, Penders and Price.

At the memory, Cody's arousal ebbed. Perhaps it was just as well.

He pushed up onto his elbows. "Ma'am, I don't mean to be rude, but up until a few days ago, I was a married man. I don't feel—"

Marguerite was laughing.

A heat burned in his cheeks. "What?"

Her laughter, high and silvery as church bells, would have pleased him under any other circumstance, but at the moment it brought on a dull throb in his temples, an indignation born of weariness and a disinclination to be derided after all he'd been through.

"What the hell's so funny?" he demanded.

She shook her head against the laughter, put an index finger to her lips as if to shush herself. "I'm sorry," she said, her composure gradually returning. "It's just the idea of..." Her face twisted again, and she surrendered to another gust of laughter. She hugged herself and rocked forward on her toes.

Cody got up, collected his shirt and moved toward the door.

"No," she said, a hand on his arm. "Please don't leave." Laughing, sniffing. "It's my fault you thought this was about sex."

His shoulders drooped, his arms unspeakably heavy. What energy he'd recovered from the catnap at the doctor's had been beaten out of him by this pretty woman's mockery.

"Lay down again," she said. "Please."

"What the hell for?"

"I'm going to massage your back."

Cody stared at her. "Do what?"

"It'll help you feel better."

Though she barely had an accent, Cody couldn't shake the feeling they were speaking different languages.

"Lay down," she said, putting a hand on his lower back and leading him over to the bed. "I don't want anything from you, and I'm not offering anything more than a backrub."

He lay down as she went on. "You've been through a trial, that much is obvious. And since you were nice to me, I thought I'd do something nice for you. Okay?"

Cody rested his face on his wrist and closed his eyes.

He heard her splashing something on her hands, rubbing them together. Then her cool touch fell on his bare skin, and she set to massaging his back. It felt good. Damned good. But he couldn't shake the humiliating way she'd laughed at him.

"Don't see what's so funny about it," he grumbled into his wrist.

She paused in her ministrations. "How old are you, dear?"

"Old enough for you not to call me dear."

"Twenty-one? Twenty-two?"

"Twenty-four," he said and resisted the urge to tell her he had a birthday coming later in the month.

(If you live that long.)

Cody clamped down hard on the thought. It was the last thing he needed to do right now, waste time and energy fretting over hypotheticals.

"Very tight muscles," Marguerite said, her thumbs making painful arcs beneath his shoulder blades. "You're more preoccupied than I thought. What happened to you and the kid out there?"

Cody elected to say nothing. What was the point of dragging her into it?

Marguerite's fingers were strong, the pressure she exerted

bringing him nearly as much discomfort as pleasure. Still, by degrees he felt himself relaxing.

Damn, but she's strong, Cody thought. The dexterous fingers worked his flesh with such force that his body jostled on the bed. A vague current of arousal pulsed through him once more. Cody marvelled at how little it took to turn him on when in the presence of a woman like Marguerite. He put her at about twenty-six years old, but only because of her worldly attitude. Her face was fresh and unseamed, and the fragrance she broadcasted, an earthy lavender scent, made him ache to take her in his arms. He imagined her full, brown legs around him, imagined her sweaty body undulating beneath his...

He jolted and sucked in a breath. Good Lord, he'd actually fallen asleep. But if he didn't get some sleep soon, he wouldn't have the energy to oppose the devils tonight.

"It's all right," Marguerite said, tipping a bottle of clear liquid into one palm and then rubbing her hands together. "Your body's telling you it needs rest."

"My body needs to get the sheriff."

That laugh again, high and mischievous, but tinged with a jeering undertone that made him bristle.

He propped up on an elbow. "The hell's so funny?"

"If you're looking for a saviour, I'm afraid you're looking in the wrong direction. I'm surprised Doc Jackson didn't warn you about Bittner."

Cody eased himself back down. "He said the sheriff keeps late hours."

"The sheriff likes to screw my waitresses."

"He some kind of ladies' man?"

"Sheriff Bittner is the furthest thing from a ladies' man I could imagine. This isn't a brothel, but Bittner likes to treat it like one. His favourite is Eliza, though she's not half his age. I tell her not to sleep with the customers, but I can't control what she does after she leaves. Or how she fucks for money." Marguerite met his gaping look of surprise with a smile. She pushed him back down and began massaging him again. "Don't look so stunned, Cody. I'm only speaking the truth."

He sighed, his surprise dissipating. "What shocks me now is considerably different than what would have shocked me last week."

She chuckled. "You have a way of saying things. It reminds me of my father. He and my mom used to laugh all the time."

"Your mom still living?"

Marguerite lapsed into silence. He worried she might be crying, but when she spoke again, her voice was composed. "You care about the boy."

"I guess I do."

"Then let him rest. The day is early, which gives you time to think about what you must do. You're welcome to rest here. So is the boy when he awakes."

Her tireless fingers continued to knead his back and his shoulders. He couldn't remember the last time Angela had done this for him. Maybe she never had. He found himself telling Marguerite all about Angela, all about their marriage and its gradual undoing.

Which brought him to the night the devils took his wife.

Cody regretted broaching the topic almost immediately. He was sure Marguerite would scoff at him – or worse, decide to chuck him out of her room – but to his surprise she did neither, only listened to him with an inexhaustible supply of patience.

When it was done, Marguerite said nothing. Cody waited as long as he could, and when it became apparent she wasn't going to comment, he said, "Some yarn, huh?"

"They sound like animals."

Cody swallowed. "So you believe me?"

"Does that surprise you?"

"*I* wouldn't believe me."

"A man wouldn't make a story up in which his wife humiliates him."

"And gets herself killed in the bargain."

Marguerite's fingers paused while she seemed to consider. "You're sad she died?"

"Was murdered, you mean. Of course I'm sad. I mean, it wasn't like we had much time left together as it was. I guess in a lot of ways we were already separated. But that doesn't mean I wanted her to die. Especially not at the hands of such…"

"Actors?"

Cody grunted. "That's what they call themselves anyway."

"Do you think they'll come here?"

"There's a good chance. They'll love that fancy stage of yours."

"My father thought Mesquite would grow. I even had a limelight brought in from the East, thinking we'd have big shows here."

"Their show's not the kind you want in your bar."

"Should I go stand watch?"

"I don't think that's necessary. I've been following them for several days now, and they only travel after sundown."

"Why only then?"

"Hell if I know. Maybe because it's cooler."

Marguerite fell silent, but her fingers pushed harder and deeper into his weary flesh. It was as though her fingertips knew the way to heal each individual muscle, to take away the worry and the dolefulness and the stultifying dread he'd been feeling ever since they'd escaped the devils last night.

So he talked some more. He told her about his father, about his father's ranch in Escondido, about how it was only a few hours from here but still seemed like it was a continent away. He described the road that led to the property, the layout of the ranch itself. He told her how great a man Jack Wilson was and how Cody worried he'd never see his father again.

And Marguerite listened. She worked on him steadily, asking a question now and then, but mostly listening. After a time, she began to talk too, and it occurred to him that this was what had been missing from his marriage with Angela. The talking. When that went away, the suspicion and the resentment crept in, and eventually there was nothing left *except* the suspicion and the resentment.

Marguerite told him something of her childhood, and as she talked, a strange thing happened to Cody. He realised he liked this woman very much. He trusted her. And if he and Willet somehow made it through this ordeal alive, maybe she'd want to spend more time with Cody too.

Her fingers kneaded, lulling him into a dreamy torpor. His thoughts grew muzzy. He said, "So your name used to be Marguerite Keeley?"

"What of it?"

"Nothing. Except it doesn't go together. The Marguerite and the Keeley."

"You're right," she said, a bitterness in her voice. "They didn't go together."

"What are you now?"

"I have my father's name."

"And that is?"

"Smith."

"You're joking."

"Why would I joke about that?"

"I figured it was Gonzalez or Chavez or something like that."

"My mother was born in Chihuahua. She married my father after they met in El Paso. She was a waitress."

"Was your mom as pretty as you?"

Marguerite's hands stopped moving, though she didn't remove them from his shoulders. Her breath was warm on his ear. "Are you trying to seduce me, Mr. Wilson?"

"You're too smart to be seduced."

"That's true. Unless I want to be. Now be quiet for a while so I can work out these knots from your back."

Marguerite graduated from his shoulders to his upper arms. Her thumbs and index fingers probed deep into his triceps, made him aware of just how sore they'd been from holding Sally's reins all night. He yawned. Man, he needed sleep.

What you need is a pair of testicles, a voice within him chided. *A beautiful woman massaging oil into your back and all you do is nod off? Easy*, Cody thought. *Take it easy.*

But the voice would not be deterred. *Something wrong with you, boy? You don't try something now, you'll never forgive yourself.*

Cody took a breath. "What you said earlier."

"Mm?" Marguerite said without a break in her attentions.

"About wanting to be seduced."

"Ah. That."

"I was thinking—"

"I don't."

"Oh."

She chuckled softly. "You're a very handsome young man, Cody. But you're still just a boy."

"I bet we're the same age."

"That doesn't mean you've had the same experiences."

"I've been around."

"You can forget about sleeping with me."

He sighed. "All right."

She began rubbing one of his hands. This he knew no one had ever done to him before. It felt exquisite. It was as though her fingers were stones dropped into a pond that sent slow ripples of pleasure through his entire body. Pleasure and relaxation. Even his facial muscles were going slack. Marguerite moved around the bed and began kneading his other hand.

"Can't fall asleep," he murmured.

"Do you trust me?"

"Course I do."

"Then go to sleep. I'll wake you by two o'clock."

Reluctantly, because he couldn't stop himself, Cody complied.

CHAPTER TWELVE

His first thought upon waking was a languid hope he could sleep just a little longer. In his dream Marguerite was oiling her entire nude body and undulating on top of him. He was naked too and on his back, but no matter how he tried to push his engorged member inside Marguerite's warmth, her slippery body always glided up or down so that he remained constantly and achingly erect and burning for her. Lying there on the cosy featherbed, a soft sheet draped over him, Cody scrunched his face in concentration, verily begging sleep to descend on him again so he could consummate his dream tryst with Marguerite.

But when it became apparent he wouldn't be able to doze again, Cody grew aware of how quiet the room was and how different the light seemed to be beyond his shut lids. He opened his eyes and glanced about the bedroom, bewildered and instantly afraid.

The sense of wrongness increased rapidly as he pushed onto his palms and stared at the window. The curtains had been drawn, but they were sheer. Further, the shutters were unfastened, yet the light slanting through the windowpanes was a muted orange, the kind of light you got at midafternoon, not late morning.

Cursing, Cody scrambled out of the bed and crossed to the window. Not only had the sun advanced toward the west – it was three o'clock at the earliest – but the outer door to the doctor's office hung slightly ajar, as if someone had left there in a hurry.

Cody was dressed and down the stairs in an instant, his heartbeat a painful stutter in his chest. *So stupid*, he thought as he rushed through the unoccupied ground floor of the saloon, *so stupid and so goddamned clumsy*. Cody burst through the doors into the punishing orange glow of the New Mexico sun. He hurried across the dusty thoroughfare, thinking, *It isn't evening yet. They won't have come.* But with a sinking dread, he noticed that Sally was absent from her hitching post.

Cody approached the door of Doc Jackson's office at an awkward run, a sense of misgiving so strong it nearly strangled him lending speed to his limping gait. Movement in the street in front of him drew his eye, and he saw with little surprise he'd nearly trodden on a large vinegaroon, another unwelcome reminder that nightfall was fast approaching. The sluggish black creature hardly moved as Cody stepped over it. He stumbled up the porch steps and almost rammed the door with his forehead. He gathered himself, leaned panting against the door and glanced around to see if his behaviour had aroused suspicion. An elderly couple eyed him warily from down the street, but other than that he'd been ignored. That was good. He had no idea why it was so, but he didn't want to draw attention to himself. The less people focused on him and Willet, the easier it would be to surprise Price's gang tonight if they showed up in Mesquite.

Of course they'll show up, the cynical voice told him. *You think they're gonna let you and Willet live after what you two did?* Cody realised the old couple were still staring at him. Throwing a nod in their direction, Cody twisted the knob and stepped inside Doc Jackson's office.

It was dark in the office. He was reminded of how dark it'd been upon waking in Marguerite's room, and he fought off a hot surge of self-condemnation for having been asleep this long.

He didn't remember drawing down the blinds in here, but that could have been the doctor shielding Willet from the blazing sun. Still, the sight of them, yellowed and wrinkled like the skinned hides of diseased cattle, made invisible fingers of dread clutch his throat.

Cody stepped closer and saw what was on the examination table.

The whiskey and the bacon gushed up his oesophagus. His whole body shook with revulsion at the sight of the splayed arms and legs, the ribcage pried open and jutting at the ceiling like the carcass of some butchered animal. Cody lurched against a cabinet and upset a jar of some clear liquid. He gagged as a cloud of flies erupted in angry surprise. They buzzed around the ruined torso a moment before returning to their feeding.

"Aw, Christ," he said, a forearm shoved over his mouth. He'd been so stupid, so much less than Willet deserved. Cody willed his body to venture nearer, but it wouldn't obey, would only stand rooted where it was, distraught and shaking, as the carrion flies siphoned the dead boy's blood.

What an idiot Cody'd been to assume they wouldn't come until nightfall. What kind of superstitious garbage had compelled him to believe that? Chances were they were still inside this building somewhere, likely right next door in the doctor's living quarters, roasting the man's legs for a late-afternoon snack. Cody realised he was making a high, keening sound in his throat, the noise a child might make under the covers while hiding from monsters. *Got to go*, he thought helplessly. *Got to go now*. But even that escape was denied him. He couldn't go anywhere, couldn't even move.

Get ahold of yourself, Jack Wilson commanded.

I can't, Dad. I just can't. You raised a coward, I'm nothin' like you. I'm—

The thought broke off as he noticed something for the first time. Frowning, Cody edged closer to see if it'd been a trick of the dim light. The boy's head was turned away from him so that he was spared a good view of the face, yet what he beheld was spattered with dark red gore. He told himself it was the panic, that he was fooling himself into seeing things that weren't there, but...wasn't there too little hair on the corpse's head? Under the crimson patina of blood, wasn't the face too wizened, too large?

"Holy God," Cody said, stepping around the table. It wasn't Willet who'd been eviscerated. It was Doc Jackson.

A huge exhalation pushed out of him, and he was forced to steady himself by leaning against the examination table. Something sticky squished under his fingers, and though he knew he should have been disgusted by it, the fact that it wasn't Willet's blood made it somehow bearable. Swallowing, Cody peered down at the ruined face, realised at once how they'd taken the man's eyelids, sawed a giant hole around the mouth so that it gaped obscenely at the ceiling in a lipless grin.

Whatever relief he'd felt disappeared in a wind of terror.

They were surely still here.

Cody pushed away from the table and had gotten halfway to the door when he remembered Willet. If the boy wasn't here, where was he? Where the hell had they taken him? Cody glanced at the door to the doctor's quarters and suddenly knew the devils were in there. Had they done the same to Willet as they had the doc? Were they, even now, slicing through the skin around his mouth to—

A voice behind him said, "Don't move."

Cody uttered an involuntary yelp and spun around. The man in the front doorway was large and unfamiliar, his round upper body all but blotting out the outer light. How the man had ever managed to slip inside without Cody noticing, he'd never know. Cody raised his hands to show he meant no harm, but the man tensed, shoved his wavering pistol forward and shouted, "I said don't fucking move!"

The fear in the man's voice broke through Cody's jumbled thoughts. He said, "All right. Just put the gun down."

The man – he was as tall as Penders and as fat as the other was strong – watched him several more moments, evidently contemplating shooting him anyway. Cody tried to swallow, but his saliva had evaporated. A shifty grin lifted the man's sagging jowls. Cody decided he liked the man better when he'd been frightened.

"Turn around," the man said.

Cody knew he had to do it, but still he hesitated. There'd been something deeply unsettling about the man's voice. There was something hungry in it, almost lustful.

Without knowing he was going to speak, Cody asked, "Did you do this?"

The man's grin went away. "Don't you speak such filth. *You* did it, you goddamned monster."

Cody relaxed a little. He knew he should've been alarmed by the accusation, but knowing the man holding a gun on him hadn't murdered the doctor meant he likely wouldn't kill Cody either.

At least Cody *hoped* it meant that.

The man said, "You don't turn around now, you won't make it to trial."

Cody nodded, did as he was told. Marguerite would vouch for him. She'd tell this bastard the truth, and then Cody could commence his search for Willet. Christ, he hoped the devils hadn't killed the kid already.

The sound of creaking floorboards told him the man with the gun was stepping closer. Cody asked, "Can I put my arms down now?"

"Sure you can," the man said, his voice still rife with that disquieting hunger.

"I know how it looks," Cody said, "but I didn't do this. You can ask—"

"That'll be enough," the man said from directly behind. Hell, any closer and they'd be lovers.

"Can I ask who you are?" Cody said.

"Sheriff Robert Bittner," the man said. Cody caught a whiff of the man's breath, a stomach-churning stew of curdled milk and tobacco juice. As if to confirm this suspicion, the man spat a hot stream of spit at the back of Cody's head. Cody grimaced as it crawled down his neck and disappeared beneath his collar.

"Hold still," Bittner said, and before Cody had time to ask how come, something hard smacked him in the base of the skull.

PART TWO
BLOODBATH IN MESQUITE
CHAPTER THIRTEEN

He twitches awake and realises he can't breathe, not even a little. The substance filling his airway is brown and gritty and it's all around him. He's in a pit of quicksand, the terrible stuff towing him lower, lower, and no matter how he gasps, his lungs only pack tighter with it. Cody's chest is leaden, an unoiled machine that'll never function again. He's sinking lower, lower still, no air—

Cody gasps and flails his arms, free of the dream. Then he's falling again, only this time it's really happening, because the rest of his senses are liberated from that muffling veil. Then, right as he opens his eyes, two things happen in quick succession: his right hand upsets a container, the liquid within sloshing over the side of his leg; and his knees thud painfully on the stone floor.

Cody opens his mouth to cuss, but the drawing apart of his lips triggers an unholy gonging in the base of his skull. He hears laughter to his left and all at once it comes back to him: the doctor's corpse, Sheriff Bittner, the knock on the head—

—Willet missing.

Cody managed to open an eye and take in the sight of the heavyset lawman slouching in a chair across the room, his feet resting on a wooden barrel sawed in half. Bittner nodded, his puffy face bisected by one of the cell bars. "I was plannin' on emptyin' that pan later on, but you went and saved me the trouble."

Cody smelled it then, the vile, sulfurous stench of old urine, the rusty metal container lying on its side after having vomited its contents all over Cody's pant leg. Wiping his hand on the dingy fabric of the cot off which he'd just tumbled, Cody said, "I don't suppose the piss is mine."

The sheriff tilted his head, folded his hands in his lap. "Course it wasn't yours, Wilson. Just how the hell'd I have done somethin' like that? Take your peter out for you while you slept? Give it a good shake when you was done? Jesus, you must think I'm some kinda pervert."

Cody noted the ill-fitting brown hat, too wide at the brim, the crown too snug, so that the Stetson perched impatiently atop the sheriff's head like it couldn't wait to return to its rightful owner. The man's facial hair resembled a furry brown horseshoe someone had hung on Bittner's lips. But it only accentuated the drooping jowls it was no doubt meant to conceal. To the fat man's left stood a slight, almost delicate desk with tall, slender legs. The man and the desk looked incongruous next to one another, which furthered the surreal fog Cody found himself in.

Cody winced. The throbbing in his skull was so severe he was certain he'd puke. Too bad the sheriff wasn't closer so Cody could expel the contents of his stomach all over the man's ugly face.

A scuttling noise echoed behind Cody. With an effort, he craned his neck around and saw a cockroach the size of a scorpion crawling a few inches from his left boot. He eyed the insect with distaste but didn't have the strength to crush it.

Bittner said something but Cody was too miserable to catch it. He closed his eyes against the black clanging in his brain. The sheriff had really rung his bell good.

Something clattered against the bars. Cody looked up in time to see the fat man striding toward him. "Whyn't ya answer me?" Bittner demanded.

Cody watched him bend over and retrieve the object he'd hurled to get Cody's attention, a ring full of keys. Before Cody had time to contemplate the idiocy of this risk, the sheriff was barking at him again. "That piss belonged to Luke Lind, who's a drunken waste of life." Bittner grinned and tapped the ring against his leg, its keys clanking together dully. "How's his piss smell?"

Cody knew he should feel indignant, knew he should fire back at this waddling sack of wind, but all he felt was a deep weariness and a desire to be left alone.

Of course you want to be left alone, a familiar voice said. Confronting the man would take balls, which you don't have.

Aw, Christ, he thought. *Not her. Not now.*

Then when? Angela persisted, exulting in his misery. *Just when will it be time for you stop being a frightened little boy and stand up for something?*

Cody grimaced. Oh, how he wished she'd shut the hell up. But the worst of it was, she was right. He had been a coward. In his cattle business, in his fights with Angela, that night at the Crooked Tree, then two nights ago at that doomed family's ranch...

"No," he said aloud. "Uh-uh." He shook his head in wide pendulum sweeps, but he couldn't banish the flood of memories, the laughter and the moaning and the carnage and the wails. On all fours, Cody squeezed his eyes shut and did his best to stifle a whimper.

"You like sittin' that way?" Bittner asked. "Or's that how you made the boy sit?"

Cody gazed up at the sheriff, perplexed, but had to look away after a moment. He couldn't bear that raunchy grin any longer.

That's right, Angela murmured from somewhere in the gloomy recesses of his mind. *Look away, Cody. It's what you were always best at. You were made to flinch, weren't you? In that land deal with Albertson, he threatened to freeze your credit at the bank if you refused to sell, so you did as you were told, let him buy half our acreage for a song. Anything was better than staring someone down and letting the stakes rise.*

His fingers balled into fists, his leg muscles going so tight they became one big cramp. *No, goddammit*, he wanted to shout, *it wasn't like that. We got fair value on that land, and anyway, Albertson was head of the bank board. What the hell was I supposed to do? Call his bluff? Let them take our credit away, lose all our land? Tell them, 'Hey I'm sorry, common sense dictates I should take your reasonable price and pocket the money, but my wife turns everything into a test of my manhood, which is why I've gotta refuse'?*

Angela's voice came back, louder this time; he could almost see her standing above him in the cell, arms akimbo, her pretty face twisted in caustic disdain. *Test your manhood? That's a riot. How the hell can you test what isn't there? Albertson took you to town with that deal and you know it. Barely enough to get us to San Fran and back. Had to stay in that seedy inn miles away from the nice places, eat at the cheap seafood dives rather than the ones where the women dress up fancy.*

"That's right," Cody murmured, "and I did it all for you, you ungrateful bitch. If we'd've saved the money instead of spending it the day we got the check, we could've bought you a *dozen* dresses."

Cody stopped, realised he'd been talking to himself. He looked up at Bittner, who eyed him with a blend of fascination and suspicions confirmed. "Godamighty," Bittner said. "I wouldn'ta believed it if I hadn't heard it myself. You really are as crazy as they say."

Cody made a face at the sour tang in his mouth. "As who says?"

Bittner rolled his eyes as if the question had been an absurd one, seemed on the verge of responding, when a noise from the next room got his attention.

Bittner's sagging cheeks rose in a smile. He gestured that way and gave a little shrug as if to say, *Speak of the devil.*

The door opened and Adam Price walked in.

Price stepped through the doorway and brushed at his sleeve. With a cold rush of dread, Cody saw it was the same costume Price wore for his performances.

"You got the boy with ya?" Bittner asked.

Cody noticed with little surprise that the sheriff had instantly turned deferent in Price's presence. When Price didn't answer, Bittner went on, "What'll ya do with him? Take him back to his folks?"

"Unfortunately," Price said, his strange, tenebrous eyes rising to meet Cody's, "Mr. Wilson murdered the boy's parents. His siblings and grandparents as well."

Cody pushed unsteadily to his feet. "That's bullshit and you know it." His vision swam with grey, and he staggered forward to steady himself on the bars.

Bittner's teeth showed, two discoloured rows of tobacco-stained nubs. "You keep your mouth shut, you murderin' bastard."

"Check the valley," Cody said. "You'll find what's left of the boy's grandpa. They spitted him like a goddamned hog." When Bittner's flinty little eyes only glittered with hate and condemnation, Cody squeezed the cell bars harder. "I'm telling the truth, dammit. I mean, Christ, head back to the Blacks' ranch north of Las Cruces. You'll find the whole clan smouldering in the fire the devils set. They make it look like an accident, and people are too damned stupid to investigate."

Bittner threw back his shoulders, his corpulent belly straining against his shirt. "You callin' me stupid, boy? I hope to God you ain't callin' me stupid."

"I didn't mean——"

"And just how the hell you know a thing like that?" Bittner asked, striding nearer. "Just how'd you know what became of that boy's granddad?"

"It's obvious enough, Sheriff Bittner," Price said. And though his expression was bland, Cody detected a hideous glee in Price's dark eyes. "Mr. Wilson here became incensed with certain members of my troupe when his wife took a more than professional interest in them."

Bittner chuckled. "'More than professional interest.'"

"Listen to me," Cody began.

But Price was going on. "What consenting adults do is none of my business. I'm merely our group's manager and lead actor, not its chaperone. Any marital problems Mr. Wilson and his wife had are irrelevant."

"That right?" Bittner asked in a wheedling voice. He waggled his eyebrows at Cody. "You two had you some marital problems?"

"They killed her," Cody said.

Bittner's vast belly shook with laughter.

But Cody persisted. "They talked her into leaving me, and when they had her outside town limits, they butchered her in their coach and drank her blood."

"'Drank her blood,'" Bittner repeated.

"Drank it, then ate her flesh and dumped what was left in an arroyo." Cody threw a nod at Price. "Hasn't been any rain since then, so her remains might still be there."

Some of Bittner's mirth gave way to incredulity. "Now just how dumb you think I am, boy? You peddle some fairy tale about bloodsuckers and women gettin' spells put on them, and you expect me to buy it?" He glanced at Price. "Christ Almighty, Mr. Price, this little shit must think I'm the dumbest lawman in the whole goddamn state."

"They're monsters, Sheriff Bittner," Cody said, his voice growing thin. "You gotta believe me."

Bittner drew his gun, a Walker six-shooter, and levelled it at Cody's face. "I don't listen to kid-chasin' sonsabitches who ride into my town and kill decent folks."

Cody turned to Price, who appeared to be studying his fingernails.

Bittner went on. "Doc Jackson always did have a bleedin' heart. I tole him it'd come back to bite him in the ass someday, but I never thought it'd happen like this." Bittner cocked the hammer of his six-shooter. "Poor bastard tries to patch you and the boy up, and how do you pay him back?" Bittner's tongue flicked out, did a quick revolution around his lips. "I ain't never seen nothin' so awful. His goddamned ribs looked like they'd been ripped apart by two teams of horses. I'll never forget the sight of his blood everywhere...all them flies..."

"His fanciful claims about cannibalism are only one problem with Mr. Wilson's story," Price said smoothly. He folded his arms, the dark cape he wore slithering behind him. "You say you saw us discard her remains in an arroyo, is that correct?"

"Saw it with my own eyes."

Price smiled. "Sheriff Bittner, why would a husband allow his wife's body to lie uncovered in a gulch? If he were as devastated as he'd have you believe, wouldn't he have given her a Christian burial?"

"Well?" Bittner said, still holding the cocked gun at his side. "What say you, Wilson?"

Cody said, "Ask Willet about it."

Bittner shook his head. "You ain't goin' near that boy again."

Price nodded. "I've taken custodianship of the child, Mr.

Wilson. You've done quite enough damage to his fragile psyche."

"Go to hell, Price!" Cody growled.

Bittner said, "Boy, I'm warnin' you."

"*Ask Willet about it,*" Cody shouted. "Ask Price here where his men are, how Willet shot one of the devils in the face and how I damn near tore another one's head off."

Bittner's gun was rising. "Shut up, Wilson!"

"*Ask* him, goddammit!"

Bittner aimed the gun. "You say another word, I'll put one in that nasty gob of yours."

Without taking his eyes off Cody, Price said, "I wonder if I might have a word with Mr. Wilson alone?"

Bittner frowned. The expression made his already slack face appear even dumber. "Don't see why."

Price turned, and though Cody couldn't see the change in Price's face, he could guess how angry Price looked from the way the sheriff wilted. Price said, "I know you don't see why, Mr. Bittner, which is why I want you to leave immediately."

Bittner flinched like a child about to be slapped. Then he left the room with ten times the celerity he normally exhibited.

Price faced Cody, his features serene again. "Amusing person, the sheriff. He pretended to be aghast at the tale we told, but I suspect he was secretly envious of you and your exploits. Particularly where the little boy was concerned. There are noxious compartments in the sheriff's tiny brain."

"Where is he?" Cody asked. "What'd you do with Willet?"

"Nothing yet. We tend to wait until moonrise to dine, as you've no doubt noticed."

"You hurt him, I'll kill you."

Price's eyebrows went up, his alabaster face full of delight. "That's quite a boast, Mr. Wilson. I'm surprised you had the nerve to utter it."

Price approached, the actor moving with the grace of a dancer. Cody was acutely aware of the disparity in their heights. Cody was five foot eleven in boots, but Price was half a head taller, not to mention broader around the chest and shoulders. Price's loosely curled brown hair shimmered in the dusky light slanting across the room.

"You don't scare me," Cody said, but even as he said it he knew how pitiful he sounded.

Price's returning smile was gentle, almost loving, and that was somehow the most terrible thing of all. Price's face altered again, appeared momentarily troubled. Then he snapped his fingers and stepped away from the cell. "My goodness, Mr. Wilson, I nearly forgot! There's someone here who wants to see you."

Cody had a momentary and completely illogical moment of hope that Willet would come through the door, but the thought vanished as swiftly as it had come. The ursine shape trudging toward him was Willet's antithesis.

Shit, Cody thought. *Penders.*

So the man had lived after all.

Steve Penders's wide brow, Cody noted with alarm, was pinched with barely contained rage. He wore the same peasant's garb he wore for the play, and he moved with the same easy grace that had so surprised Cody that first night at the Crooked Tree. If he'd sustained any lasting injuries from the fall into the valley, he was sure as hell doing a good job disguising them. If anything, he looked livelier than he had last night when he'd climbed naked up the rock face.

Price put a hand on one of Penders's massive shoulders. The men were just about the same height. "A frightful fall Penders took last night," Price said. "'Twas a good thing most of his bleeding was internal. It's easier to transfuse that way."

"Transfuse?" Cody asked. He was dimly aware of backing away from the bars. Penders looked strong enough – and furious enough – to bend them like reeds.

"Blood has regenerative powers," Price said. "As long as there's a fresh supply on hand – the boy's mother, in last night's case – we're able to drink ourselves back to health."

One mystery solved, Cody thought. He hadn't held much hope in Willet's mom being left alive, but hearing it confirmed was still a blow. God, the poor kid.

"Yes," Price said, as if reading Cody's thoughts, "the woman did give out in the end. Yet even if she had possessed more blood to lend to our cause, I doubt it would have helped Dmitri."

So Cody *had* killed one of the twins. He knew it was silly to doubt what he knew to be true, but seeing Penders walk through that door had been like seeing Lazarus rise from the dead.

But at least you got Dmitri, Cody thought.

"I'd be careful not to betray too much merriment, Mr. Wilson. Dmitri's brother is inconsolable. In fact, Dragomir's been so wild since his brother's death that we forced him to remain back at the inn until the show tonight."

Cody's mind raced. Before he could ask the question that had arisen, Price put one hand on his elbow, the other on his chin, and leaned forward confidingly. "Dragomir aims to eat you alive, Mr. Wilson. He made me promise him we'd let him kill you in the slowest, most excruciating manner imaginable. So of course I had to acquiesce to his wishes." Price smiled benevolently. "Few bonds are as strong as brotherhood."

A chill whispered down Cody's spine. He could picture Dragomir Seneslav pacing up and down his hotel room, waiting to get his hands on his brother's killer.

Penders grasped the iron bars. "Dragon's gonna have to get in line."

"Patience, Steve," Price said. "Remember we have a show to perform."

A memory of Penders having his way with Angela on the stage of the Crooked Tree flitted through Cody's mind, and without thinking he said, "How you gonna do your act with only three people?"

"Don't you mean four?" a voice said from the rear of the room. Penders and Price moved aside to regard the speaker, who leaned against the back wall, his porkpie hat tilted jauntily back to reveal an arrogant, intact face.

"Howdy, old friend," Horton said and dropped Cody a wink.

Cody's stomach plummeted. It was impossible. *How can you have a face again?* Cody wanted to ask. *I watched Willet turn it into a bloody stew. And now...there's not a mark on it.*

But that wasn't quite true, Cody realised as Horton drew closer, his cocksure strut as infuriating as ever. There were marks on his face, only they were subtle and tough to see unless the lighting was just right. There was a brilliant spray of evening sun still blazing over the horizon, and as Horton took his place beside Penders just outside

Cody's cell, Cody could see the faint white lines crosshatching Horton's face. They looked like ordinary scar tissue, only that kind of scar had to develop over time. The ghostly latticework webbing Horton's face might have been there for years, but Cody knew better.

But how? he almost screamed. *How can a face regenerate so quickly? How can what was obliterated less than twenty-four hours ago be damn near normal already?*

You know how, a voice answered. *You know how, but you don't want to admit it.*

Cody steeled himself against the knowledge, suspecting in some protected and secret region of his mind that if he did succumb to the truth, if he did credit his perceptions and all the evidence and follow it until he reached a conclusion, if he did open himself up to an idea that was not only patently insane but borderline blasphemous, the world in which he had always lived would be plunged into chaos.

Hasn't that already happened?

No, he thought weakly. *No...*

"You'd be better served by accepting it, Mr. Wilson."

Cody shot a sickly look at Adam Price, who was standing wide-legged with his fingers laced before him. Price's smile was small, but it was there.

My God, Cody thought. *Can he read minds too?*

"Scared yet, Wilson?" Horton asked.

Hell yes, I'm scared, he thought. *But I'll be damned if I admit that to you, you wife-murdering bastard.*

Of course, Cody didn't know which one had actually done the killing, for he'd been outside the black deathwagon when it was happening, too scared and sick and hurt to bust open the doors and see the devils pawing her again. Yes, he'd heard her screams, and yes, he'd recognised them for peals of anguish rather than moans of pleasure, and maybe a better man would've gone in there to do something about it, but all he could think at that moment, the moment when the deathwagon started shuddering with the carnage occurring within, was that he would be killed too if he intervened. But just as strong in him – and this was the part for which he never thought he could forgive himself – was the wounded rage still poisoning him in that moment, the diseased and ignoble belief that

Angela deserved what was happening to her, that her vicious and continuing betrayal of her husband had earned her a death sentence.

Price glanced back at Bittner, who had appeared at the door and was watching the confrontation with what looked like a mixture of awe and elation, and said, "Sheriff?"

Bittner blinked at Price. His mouth worked a moment before he said, "You want me to leave again?"

"I do."

Bittner nodded, backing through the door slowly.

"And Sheriff?" Price said. "If you open that door again, I'll gut you and roast your liver for supper."

With more agility than Cody would've believed the man was capable of mustering, Bittner hopped back and slammed home the door.

Price stepped toward the cell. "Penders, Horton. Would you please join Dragomir back at the inn?"

A braying terror exploded in Cody's mind. "What inn?"

Price's smile widened. "You know which one, Mr. Wilson."

CHAPTER FOURTEEN

Cody clutched the cold iron bars. "What'd you do with her?"

Penders had been moving toward the door, but now he stopped, shot a fierce look at Cody. "Don't tell him, Mr. Price. He don't need to know."

Cody noticed a dark smear of crimson on the forearm of Penders's grey shirt. "What did you guys do to my horse?" Cody said in a tight voice.

Penders winked. "The old girl was tasty."

Cody's stomach roiled. *Oh, holy hell*, he thought. *Poor Sally.*

"I'll join you in a moment, Penders. You and Horton need to prepare for our performance."

As the door closed and Cody was left alone with Adam Price, a horrible certainty descended on him. Cody paled. "You aim to put Marguerite in your show, don't you? You aim to bewitch her the same way you bewitched Angela?"

"Mr. Wilson, I assure you we never *bewitched* anyone."

"Angela wouldn't have done that on her own."

Price gave him a penetrating look that Cody found unbearable. "We both know better, Mr. Wilson. Your wife was practically aching for an excuse to transgress. We merely provided her the opportunity she was seeking."

Cody lunged at the bars. "Fuck you."

Price loomed closer. "Would you like to hurt me, Mr. Wilson?"

Cody licked his cracked lips. The man

(*he's not a man*)

was within grabbing distance now. If Cody wanted, he could seize a handful of those glossy brown locks and rip them out at the roots. If he wanted

(*you'd be dead within seconds and you know it*)

he could wipe that shit-eating grin off the bastard's face…

Price's face began to change.

Oh, holy God, Cody thought. *I'm not seeing this.*

But he was. Price's chiselled, too-pretty face was now stretching, thinning, the jaw and the teeth elongating, the skin at the man's temples pulsing with unnatural rapidity. Cody thought of his stepmother making bread, the way the dough would attenuate; the bread had the same pasty colour that was overtaking Price's face now, the skin growing bloodless. But the eyes...Jesus Christ, the eyes were glowing in their enlarged sockets now, an unnatural, iridescent orange that reminded Cody of the gaslights he'd once seen as a very young child in an Albuquerque hotel, a phantasmal orange hue that made him think of ghosts, that had kept him up the night he and his father stayed there despite the fact that the bed was the most comfortable one he'd ever lain in.

Cody drifted backward and averted his eyes.

"Few get to see me this way," Price said, only it wasn't Price's voice anymore. "The ones who do are the ones who suffer most."

"You...you've got an accent," Cody said breathlessly. He stared down at his shoes, telling himself that no matter what that thing said, he wouldn't peer into those glowing orange eyes again.

"*Yes*," the Price-thing said. The voice was guttural, like steel scraping stone. "Now you have to believe it. It's good for you to learn the truth now. While there's still time."

Cody's voice was scarcely a whisper. "Time for what?"

"Time for you to fear the night."

Cody's whole body began to shudder. He couldn't help it. He realised he was going to wet himself soon.

"*Look at me.*"

Cody shook his head, felt the room begin to tilt.

"*LOOK AT ME, CODY WILSON!*" the voice thundered.

Though the last thing in the world Cody wanted to do was to peer into the monstrous white face again, his head rose up and he did it anyway.

The creature held Cody for an endless moment with its glowing orange eyes.

Then, miraculously, Cody found his voice. "Where the hell do you...what *are* you?"

"*You know what I am,*" the creature growled.

Where Adam Price had been now stood a creature at least a head taller. The face had elongated even more, but it was only in proportion to the rest of the ghostly white frame. Arms as long as broomsticks, a neck that was longer but that also pulsated with tendons and a hundred tiny muscles that twitched and jumped. Cody shuddered at the sight of Price's tongue – long, black and cloven like a serpent's – as it slid out slowly between the chalky lips.

Cody had crowded against the stone wall at the rear of his cell. The creature merely held him with its incandescent eyes, and Cody found he was unable to look away.

"You have killed one of mine," the creature said.

Cody sought for his nerve, but found he had none. Those unblinking eyes penetrated into his cowering, quivering heart and rendered speech impossible.

The creature that no longer looked much like Adam Price continued. "The twins have been with me since the 1600s. They were with me in the motherland. In Hungary. In Austria, Switzerland and France. They refused to abandon me when things once looked very bad in northern Germany. And now Dmitri is dead."

Cody's head spun. He struggled to make sense of Price's words, but the infernal eyes effaced all thought. He could scarcely breathe.

"I have never lost a servant *until I was ready to let him go,*" Price said, his low voice a throaty roar. "*I will punish you, Cody Wilson. You will weep blood.*"

Through the churning terror that entombed him, Cody had a quick recollection of the play, *The Return of the Maiden Carmilla.* Though Price never looked like he did now during the play, there had been a similar aura of malice oozing out of him, first as he pursued Angela and then at the end when he and the Seneslavs acted out the fight against Penders and Horton.

"You lost," Cody whispered under his breath.

Price's slow grin was an obscene, grisly rictus. "That was a play."

"But you still lost in the end. Men like you always do."

"Perhaps you'd like to face me now, Mr. Wilson. While the others are out of the room."

Cody tried to conceal the leap of terror Price's words had wrought within him. "How am I supposed to fight you when I'm in this cell?"

Wordlessly, the vampire stepped over to the barred door. Price extended a cadaverous index finger, out of which sprouted a black fingernail as long and sharp as a pocketknife. The tip of the nail twitched toward the keyhole. Cody watched in astonishment as the cell door swung open.

"Come forth," the vampire rasped.

Cody did as he was bidden despite the way his heart galloped in his chest. He passed through the cell doorway, then angled to the right, as far away from Price as he could get.

Cody turned and regarded the vampire, who eyed him with sardonic contempt.

"You have me all alone," Price rumbled. "Now best me."

Cody looked around. "I don't have a weapon."

Price opened first one side of his sleek black frock, then the other. His serrated, icepick teeth garbling his speech, Price said, "Nor do I."

When Cody made no move to attack, Price gestured toward the cell. "Would you like to take refuge in your sanctuary?"

Cody's breath came in insufficient heaves. He clenched his fists, waited for inspiration to strike, but the only thing that struck him was an insane urge to run. If only there were some place to run *to*...

Price's orange eyes glowed, the vampire suddenly enraged. "*Are you not a man? Have you no dignity at all?*"

Cody felt a dull heat kindle at the nape of his neck.

"We take your wife from you," Price said, his orange eyes blazing. "We humiliate you before an entire town. You follow us like some obsequious cur who follows its master even after it has been turned out of its home. You witness the murder and the butchery of untold victims." Price stepped toward him, the tendons of his neck thick and corded. "Yet you still cannot muster enough mettle to strike me?"

Cody strode at Price, cocked a fist, swung. But the moment before Cody's fist slammed into Price's face, Price whipped his head aside, seized Cody two-handed by the shirtfront, pivoted, and hurled him through the air. Cody collided with the stone wall and landed on the desk. The impact snapped the spindly desk legs like brittle twigs, and Cody, riding the desktop like a child's sled, came crashing down on the unforgiving floor.

Price chortled, but Cody scarcely noticed it. His hand, as if directed by some primitive survival instinct, had closed on one of the slender desk legs. Cody regarded it in mute desperation. The bottom of the desk leg was circular, but the broken end had been splintered halfway down its length, leaving the upper tip as sharp as an arrowhead.

Or a stake.

Cody began to rise.

"Resourceful," Price remarked. "No wonder you were able to best Dmitri."

Cody said nothing, only clenched the short spear as tightly as he could, his eyes flicking repeatedly to Price's chest.

"Perhaps you'd like some help," Price rasped. And Cody watched with a mixture of suspicion and bemusement as Price spread his frock coat and tore open his white shirt. The vampire tapped his bare chest with an index finger. "Here. I will give you one opportunity."

Cody's eyes narrowed. "You're bluffing."

"*Do it now!*" Price roared.

With a savage grunt, Cody slammed the makeshift spear into Price's chest, the shard of wood sinking easily into Price's flesh. The splintered desk leg was over three feet long, and at least a third of that slid into the centre of Price's chest before the friction of the vampire's ribs, lungs and tissue brought it to a halt. Price staggered backward into the door, beyond which Sheriff Bittner was hollering to see if everything was all right. Cody was about to scour the jail for some previously undetected escape route when the sight of Price sliding the spear out of his chest made Cody's hope congeal.

Cody stared in mute dismay as the desk leg was drawn slowly out of the vampire's chest. Cody gaped at the smear of crimson on the wood. "How the hell can you—"

"It's only a play," Price said. "Do you really believe we would divulge a means of destroying us? After all you've seen these past several days, I can't believe you'd be so naïve."

With an effortless tug, Price extracted the stake from his chest. A steady trickle of blood issued from the hole, but the vampire behaved as if he were in no pain at all. Price chucked the bloody table leg aside.

Price flung Cody through the cell doorway and landing on the urine-stained floor. The cell door snicked shut behind him. Cody turned in time to see Price moving toward the door. The vampiric features were metamorphosing into human ones again. Despite the gaping wound in his chest, Price behaved as though nothing extraordinary had just occurred. The vampire buttoned up his frock coat, brushed his long brown curls out of his eyes and grasped the doorknob, which quivered in his grip. Bittner was rattling it from the other side and shouting angry curses through the door.

Price glanced down, taking stock of himself. Unhurriedly, the vampire straightened his coat, palmed sweat from his forehead and undid the door bolt.

On the instant Bittner came blundering in, the overweight man moving with the graceless energy of a frightened heifer. "What the hell's happening in here, Price? I thought I heard—" Bittner broke off, noticing the vermilion trail Price had left. "Say, you're bleeding."

"It's nothing," Price said.

"The hell it is," Bittner said. "You're bleedin' like—"

"*Sheriff.*"

Bittner shut up fast. He regarded Price with immediate trepidation.

Price went on in a calmer tone. "You will guard Mr. Wilson until the show tonight. At that time, you and your men will escort him to the saloon for our show."

A stupid, childlike grin spread on Bittner's face. "I can't wait to see it, Mr. Price. I bet it's grand."

Price's eyes locked on Cody's. "'Grand' doesn't begin to capture its glory, Sheriff Bittner. This will be our greatest performance ever."

And with that, Price went out.

CHAPTER FIFTEEN

According to the clock hung above the finely crafted mahogany bar at Marguerite's, it was nearing ten o'clock. A gaunt old pianist plinked out some maudlin song with inexpert enthusiasm, yet you could scarcely hear the out-of-tune upright piano over the noise generated by the drunken patrons. A barber's chair sat untenanted beside the piano, despite the fact that damn near every man present tonight was in dire need of a shearing. In the main gathering room, there were nearly sixty men drinking whiskey – the kind Cody's dad referred to as tarantula juice – swapping jokes and trying to one-up one another. Most of the patrons, Cody noticed without surprise, were armed. Despite the fact that the shoes on many of them were little more than tired scraps of leather held together by fraying thread and blind faith, these men still had ample funds to keep themselves in whiskey and firearms. Cody wondered how many of them had children and how well those children ate.

There was only one waitress present, a harried young woman with lank black hair and a permanent expression of nervous tension carved into her face. Cody couldn't blame her for being nervous. Marguerite and Eliza were nowhere to be seen, so not only did the young woman have to serve drinks to the entire assembly of ruffians, she had to pour them as well. Several men shouted complaints about her tardiness every time she passed. Cody thought it just as well that the drink service was delayed tonight. It wouldn't hurt the patrons of Marguerite's to slow down their alcohol consumption, and a bit more sobriety could only enhance the overall mood in here.

Thinking of Marguerite, Cody's eyes happened on the doorway beyond the bar that led to the kitchen. It was closed. Frowning, Cody glanced over at the stairway leading to the second storey and saw with surprise that a steel accordion gate had been extended there, effectively closing off the upper floor. His frown deepened.

Was it common practice for Marguerite to block that passageway, or did it have something to do with the devils and their show?

The men ceased playing cards and billiards when Horton peeked around the curtain's edge and announced the play would begin shortly. If Horton spotted Cody in the audience, he didn't let on.

Cody sat in the third row – there were six rows total – between Sheriff Bittner and the deputy named Boom Catterson. This man was plumper than the sheriff, though not nearly so tall. Like Sheriff Bittner's, Boom's hat was ill-fitting, but unlike the sheriff, Boom did not sport a brown Stetson. Instead, the sweating, clean-shaven man favoured a prim grey bowler hat with a green feather tucked into its band.

If it were only these two men, Bittner and Boom Catterson, guarding him, Cody would feel confident in surprising them and either escaping through the doors or disarming one of them to make it a fair fight.

But Slim Keeley was another matter.

Marguerite's ex-husband stood a short way off, leaning against a wooden post. There were complex spirals and curlicues inlaid in the post, no doubt the work of Marguerite's father. Cody pictured the man sweating over the woodworking, the carpenter putting in long hours to create a design that few would ever appreciate.

Least of all a man like Slim Keeley.

Keeley's horsey face was pinched in a perpetual squint, one Cody figured the guy had spent long hours practicing in the mirror. Slim smoked one cigarette after another, rolling the next one before the first was finished. Slim would lean like that, his tall frame performing each duty with studied casualness, his hands in languorous but constant motion. The rolling of a cigarette. The tossing aside and the grinding of the butts with a bootheel. The lighting of the next one. An occasional sip from a silver hip flask.

Gradually, as though he'd been aware of Cody's scrutiny the entire time, Slim Keeley swivelled his head and squinted at him. The man's black Stetson shadowed his eyes, but beneath that Cody thought he discerned the ghost of a smile.

Cody turned back to the stage, unaccountably and totally enraged.

"Slim don't like you much, does he?" a man in front of Cody

said. The man was sloppy, the black beard surrounding his wet russet lips reminding Cody unpleasantly of a wild tangle of pubic hair wreathing some woman's labia.

Cody met the man's mordant stare and considered telling him to go hump a goat.

But Sheriff Bittner reached forward and clapped the man on the shoulder. "This here's Deputy John Ebright. Unless you want him to whup your ass the way Slim did earlier, I recommend you show him the respect a man in his position's owed."

Cody gave a faint shake of the head. "His position? Sheriff Bittner, I don't call being your lackey a position of much prestige."

"Careful, Wilson," Bittner said. "John's a hell of a shot with them Schofields."

Cody let his gaze wander down to the man's hips, where, sure enough, there hung a pair of .45 calibre Schofield pistols. Cody said, "My dad's got one of those."

Ebright had turned most of the way around in his chair, and now he patted the grips of his guns. "I got two. And I don't give a shit what your dad carries. This is the same gun Virgil Earp used against the Clantons."

Cody nodded. "I expect Virgil only owns one Schofield. A good shot like him wouldn't require two guns."

Ebright's swollen red lips spread in a nasty grin. "I carry the extra one just in case a kid-fucker like you comes to Mesquite. Kid-fuckers deserve to eat more lead than the average criminal."

Soft laughter to Cody's left. It came from Slim Keeley, who tipped John Ebright an approving wink and commenced rolling a cigarette. Cody remembered the way the son of a bitch had waylaid him earlier, not even giving him a chance to defend himself. He wanted to call the cocksucker over here now, challenge him to a fair fight.

With an effort, Cody held his tongue.

As the minutes ticked down and the crowd of smelly men became restless, Cody's thoughts tended more and more toward Slim Keeley. It was a fool's pastime, he realised, to waste his mental energy on the tall deputy, but now that the image had grabbed ahold of his mind, it bored in with the obduracy of a nightmare: Slim Keeley mounting

Marguerite several years ago on the same bed on which Cody had lain earlier today. Marguerite gloriously naked, offering herself up to her husband. Keeley thrusting up into Marguerite and making her bite her wrist to stifle her cries of pleasure.

Why are you torturing yourself with thoughts like that? Cody's father asked. It had been a common litany around their ranch when Cody was growing up. Cody would become obsessed with some perceived wrong he'd committed and brood about it instead of letting go of it. Once, at around the age of eleven, Cody had gotten runner-up in a spelling contest and had proceeded to rip his hair out in clumps. For weeks Cody had lost sleep over it, convinced he was a worthless simpleton who'd never be as smart as his father. When Jack Wilson assured his son that the spelling of *hippopotamus* would have no bearing on Cody's success in life, Cody had informed him that it wasn't the misspelling that haunted Cody to such a degree – it was the fact that Cody had *known* the word but had forgotten it under pressure. And wasn't the ability to do well under pressure, the eleven-year-old Cody had asked his father, something that *would* have a bearing on how successful he'd be?

His father had smiled wearily and told Cody he didn't have to be perfect.

Inside his head, Cody had answered that his father wouldn't have put an extra *m* in hippopotamus.

Nor, Cody thought now, would Jack Wilson have married a faithless tart. Nor stand idly by while the tart humiliated him. Nor let the bastards who wrought that humiliation on him get away with it unscathed.

Cody's fists balled into tight knots.

And now he realised why he'd been brought to witness this foul drama again. He knew why Price had taken such pains to make sure he was present for what was about to take place, as well as the reason why Cody was so thoroughly guarded by corrupt lawmen. For what Cody would witness tonight might indeed drive him crazy. Hell, he recognised how close to madness he already was. Bone weary and stabbed in the leg and grieving not one loss, but two. He hadn't seen Willet since this morning, and the knowledge that the boy's disappearance was largely due to Cody's negligence sat in his belly like a coiled rattlesnake. He'd met a friend in Marguerite, who in time might have developed into more than a friend – much more – had they been given the opportunity to know each other better. But they'd only been acquainted long enough for Cody to become attached to her, and that too harkened back to his father's wry cracks about him: "Boy, you fall for every pretty thing you see."

The words had been spoken in jest when Cody was but a boy, but when the tendency toward infatuation, if anything, became magnified with age, the jest turned into a fret and finally a caution. His father had spoken loudest when he'd met and fallen for Angela McCarrick: "You always have been one to make plans before you even courted a girl."

But Cody, wildly smitten and more than a little aroused by the mere thought of the leggy blonde from the other side of Escondido, had told his dad to mind his own business. Then to mind his own *damn* business. And from there things had deteriorated between them.

In retrospect, he could see Jack Wilson had been dead-on about Angela, but he suspected the man would happily approve of Cody's courting Marguerite. The fact of this – the notion that his father would recognise in Marguerite exactly what Cody saw, the quickness of Cody's affections toward her be damned – somehow made what was about to happen so much worse. And this too, Cody was bitterly certain, Adam Price understood.

When the kerosene lamps dimmed and the hoots and catcalls erupted around him, Cody steeled himself as best he could for the opening scene. The play would begin as it always did, with a pretty young maiden making her unsuspecting way through the forest. Tonight that maiden would be played by Marguerite. Debasing her while Cody bore witness was the last thing the devils had planned before they finally murdered him. Of this Cody had no doubt.

But when the brilliant limelight illuminated the maiden onstage and the crowd of men sighed in happy lust, Cody was spared the ultimate indignity of seeing the woman he'd just begun to hold dear made the plaything of the devils. The woman wearing the virginal white dress was someone he'd been sure he'd never see again.

The woman was Angela.

"Holy hell, that's one fine lady!" a slurry voice called out from the dark crowd.

There came a smattering of assent from the glassy-eyed audience, but mainly the men just watched, gape-mouthed, as Cody's once-wife strode unselfconsciously across the stage. Though the white dress sheathed her all the way to her ankles, the sultry way she walked marked her as one of the devils.

Converted, Cody thought. *She's been converted to the darkness, been made a willing member of their bestial cult.* Though she was more beautiful than she'd ever been, she wore her otherness like a new, tainted skin. And going back to the night of her supposed death, Cody understood how easily they had fooled him.

After awakening from the brutal face-stomping Horton had given him and finding the bastard still screwing Angela, Cody had staggered to his feet only to be pummelled by Penders, who'd been stationed just inside the bedroom to stop Cody from interrupting the festivities. Or Penders was simply watching the pair have sex. Regardless, the beating Cody received at the hands of the huge man had been far worse than the stomp he'd gotten from Horton, and this time he'd lost consciousness for several hours.

When he awoke, it was well past ten o'clock, which meant the second and final Tonuco performance of *The Return of the Maiden Carmilla* had already begun. Though the clanging in Cody's head was savage enough to make him want to stick a gun in his mouth, he got up again and soldiered through the pain and humiliation as well as he could.

Cody packed the saddlebags with some necessaries, went out and mounted Sally. And though every step the old mare took sent glancing spires of pain through his skull, he was able to reach his neighbour's ranch by ten thirty.

Ethan Griggs was a gentle soul in his late fifties who cared more for relaxing with his family than he did making money, and as a result, his humble little ranch had never prospered. Three of the man's children and three times as many grandchildren all somehow lived on the ranch, and outside of being cramped, they seemed to get along fine. On many occasions Griggs or one of his progeny had done Cody a good turn, so Cody knew he could count on the man for help. Bailey Griggs, Ethan's youngest son, would often kid Cody about purchasing Cody's ranch so Bailey's own brood could have some room to breathe. And had Bailey Griggs the funds to do so, Cody might have actually considered it. But like his father, Bailey barely scraped by.

It was Bailey who answered the door when Cody showed up that night to ask for help taking care of his cattle.

"How long you figure on being gone?" Bailey had asked.

Cody had answered that he had no idea, which was true enough. He didn't mention the possibility that he might commit murder that night or be killed himself, and therefore might never be returning to reclaim his stock. But time was wasting, and he sure as hell didn't feel like explaining the whole thing to Bailey Griggs. So Cody told him it might be awhile and that he'd compensate him fairly for looking after his ranch. And with Bailey and his wife Esther watching after him, Cody rode off toward town.

He figured the play would end sometime between eleven and midnight, and it was likely that Angela and the acting troupe would be pulling out of Tonuco shortly after that. Somehow, he managed to reach the outskirts by eleven. He tethered Sally to a gnarled old juniper tree just outside of town and waited, though out in the open as he was, the febrile New Mexico breeze did his headache no favours. Crouched on a hillside, he figured he and Sally were hidden well enough to go unnoticed. On the far side of the road, the terrain dropped off severely into a rocky arroyo.

Just after midnight, he heard the sable coach approaching. Moments later, the six quarter horses appeared, their sinuous muscles flexing and their bodies black as pitch. The figure leading the coach was likely Horton, but Cody wasn't certain.

Suddenly worried they'd be seen, Cody untied Sally and led her as far up the hillside as he could. Tethering her again, he hustled back toward the road and hunkered low in the hope of catching a glimpse of Angela through the coach windows. He was armed, of course, but he had no real intention of taking on the whole troupe – at least not yet. So it was with a nasty jolt of surprise that he watched the sextet of black quarter horses pull up only thirty or so yards from where he'd hidden. It was a further surprise to see Angela step out of the coach and scamper up the hill toward him. For a brief and hideous moment he was sure she was aware of his presence. Then she'd turned her back to him, hiked up her dress, squatted and taken a piss in the gravelly dust.

Shaking with nervous energy and unaccountably embarrassed despite the fact that he'd seen this woman naked countless times, Cody had regarded the .32 in his right hand until she'd finished and stood up again.

He'd seen Angela climb into the black deathwagon, had watched in sick humiliation as the many hands of the devils had groped at her from the shadows of the coach and drawn her greedily inside. When the coach door knocked shut, the prurient laughter within gave way to vile rutting noises – rapturous moans from Angela and porcine grunts from the men. Even as the unseen spectacle unfolded within the black coach, Cody had wondered how many of the men were at her, how one woman could take on five of them at once. But that thought scattered when Angela's moans spread into wails, and the easy rocking of the black coach became an arrhythmic thrashing. The door was thrust open, and despite the late hour, there had been enough of a moon for Cody to see gouts of blood splashing out of the opening. It had been Penders who'd appeared bearing what looked like the remnants of a slaughterhouse kill. The gory mass of bones and flesh and viscera clutched to his broad chest, Penders had crossed to the drop-off and heaved it all into the gorge. Cody hadn't bothered checking to make sure the remains were Angela's because he had no reason to believe they *weren't* hers.

But now in Marguerite's saloon, watching Angela cast fearful glances into the stage forest – the same portable set the devils used in all their shows – Cody understood how easily he'd been fooled. He could imagine Angela in there with the devils while Horton drove the team and Penders disposed of the slop. Had she been snickering at Cody while they hoodwinked him? Had Price or one of the Seneslavs been screwing her at the same moment Cody mourned her death? He figured yes on both counts.

And whose remains had it been that Penders had dumped? Did it matter? In the days since Cody'd first encountered the devils, he had seen them kill indiscriminately. Men, women, the very old, the very young. It didn't matter. And thinking about Price's ghastly transformation...the ageless evil in those infernal eyes...Cody suspected Price, at least, had been doing this sort of thing for much longer than anyone might believe. Thousands of years? Longer?

And right on cue Price came skulking from the darkness and onto the stage. But where before he'd been flanked by the Seneslav twins, there was now only one brother – *The Dragon*, Penders had called him – creeping to his left, near the edge of the stage. Adam Price and Dragomir Seneslav were almost upon Angela, whose back was dutifully turned, when Dragomir's colourless eyes performed a quick scan of the audience.

And fixed on Cody.

The effect was instantaneous. Dragomir's role as a servant to Adam Price was forgotten, and in its place arose an unreasoning hatred. Had Sheriff Bittner, John Ebright, Boom Catterson and that bastard Slim Keeley not been watching Cody, he'd have bolted the moment the Dragon locked eyes with him. But there was no way to escape without being gunned down by one of the lawmen, and Cody suspected that even if he did evade Bittner and his deputies, Dragomir would run him down and rend him to pieces before he breached the doorway.

Dragomir looked for a moment like he might do exactly that. He even began to transform, though Cody was sure that the yokels surrounding him counted it as part of the show. The square underjaw began to elongate, the muscles there hopping and bulging. Dragomir stepped toward Cody, but Price turned and hissed something at him. Dragomir paused, mouth still opened unnaturally wide, the eyes glowing the way no human eyes ever could, but he didn't make a move to relent. Price strode toward him, his expression hard, and clamped a hand on Dragomir's shoulder. He muttered something again, this time in some foreign-sounding language Cody had never heard before, and the change in Dragomir began to reverse itself.

A relieved exhalation seemed to ripple through the audience.

A man in front of Cody turned back to Sheriff Bittner and said, "Some show, huh, Sheriff?"

Bittner's voice was laced with poorly concealed relief. "I expect so."

The man in front of them giggled, a high, juvenile sound, and leered at Boom Catterson. "I damn near shat myself when that guy's eyes turned orange. How about you, Boomer?"

Before Boom could reply, Bittner said, "That'll be enough, Luke."

The one named Luke giggled again, unabashed, and turned back to the stage. Cody frowned a moment, flailing for a scrap of memory, and soon he had it. Luke Lind, the man's name was. Cody had spilled the drunkard's urine all over himself in the jail cell. Lind turned, grinning, to the guy next to him, and Cody caught a glimpse of the man's missing front teeth. The pitted, unwashed skin. The nose hair so long Lind could braid it if he had the urge.

Studying Lind, Bittner mumbled, "That bastard's got the brains of a two-year-old." Bittner glanced at Boom Catterson, who was still staring uncomfortably at Dragomir. Cody noted the large beads of sweat on Boom's bald forehead. He'd taken his silly bowler hat off and now sat fondling it in his lap.

You know, don't you? Cody thought. *You know something's wrong, but you're too scared to say it. Don't want to lose face in front of Bittner or Slim Keeley. But you suspect.*

Onstage, both Price and Dragomir were closing on Angela again, but this time she whirled before they got too close and let loose with an earsplitting shriek. Cody knew her well enough to know she was enjoying every moment of this, but to the men in the audience she was every bit the scared virgin she was meant to portray. Before Price could grab hold of her, Angela bounded offstage. Price and Dragomir followed, and moments later the lights dimmed.

It was too dark to see precisely what was happening now, but Cody made out the vague forms of the devils rushing around, changing scenery, the forest giving way to an old barn.

A couple minutes later the lamps were rekindled to reveal Horton, shirtless, shovelling invisible hay with a pitchfork. Like she had that first night at the Crooked Tree, Angela appeared shortly after, throwing frightened glances over her shoulder. They exchanged approximately the same lines as they had in Tonuco, Angela telling Horton about the vampires pursuing her.

Then things began to diverge from the play Cody had witnessed before. Rather than shielding Angela as Price and Dragomir approached, Horton merely moved upstage and pretended to peer into the darkness. Coming back to her, Horton shook his head and told her everything was clear; there were no monsters headed their way.

"Then I suppose I owe you a debt of gratitude," Angela said, her manner instantly changing.

Here we go again, Cody thought.

Angela reached back, untied a string between her shoulder blades, and suddenly the whole dress was pooling around her feet, leaving her completely naked.

"Godamighty," Bittner whispered.

Cody slumped back in his seat, glanced around at the men so he wouldn't have to watch the happenings onstage. Cody saw in the men's faces what he figured he'd see. Most of them were ogling Angela's naked body; here and there Cody could discern guys elbowing their neighbours and prodding each other to make sure they really were seeing what they thought they were seeing.

At least it's not in Tonuco, Cody thought. *At least it's not in front of the people I went to church with and did business with.*

He threw an incurious glance at the stage and discovered without much surprise that Horton was naked now and that Angela was wrapping one sinuous leg around him. The pagan aura of the scene was only enhanced by the glare of the limelight directed at the pair from above the stage.

"Holy shit," Luke Lind said.

Cody looked away as Angela leaned back and began to undulate with Horton.

"That ain't proper!" someone nearer the stage called out, and a dozen voices promptly shouted the protester down.

As one, the all-male audience leaned forward while the pair on stage copulated, and though there were a few appreciative comments, most of the men simply stared in rapt, aching silence. Cody eyed Boom Catterson, who was one of the only men not gawking, who was instead studying the bowler in his lap. To Cody he looked like a chastened little boy engaged in an act of contrition. The man was sweating so badly he looked like he'd been submerged in a vat of cooking oil.

Angela was moaning, and so was Horton. Evidently they'd abandoned the vampire angle of the scene. They were no more concerned with Adam Price and Dragomir Seneslav than they were with contracting venereal diseases. Cody turned to his right and noticed with grim disgust that Sheriff Bittner had also removed his hat, but that he'd done so to conceal the hand he'd snuck inside his trousers. Cody looked quickly up from Bittner to spy Slim Keeley still leaning against the carved post, still smoking a cigarette. The man behaved as though there was a live sex show at Marguerite's every night.

Cody's thoughts turned again to Marguerite. What had they done with her? Was it possible they still planned to use her in this abominable farce?

After an interminable session of fucking, the stage lights winked out.

At first there was only dry-mouthed silence, but soon a scattered applause began to sound. It didn't take long for the applause to swell, and before Cody knew it, the whole assembly had risen in a bellowing, hat-tossing ovation.

Good God, he thought. *They act like they just witnessed something wonderful. If they only knew the truth about Angela and Horton. If only they knew that both of them were monsters.*

The clapping began to dissipate. Cody realised at once he'd missed a potential opportunity to escape. When would the lights be out again, the whole audience distracted? He chided himself for his inaction. He turned and had begun to measure the distance to the door when he became aware of someone watching him. Cody narrowed his eyes to peer through the murk until he distinguished who it was.

Slim Keeley. Of course. The tall man was watching Cody as though he knew everything that had gone on since the devils first arrived in Tonuco. Was it possible? Could Adam Price and the rest have spilled everything to the sheriff and his deputies just so they'd know how agitated Cody might get when Angela performed her whore routine again?

It was entirely possible, he now realised. Likely even. Goddamn them. Goddamn Price and Horton, goddamn Keeley and Bittner.

They were all against him. They didn't care about Willet. They didn't care about Marguerite.

With another nasty jolt, Cody realised that Keeley probably knew about Cody's crush on Marguerite too. How? Who the hell knew? But the knowledge in that gaze was more than sheer mockery – it was gloating. Sneering, unmitigated gloating.

"And now," a voice interrupted, nearly making Cody cry out in surprise, "we introduce a new actress into our production. A lovely young thing with whom many of you will be familiar…"

And here it is, Cody thought. *This will make it perfect. Marguerite will come out and Penders will bang her or Price will or maybe even Angela. Who gives a damn? I'll be dead soon anyway. Why not get it over with now before they inflict yet another degradation on me?*

Cody had started to rise when a new figure sauntered out onto the now-illuminated stage, but he froze halfway to his feet.

"Sit yourself, Wilson. Before I whup your skinny ass."

Cody scarcely registered Bittner's words or the rough grip on his forearm. His mind raced while he struggled to calculate how this new development altered things.

"I said sit *down*, boy. Before I shoot your ass dead right here."

He hasn't noticed, Cody thought. *He hasn't even looked yet.*

Boom Catterson leaned across Cody and said in a low voice, "Bobby?"

"Shut up, Boom," the sheriff spat. "This pissant is hard of hearin'."

"But Sheriff—"

"Goddammit, Boom!"

"*Atta girl, Eliza!*" a voice from the crowd called, and Bobby Bittner finally turned toward the stage. His mouth fell open.

The one named Eliza, the barmaid whom Marguerite had dubbed Bittner's favourite, was strutting across the stage toward Penders.

And unbuttoning her dress.

CHAPTER SIXTEEN

Bittner got up immediately.

"Show us them titties, 'Liza!" another patron called.

Moments later, she did, the front of her light green dress peeling open to reveal small but lovely breasts. They were damn near phosphorescent in the glare of the limelight.

Luke Lind whirled and leered at Sheriff Bittner. "It's about time the rest of us got to see those sweet little dugs!"

Bittner balled his fists. "Shut yer fuckin' mouth, Luke."

Cody glanced beyond Bittner's tensed form and saw that Keeley was eyeing the sheriff too, a pensive look contracting Keeley's features. Not worry, but something more guarded and alert than Cody had seen in the man's face thus far.

Penders met Eliza in the middle of the stage and took hold of the dress, which was bunched around the young girl's slim midriff. Cody figured her for twenty at the oldest, likely younger. She wriggled happily as Penders dragged the dress down her legs, revealing a nubile white body that showed no sign of Sheriff Bittner's slimy depredations.

The crowd hooted at the sight of the girl's scarlet thatch of pubic hair, her tight little bottom. Many of them stood, gesticulating toward the stage as though confirming for their companions that what they were witnessing was in fact real.

Bittner stood immobile, his mouth working mutely. He cast unbelieving looks at the men around him. Cody sank back into his chair, eyeing the Walker six-shooter on Bittner's hip. The damn thing was a flap holster, else Cody would've been able to remove it easily. Still, he wondered if Bittner would even notice, so great was his bewilderment.

More of the men stood up, and more delighted whoops erupted from the audience. Through the shifting crowd, Cody could see that

Penders had the young girl draped over a table and was ramming her from behind. She cried out as he thrust into her, but she didn't sound unhappy.

Bittner, however, was livid.

John Ebright stood and made as if to hold the sheriff back, but Bittner shouldered past him with a muttered oath. The sheriff waded forward, knocking a wooden chair over and shoving Luke Lind out of the way. Lind bumped into a man nearly as big as Penders and whose shaggy head of hair reminded Cody of the illustrations he'd seen of grizzly bears back in grade school. Lind threw up his hands, palms outward, to mollify the big brute, but Grizzly seized him by the shoulders, pivoted and hurled him into a group of unsuspecting audience members. Cody reckoned Lind's flying body took out at least four men. The ones who'd been knocked down collided with several others, which of course led to half a dozen scuffles.

Bittner stalked forward, oblivious of the pandemonium he'd created, until he'd jostled his way to the stage. Now that the path had been cleared, Cody could clearly see Penders tupping the red-haired girl with barbaric abandon. Eliza was howling with pleasure. Or perhaps it was agony. From the sounds she was making, it was difficult to tell. And despite the scattered brawls that had broken out, most of the men in Marguerite's saloon were still transfixed by the sex show.

Cody tensed as John Ebright came forward to stop Sheriff Bittner. Boom Catterson sat there in mute dismay. Without further consideration, Cody whirled and climbed over the wooden chair he'd been sitting on. The men behind him parted wordlessly as he passed, too entranced by the sight of Eliza to notice the prisoner escaping. Cody had gotten past the back row of men and was preparing to sprint toward the front door when a shape materialised to his right. Cody didn't even get an arm up to fend the man off before Slim Keeley slammed him against the wall, one of the man's forearms pressed against Cody's chest, the other holding his long-barreled Colt Peacemaker to the underside of Cody's jaw.

"Bittner gets distracted too easily," Slim said in a low, drawling voice. The circular tip of the Peacemaker dug into Cody's flesh. "Pussy can do that to a man."

Cody struggled to breathe. "You gotta let me go."

Slim's hateful face swam nearer. "I'm listenin'."

The pungent odour of tobacco smoke surrounded Cody like a shroud. He searched Slim's face for some trace of human emotion, some semblance of compassion, but all he found was the same deadly calculation he'd seen in the man's features all evening.

Still, Cody had to try. "Don't you care that they've got your ex-wife?"

A venomous smile twisted Slim's scar of a mouth. "Is the fact that you pine for her supposed to make us buddies or something?"

Cody shook his head, grappled for the words. The gun in his jaw bit deeper.

"Naw," Slim said evenly. "I don't think you two did sleep together. You wouldn't have been man enough for Margie."

"They'll kill her," Cody said. "They turned my wife into something..." *God*, he thought. *How to phrase it and not sound deranged?*

But he realised Slim wasn't even listening.

"You want to hear what kind of a lay she was, boy? Whether Margie likes it rough, wants you to slap her around a little?"

Beyond Slim's sneering face, Cody saw Bittner climbing onto the stage. There was a roar of protest from the crowd, and a dozen sets of hands pawed at the sheriff to impede his progress. Penders was slapping Eliza's milky buttocks now and thrusting into her with such force that he appeared to be trying to kill her rather than merely to couple with her.

Bittner's voice shrilled above the crowd for them to *Get back, get back*, but the men refused to relinquish their hold on him. Bittner lashed out, caught one man in the forehead with the butt of his Walker. Someone suggested that Bittner be shot. No one drew on the sheriff right away, but someone did land a wild haymaker on his jaw. Stunned, Bittner pistol-whipped the man, splashing blood against the stage front, and then several patrons went for Bittner. Bittner was demanding that they leave him alone, but his voice was swallowed by the angry mob. Someone pulled a knife. The cacophony was great enough now to draw Slim Keeley's gaze away from Cody.

With one motion Cody ripped his head away from Slim's

Peacemaker – the steel notch of its sight carving a narrow rut in Cody's jaw – and pumped a knee into Slim's groin. The tall man doubled over, but rather than scurrying for the door, Cody swung both elbows down into the middle of the man's back. A gunshot exploded and Cody lunged away instinctively, sure the shot had come from Slim's Colt. But as Slim hit the floor and his gun skittered away under the chairs, Cody heard another shot and looked up to see Bittner firing into the crowd. One man had already fallen, gutshot by the sheriff, and another was pinwheeling his arms as he staggered backward into the stupefied cluster of onlookers. Onstage, Penders had stopped punishing Eliza and was now striding toward Bittner, who had his back to the huge, naked man. Eliza was standing erect, watching after Penders in what might have been disappointment but making no move to cover herself. Bittner fired again, and a third man went down, but now Cody could see others in the crowd reaching for their pistols, their shock at the sheriff's jealous rampage having begun to abate.

As the man sworn to protect Mesquite's populace continued to massacre innocent townspeople, everything went haywire. Penders neared Bittner. Evidently remembering her former allegiance to Bittner, Eliza darted at Penders, perhaps to prevent him from harming the sheriff. The red-haired barmaid slapped Penders in the middle of the back, but the moment she did, the huge vampire whirled, seized her by the throat and began to squeeze. Eliza's bare legs scissored wildly, her face going a brilliant red. Like it was nothing at all, Penders wrapped his free arm around her waist, jerked up on her neck, and then her head was tumbling from her body like a weed someone had yanked. Her headless body slumped against Penders, a happy fountain of blood bathing the front of the huge man's naked body.

Several men screamed in terror.

But like many of the patrons, Bittner was too busy to even notice Eliza's death. Bittner shot a man in the throat, caught another in the forehead. From the crowd to the sheriff's left emerged a little man with a black handlebar mustache. The man's eyes were huge and murderous, but he was having trouble extricating his gun from his leg holster. Just as he jerked the gun free and made to end Sheriff Bittner's odious existence, another shot exploded and the left side of the little man's face disappeared in a scarlet haze. A splatter of flesh and bright red blood hit the burnished wooden stage, and the little man fell. On one side of his mouth, the handlebar mustache still sprouted like a furry caterpillar; on the other his tongue lolled out of the yawning cavity of his missing cheek.

Everyone in the bar turned to see who had shot the little man. Cody just had time to glimpse John Ebright's surprised face before spinning and hustling toward the door.

Cody knew Slim Keeley was scuttling toward the Colt, knew that Slim would recover it any moment and turn it on him. Cody was two strides from the door when he saw that someone else had gotten it into his head to leave before the violence got any worse. But the blond-haired man staring out the window next to the front door wore a look of horror. He was backpedalling now and had both arms out in a warding off gesture. Cody nearly slammed into him. He looked up and saw what had spooked the man so badly.

Angela's elongated, vampire's face chortled at them through the window. Cody dropped to the floor just as the Spencer rifle she was pointing went off and the blond-haired man flew backward.

Movement in Cody's periphery jerked his attention away from the twitching blond-haired man. Slim Keeley had indeed retrieved his gun, and he was absolutely coming for Cody when he saw the blond-haired man's chest open up and the Spencer rifle on the other side of the window that had done the shooting. Cody thought for sure that Slim would shoot him anyway, though he had a fleeting hope Slim might instead turn his Colt on Angela.

But Slim did neither thing, opting to take cover behind one of the ornate wooden pillars instead. And a good thing too, for the moment he ducked behind the post, Angela fired again and nearly took off Slim's face. The splintered wood and sawdust kicked up by the Spencer's slug blinded Slim for a moment, which gave Cody time to scuttle into the crowd again. *That's the first nice thing you've done for me in a long time, Angela,* he thought. *Thanks for your help, you unholy bitch.*

Cody crawled forward as another gunshot erupted. He gained his feet in time to see Grizzly pistol-whipping a man adjacent to the stage – poor Luke Lind – and then hulking toward Sheriff Bittner, who was now training his gun on Penders.

Evidently deciding that the sheriff would have to deal with Penders and Grizzly on his own, John Ebright had taken cover within the crowd to the right of the stage. With a strident yelp, Boom Catterson sank to all fours and clambered under his chair. Another gun fired, but Cody had no idea from whom the shot came or if it hit anyone. Rather than scattering or heading for the exits, the majority of the audience had simply hunched down so they could still view the goings-on without being killed, while others had followed Boom's lead and taken refuge under their chairs. There were three or four fistfights raging, but what nobody apparently realised was that the real villains were not the ones with guns. That is, unless you counted Angela. The ones the men should have been worried about had just appeared on either side of the stage: Dragon Seneslav and Billy Horton.

And of course, Steve Penders, who was beginning to transform.

"What the hell's going on here?" Sheriff Bittner asked, finally noticing the vampires and Eliza's headless body.

Then the limelight winked out.

And the screaming began.

★ ★ ★

Though the stage lights had been extinguished, there was still enough illumination from the scattered kerosene lamps to see Penders reach for Sheriff Bittner. In the faint orange light put off by the lamps, Steve Penders's blood-slicked face was now a grisly mixture of anticipation and implacable hunger. He no doubt would have killed Bobby Bittner at that moment had someone not fired a gun at him from less than ten feet away. The slug caught him in the throat, and though the tissue there reacted the way human skin was supposed to, the blood that trickled forth from the wound seemed too sparse. And too dark.

Penders glanced at the man who'd shot him, and through the darting figures Cody was able to see that Boom Catterson had finally crawled out from his hiding place to defend his sheriff.

Wrong time to find your courage, Cody thought in the moment before Penders leaped.

Cody couldn't help remembering the night before, the manner in which Penders had clambered up that almost sheer rock face to grab at him and Willet. The huge man's agility was uncanny. Then again, Penders wasn't a man, was he?

When his body slammed into Boom Catterson, the absurd bowler hat went tumbling sideways and the short man was driven back more than a dozen feet, smashing into chairs and an onlooker who'd taken too long to get his ass moving. Boom opened his mouth to scream, but before he found his voice, Penders buried his monstrous, goblin-like face in the man's throat. The only sound that escaped the convulsing deputy was a meaty gurgle, but that might have been Penders's animal noises as he tore through the man's windpipe.

Briefly, Cody toyed with the idea of going for Catterson's gun, which lay a few feet from where the deputy was being eaten, but at that moment, the guy who'd gotten knocked down by Penders began to squeal in pain or terror or both. Screwing up his eyes, Cody saw why.

Without looking up from Boom Catterson's ruined neck, Penders had shot out a hand to seize the man before he could scuttle away. The poor bastard, who'd been trying to sneak to safety on hands and knees, shrilled out a scream that would have been comical under other circumstances. Penders dragged him backward by one skinny ankle. The screaming man flopped over on his back and began kicking at Penders with his free leg. One kick caught Penders in the side of the head. Penders swung his bloody face up and roared. The man's screaming devolved into hysterical sobs. Then Penders reached out, grasped the man's tongue and ripped it out of his mouth. The man jittered, a tide of bloody froth spilling from his lips. Instead of consummating the poor bastard's injury and ending his suffering, Penders took a bite out of the tongue very much the way a normal man would chew on a chicken leg. Meanwhile, the man choked on his own blood.

Horton made a beeline for the first victim he could find, which turned out to be Luke Lind. The unfortunate son of a bitch never even saw the vampire that killed him. One instant Lind was gaping at Boom Catterson's dead body in horror; the next Horton had him facedown on the viscous floor, his powerful fingers prying open the man's back like a pair of shutters. Lind's high-pitched scream devolved into a wet moan. Horton pulled apart Lind's rib cage and buried his face in Lind's exposed lungs. Soon, the only thing still moving on Lind's prostrate body was his right foot, which twitched arrhythmically while Horton fed.

Shots sounded near the foyer. Cody glanced that way and through a shattered window saw that Angela had culled at least two more men with the rifle, while another two or three were now returning fire. Her tenebrous form jolted as the slugs tore into her, but she did not go down. More men joined the assault on the vampire woman serving as their jailer, but before they could surge too near the door, another shape – Price, Cody realised – came knifing out of the shadows to take them down. Cody saw Price knock two of their heads together and watched him take a chomp out of another man's neck before he returned his attention to the stage.

Where Dragomir Seneslav stood glowering at Cody.

Cody immediately went for Boom Catterson's gun – not because he knew exactly where it had fallen and certainly not because he'd gotten over his fear of the massive Steve Penders, who was still rampaging in the vicinity of where the gun had fallen. If anything, Cody was far more terrified of the giant than he'd ever been. But Penders's back was to him – he'd abandoned the severed tongue and was now holding aloft a bellowing, white-haired man who was pretty good-sized himself – and Cody knew if he delayed any longer Dragomir would pounce and begin taking his sadistic revenge.

In the damnably paltry light he scrabbled under the chairs, praying he'd happen upon the gun. His fingers encountered cigarette butts, spilled ashtrays. He upset a half-full spittoon with an elbow. And despite the lukewarm slime that coated his fingers and made him want to retch, he kept at it, crawling around like a blind toddler and hoping against hope he'd locate the gun before Dragon or Penders found him.

His eyes caught a bluish glint a few feet ahead, right beside someone's dead body. *Oh my God*, he thought. *There it is!*

Cody scrambled forward and had actually slapped his fingers over the handle of Boom Catterson's Walker when a bootheel stomped down on the back of his hand. Excruciating pain exploded up his wrist, then grew even more severe as the boot made cruel, grinding arcs on his flesh. Whoever owned the boot was putting his whole weight on Cody's hand, mashing it slowly like it was a cigarette that refused to extinguish. Mouth drawn open in an agonised grimace, Cody pawed at the blue-jeaned leg, exerted what force he could to extricate his hand or at least alleviate the awful pressure on it. Jesus God, he could feel the skin splitting now, the top layer of his hand tearing like wrapping paper.

Grimacing, Cody glanced at the dead body to his right and spotted a huge knife case strapped to the corpse's ankle. Desperately, Cody reached down and clawed at the case until he got the snap open. It didn't occur to him until the moment his fingers closed on the handle of the Bowie knife that it wasn't Penders or Dragomir brutalising his poor, ruined hand. Neither of them wore jeans.

Cody unsheathed the huge Bowie knife, got a good grip.

And pumped it into the meat of the man's thigh.

The tormentor immediately stumbled away, the abrupt freeing of Cody's mutilated hand for some reason accentuating the exquisite pain he felt. Cody howled, grasped the injured hand and gave only a fleeting thought to the Bowie knife he'd left embedded in the thigh of the man who'd hurt him. But of course he knew who it was.

Knew it even before Slim Keeley yanked out the knife, stared venomously at Cody and said, "I'm gonna cut your eyes out with this."

Cody went for the gun. This time he grasped the Walker before Slim could stop him. Cody dove sideways. The Bowie knife whistled down at him and missed his face by mere inches. Cody raised the gun and squeezed the trigger, but Slim had gotten the knife hand up and deflected Cody's wrist with it. It was awkward shooting with his left hand to begin with, and the fact that Slim had thrown off his aim made it impossible to hit his target. The shot went wild, pinged against the wall, and then Slim was lunging at him with the knife, crowding him as much as he could so Cody couldn't get off another shot. Slim swung the knife up and would have gutted him had Cody not staggered backward. Cody's shoulders bumped something large and smelly and yielding, and when he whirled, expecting to see Penders's transformed face, he was relieved to find he'd slammed into Grizzly instead. The giant paid Cody little mind.

Slim attacked again, his body better balanced this time. But Cody had recovered too, and as an orange shaft of lamplight strobed over Slim's contorted face, Cody decided what to do. Rather than firing the Walker straight into Slim Keeley's haughty forehead, Cody tore down at him with a vicious diagonal slash and watched with grim satisfaction as the hard steel barrel dug a ragged trench from Slim's temple to the bridge of his nose, the eyeball in between popping open with a wet splash. The knife stroke that Keeley had begun ended with the knife tumbling forgotten between them. Cody made a mental note to retrieve it later. If he had time.

Slim clamped a hand over his mutilated eye and wailed like a sow birthing a large brood. The tall deputy reeled toward a wooden pillar but got his legs tangled with an overturned chair and pitched forward onto his belly. Cody followed, cold all over now, and kicked Slim as hard as he could in the ass. Slim flopped over, holding his butt with one hand and his haemorrhaging eye with the other.

"Please don't hurt me no more," he was gibbering. "Please don't—"

"You were a big man earlier, weren't you?" Cody growled. "Blindsiding me in front of Marguerite? Kicking me when I couldn't defend myself?" Cody knelt next to him, holding the gun well away in case Slim should take it into his head to grab for it. "You live through this, you ain't gonna be getting much pussy now, are you?"

Raw hope bloomed in the side of Slim's face that hadn't been disfigured. "You mean you're gonna let me go? I'm sorry for what I did to you. I'm sorry for—"

Cody grasped the man's chin and squeezed. "You're a coward, Slim. You abused a good woman and got away with it because you're buddies with that dickweed Bittner, but—" Cody broke off as Slim's good eye shifted to something behind Cody.

Cody whirled, aiming the gun at whatever it was that had snuck up on him, and in the moment before his Walker fired he saw it was Dragomir Seneslav. The first slug caught the shirtless vampire in the belly. The second got him in the side just below the right nipple. Cody squeezed the trigger a third time but only heard a dull click, and it didn't matter anyway because neither of the shots had done a damn bit of good.

What did help was that Cody had instinctively fallen to his right as he fired with his left hand. The heavy chair leg Dragomir had raised above his head and brought down with the force of a sledgehammer missed Cody and crushed Slim Keeley's awestruck face. It staved in Keeley's skull and made what was left of his head look like a pile of ham someone had doused with ketchup. Some of Slim's blood spattered Cody's face, but Cody hardly noticed. He was too busy crab-walking awkwardly away from Dragomir, whose vampiric face suddenly reminded Cody very much of some fairy tale dragon's. The creature stalking him wasn't breathing fire, but dear God, Dragon didn't need to. The fire was in his lambent orange eyes and in his toothy leer. Cody toppled a chair, got his body wedged between a pair of unyielding objects and finally risked turning his head and losing sight of Dragomir a moment so he could navigate the bottleneck.

The moment he did, he knew he'd made a mistake. Rather than allowing him to get away, Dragomir snagged one of Cody's pant legs, lifted him a foot off the ground and heaved him bodily toward the stage. The room swirled like some hellish kaleidoscope for an endless instant. Then, just when Cody thought he'd land on the stage and survive mostly unscathed, the side of his head and upper body hammered the edge of the stage and he collapsed, insensate, to the floor.

Groggily, Cody peered up and spied, though the world was doing a slow, sickening leftward lean, Adam Price squeezing a man's head until the man's eyes trickled blood. The body twitched in its death throes, but the head that Price clutched remained motionless as Price licked the rivulets of blood from the man's cheeks. Price inclined his face to the ceiling, savouring the taste of the blood with a look of orgasmic joy. *Jesus Christ*, Cody thought, unable to look away. *Just like a man sampling wine at a fancy restaurant.*

Cody began to turn away, but movement in his periphery drew his attention back to Price. The king vampire had discarded his victim and had snatched the lone waitress from her hiding place under a table. The poor girl shrieked in terror. Cody's vision was gauzy from his collision with the stage, but he saw clearly enough the way the woman's yowls nettled Price, as well as the way, a moment later, Price wrenched her head sideways to silence her forever. Price bit into the limp girl's neck and began to suck.

Cody snapped alert as something clumped down on the floor beside him. It was an arm, but whose arm it was he had no idea. It had been severed so high on the victim's body that a good part of the shoulder comprised the sloppy, ragged end that, mercifully, lay farthest from Cody's face. The fingers, only inches away, twitched accusatorily at him.

Cody forced himself to sit up. His head was a hornet's nest of agony, but it was preferable to being dead. He knew if he didn't figure things out quickly, a headache would be the least of his worries.

His bleary eyes swept the crowd. He made out Dragomir and his elongated face watching him motionlessly from fifteen feet away. To Dragomir's immediate right, Horton had his face buried in the shoulder of a dead man. Cody shivered. *At least I know where the arm came from now.*

Gunshots exploded from the area near the front door. Cody glanced that way and saw that a desperate band of survivors had marshalled their forces and were pouring lead into Angela and Penders, who were barring egress. Angela was streaming blood, not only from the continual gunshots but from the glass she must have plunged through to get inside the bar. Her jaw was rimed with slick, shiny blood, and Cody understood with faint revelation that she had entered not only to prevent the patrons from escaping, but to get at them as well. Confirming this was a pair of lifeless bodies heaped near where she stood, her body jagging with the impact of gunfire.

When Cody's gaze fastened again on Dragomir, he was stunned to see the vampire was no longer leering at him in triumph, was instead joining Horton and Price in a sneak attack on the fifteen or so men who were advancing on Penders and Angela. Penders was roaring with pained ferocity, and Angela had lowered to one knee. Both their bodies were leaking from a score of places, Penders's immense gut a glimmering sack of black and red.

Rather than joining the battle in the foyer, Sheriff Bobby Bittner was retreating toward the bar. The sheriff's Colt hung forgotten at his side, on the man's slack face a look of craven stupefaction. Bittner gaped at the trio of vampires approaching the band of survivors, many of whom had stopped to reload. Bittner was close enough to warn them, to at least give the men a chance before they were blindsided by Price and his comrades. But Bittner clearly had no intention of helping anyone but himself.

Cody glanced around, his keen eyes strafing the floor for a weapon. He found it on the hip of a decapitated man. Opening the holster, Cody saw right away that luck had been with him. A double-action Smith & Wesson .38. Damn near new. Cody checked it, found it fully loaded. The poor bastard who owned the thing had gotten his head ripped off without firing a single shot.

The gun at his side, Cody rose and started to run, but it wasn't toward the gang of shooters or the vampires he hurried.

It was toward Sheriff Bittner.

CHAPTER SEVENTEEN

Bittner had reached the corner of the bar before he noticed Cody bearing down on him. The sheriff raised his Colt, but he did it gradually, almost like a man in a dream. Cody kicked the gun from his hand, reared back and let loose with a punch to the man's stubbly jaw that made Cody happy to be alive. Bittner half spun, collided drunkenly with the brass rail and stumbled sideways into the pooled darkness behind the bar.

Cody followed him, the sheriff now clambering away, Bittner's ratty eyes large and shiny in the murk. Cody had a moment of acute paranoia that Dragomir or one of the others would fall on him while his back was turned, but then he remembered Dmitri Seneslav the night before, the man's eyes widening in sudden distress. No, they'd not bother him over here, he realised. Not a single one of the devils had ventured near the bar during the entire melee. And they wouldn't either. Not only because they were engaged in a battle with a gun-toting mob, but because they were afraid of something. If Cody was right...

Bittner lay on his back, his hands outstretched beseechingly. The man's lips trembled as if he were freezing to death, but no words escaped them. At least, nothing coherent. His body hunched, he hurried over to the door leading to the kitchen, but it was just as he'd figured, locked tight. He could use the .38 to blow holes through the lock, and that'd get him through the door, but the moment he fired, the devils would be swarming over here – or at the very least, they'd be aware of his position.

No, Cody thought, rushing back to where Bittner still lay, his round body encased in a debilitating fog of terror. He had to see if his hunch was correct.

Cody's eyes flicked to the cobalt vase poised between two bottles of gin. He kept the Smith & Wesson trained on the sheriff while with his free hand he reached out and clutched the bouquet of bluebell flowers. When he knelt before Bittner, the gun in one hand and the bouquet in the other, the sheriff stared at him uncomprehendingly.

"Don't worry," Cody said, "I ain't gonna ask you to marry me."

Bittner's stupid eyes blinked, then shot wide when the shrieks began.

Cody didn't even need to rise and turn around to see what was happening. The vampires had attacked the shooters. An ugly, jeering doubt grabbed hold of him then, told him he'd missed his chance to thwart the vampires, that he could've made a difference in the battle.

But that was bullshit, and Cody knew it. Had he joined the fray, he'd be dying as surely and as violently as the rest of them were dying.

Trying to block out the wails and the gunfire, Cody said, "Sit up."

But Bittner wasn't listening, was staring at the ceiling beyond Cody, perhaps imagining the scene of indescribable horror unfolding just forty feet away.

Cody raised the butt of the .38 and cracked the sheriff on top of the head. Not hard enough to knock him out – no, that wouldn't do at all – but with just enough force to make him stop gaping like a dead carp.

Bittner blinked at him, his expression dumber than ever, but Cody seemed to have his attention. Or at least as much of it as was possible under the circumstances.

"*Sit up*," Cody growled.

This time Bittner complied.

Cody dropped the flowers, their green stems still dripping from the vase water, in the sheriff's lap.

Bittner said, "What do I want with—"

"Eat them," Cody said.

Bittner's wet mouth trembled, then formed itself into a weird parody of a smile. "The hell you talkin' 'bout, boy? A man don't eat flowers."

The gunshots were infrequent now, the gargling death wails and earsplitting screeches of terror winning out.

"I told you to eat 'em," Cody said. "Now do it."

There was only an occasional gunshot now, the whole bar resounding with the stomach-churning noises of the vampires feeding.

Bittner chuckled, a good deal of his former haughty manner returning. "You really did lose your mind, didn't you? And here I thought you were gonna kill me."

Cody cocked the hammer, placed the barrel between Bittner's thick eyebrows. The man became absolutely still except for the little weasel eyes, which crossed slightly as they stared up at the barrel of the .38.

"Eat," Cody repeated.

Automatically, Bittner reached down and found the flowers. He brought them up to his open mouth and began taking hesitant nips at them. He started to cry.

"*Faster*," Cody demanded. There were no gunshots at all now, but there was still the screaming. Plenty of it.

"I *can't!*" Bittner moaned, little specks of blue and green dotting his blubbery lips. "Stuff is so bitter I can't even breathe."

Cody seized what was left of the thinning brown hair on the man's crown. He pressed the gun against Bittner's temple and spoke in a ragged hiss. "You're gonna eat these flowers or I'm gonna put one in your brain. You think I won't do it, you perverted piece of shit?"

Very little of what Cody said seemed to register in Bittner's horror-struck mind, but the sheriff understood the seriousness of Cody's tone adequately enough. Bittner began cramming the bluebells into his mouth and munching them like a cow at pasture.

"Now swallow," Cody commanded.

With a jerking gulp, Bittner obeyed. The fat sheriff was weeping freely now.

Cody reached down, gathered another clutch of stems and slapped them against the chest of Bittner's sodden shirt. He immediately regretted it because it set off a coughing spell that made the man lean into him, regurgitating some of what he'd ingested. Cody waited, lips compressed in frustration, until the episode ceased. Then, pitilessly, he crammed several flowers into the man's quivering mouth.

"I can't," Bittner mumbled around the flowers. "I need sumpin' to wash it down."

"Shut up and eat," Cody said, keeping the pressure of the .38 steady on the sheriff's temple.

Wordlessly, Bittner continued to chew.

Cody watched the sheriff, but he was listening to the vampires. Listening hard. They seemed immersed in their ghastly buffet, the bar echoing with their frenzied smacking and the wet, ripping sound of dividing flesh. Intermittently, a bone would fracture with a dull snap.

Cody leaned over, selected a bottle and smashed its bottom on one of the shelves under the bar. The sweet smell of gin clotted the air. As the alcohol soaked into his pants and his boots, Cody listened to hear if they'd been discovered.

The sounds of feasting continued.

At length, his mouth stuffed with bluebells, Bittner said, "Why in hell'd you do that? That was good gin."

"Eat your flowers."

Bittner munched them quietly now, perhaps grown used to the taste.

Maybe three minutes had gone by when Cody switched the gun to Bittner's other temple and scooted around as quietly as he could so that he was crouching next to the sheriff. It had gotten very quiet in Marguerite's.

"What now?" Bittner whispered, eyes flitting about the darkness in terror.

"We wait a minute."

"Wait for what?" Bittner said, his voice a quavery soprano. "They're gonna find us back here and they're gonna drink our blood. Holy God, I never seen such a—"

Bittner cut off as a low, monstrous voice echoed through the bar. The language was one Cody'd never heard before, but the voice was unmistakably Adam Price's, the voice Cody had heard back at the jail when Price had transformed. Gravelly, ancient, the kind of voice you'd hear if you died and learned you hadn't been admitted by St. Peter.

Cody bit his bottom lip to stifle a scream.

Bittner's eyes weren't little any longer. They were the size of half dollars, and nearly full of white. "Holy God," Bittner murmured in his weak soprano. "Holy God!"

That's right, Cody thought. *A man like you only thinks of God when things have gone too far.*

Cody took a deep suck of air and let it out slowly, steadying himself. *Do it now*, he thought. *And do it right because you only have one chance.*

"Stand up," he told Bittner.

But Bittner didn't seem to hear him, only kept on riddling the dimness with those white, panicked glances.

Cody got the barrel of the Smith & Wesson under Bittner's jaw, drove it upward so the man had no choice but to stand if he didn't want his chin skewered by oiled steel.

As they rose, Cody took the gun away from Bittner's face and shifted it to the meat of the man's hip. He held it low enough so the vampires wouldn't see it, both their angle and the sheriff's girth impeding their view.

When Cody and Bittner had straightened, Cody was able to pick out all five of the vampires right away. It wasn't difficult. The farthest from them was Adam Price, who had wrapped his freakishly long vampire fingers around Grizzly's throat and forced the behemoth to his knees. Casually, Price strangled him. Grizzly's wild black mane of hair jittered as he entered his death throes, but Adam Price hardly moved. The vampire leader merely gazed remorselessly down at his bested foe. Beside Cody, Bittner stifled a sob as Price's fingers squelched through the distressed flesh of Grizzly's neck. The dead giant slouched forward, his blood washing over his shoulders in pulsing sheets. Rather than lapping at the scarlet froth covering his knuckles, Adam Price seemed content to watch his victim bleed to death.

With the exception of Price, all the vampires were feasting on their vanquished victims. Dragomir scooped up an emaciated man of indeterminate age and thrashed him on the floor as if he were beating the dust out of an old rug. Horton got hold of a man by the privates, and before the man could bring up his hands to protect himself, Horton ripped the crotch of his pants away, along with the man's genitals. As the man howled in torment, Cody realised it was Deputy John Ebright. A moment later Horton knelt and burrowed into the gory mess of the man's abdomen to feed.

Ebright's screams went on for a good while.

Angela and Penders lay near each other looking like mangled heaps of offal. Angela's slug-torn body was draped over an inert figure, her long, cloven tongue lapping weakly at the man's spurting throat. To her immediate left, Penders lay facedown in a puddle of blood slowly spreading from a disembowelled corpse. For a moment Cody watched, fascinated, as the bullet holes that spread from Penders's bare back like red cactus blossoms began to close and knit together.

As long as they can get enough blood in time, Cody thought, *they can rebuild their bodies.*

Unless, his dad's voice reminded him, *you lop off their heads.*

Remembering the way he'd killed Dmitri Seneslav both strengthened his resolve and brought his gaze to the two figures in the foreground. These two, Billy Horton and Dragomir Seneslav, were halfway between where Price waited and where Cody stood with his gun shoved into Sheriff Bittner's side.

Cody had once seen a pack of feral mongrels run down and devour a screaming calf. Cody had only been six at the time and too young to save the animal, but for months after he'd been plagued with nightmares of the calf's yelping and the dogs' snarling, inexorable attack. Horton and Seneslav looked very much the way those mongrels had looked, from the vicious shredding dealt by their claws to the rabid tearing of their deadly teeth. They even growled like dogs. Horton was digging his way into the side of his victim's neck, the man so recently expired that the severed arteries sprayed brightly over Horton's elongated face. Dragomir's feeding was even more violent and even more bestial; he'd buried his whole head in the guts of his victim, a ginger-haired man who didn't look old enough to be served alcohol here, much less lose his life in such a grisly fashion. The young man was undoubtedly dead though. Cody could tell that by the way his unblemished face joggled on his thin stalk of a neck. The sight of it chilled Cody to the marrow, but he knew there'd never be a better opportunity.

"Now walk beside me," he muttered, hoping Price wouldn't hear. "Nice and slow."

Bittner tensed, but did as he was bidden. Together they moved toward the end of the bar, the sheriff to Cody's left and slightly in the lead so the vampires wouldn't see the .38 jammed into his side. As they emerged from the shelter of the bar, Cody had a sudden worry. In many of the legends he'd heard, a person bitten by a vampire became a vampire. After all, wasn't Angela living – or undead – proof of that? Drawing closer to where Horton and Dragomir champed and swallowed, Cody imagined the roomful of corpses rising as one and turning their new vampiric faces toward him. Then they'd reach for him, groping, a dark ocean of them rolling toward him in an unbroken mass of slavering maws, their orange eyes rapturous and glowing...

"Dragomir!" Cody called.

The head buried inside the ginger-haired boy's guts snapped up and regarded him uncomprehendingly. Beside Cody, Sheriff Bittner moaned and stood rigid. Cody ground the barrel deeper into Bittner's side to remind the man it was there. If the sheriff bolted, everything would be lost.

The entire length of Dragomir's face was painted red. Cody caught a faint whiff of faecal matter and wondered if one of the men had shat himself or if Dragomir had merely split open one of his victim's intestines.

Recognition followed then, and Dragomir's endless bottom jaw hinged lower in obscene anticipation.

"God forgive me," Cody whispered.

Without waiting any longer, Cody reached across the sheriff's body with the broken gin bottle and plunged it into Bittner's big belly. Bittner doubled up, hands instinctively closing over Cody's wrist, but before the large man could dislodge the razor-sharp glass, Cody wrenched it down, unzipping the man's guts. Bittner let loose with a bloodcurdling shriek and began to tumble forward, but Cody released the broken bottle and, quickly shoving the .38 down the front of his trousers, hooked his arms under the man's sweaty armpits. They both almost fell anyway, Bittner's considerable weight towing Cody forward like an anchor, but because he'd been expecting Bittner to fold in on himself, Cody was able to brace them both up by planting his foot between Bittner's boots and hauling the big man backward. Bittner tottered into Cody, and for a crazy second he was sure the huge sheriff would fell them both. The image that flashed into his mind was monstrously absurd: Bittner pinning Cody beneath him like an inexpert lumberjack crushed under the weight of a falling oak. But Cody kept them both on their feet, and though he couldn't see Dragomir from his current position, he did hear Adam Price call out, "*Dragon!*"

Cody imagined the fiendish vampire visage of the remaining Seneslav twin as it saw the blood gushing from Bobby Bittner's ruined belly...the depthless hunger in those lunatic orange eyes. The temptation would be too great for the vampire. Cody heard two sets of footfalls, one undoubtedly Dragomir's, the other likely belonging to Adam Price.

Bittner still writhed in Cody's arms, a deep gurgling issuing from his throat.

"*DRAGON!*" Adam Price bellowed, but then Bittner and Cody were both driven backward with concussive force, and the world was filled with the snarling and growling of the vampire.

Cody crawled out from under the twisting bodies and beheld the sheriff's thrashing head, the blood spurting from the gaping wound in his gut.

Dragomir Seneslav had begun to feed.

*   *   *

Price was on Dragomir at once.

"*Stop it, goddamn you!*" he shouted, seizing his comrade's flexing arms and straining to detach him from Bittner's glistening entrails. Cody pushed to his feet and started to back away.

"DRAGOMIR!" Price bellowed, his grinding voice so deep and loud that it shivered the remaining windows.

Price seized Dragomir but was unable to detach him from Bittner. As the vampires struggled, the tendons in Price's straining throat stood out like telegraph cables. And though Dragomir was gripped by the unquenchable bloodlust aroused by his fresh victim, Price finally tore the vampire away.

Cody glanced to his left, suddenly certain one of the other creatures would be vaulting toward him, but Horton was still immersed in his victim's throat, and Penders and Angela still fed languidly, their damaged bodies quietly but steadily mending. Cody took a step in their direction, thinking he could maybe sneak by them and slip through one of the shattered windows, but rejected the idea almost as soon as it had come. The wounded vampires certainly *looked* vulnerable, but he couldn't wager his life on that. Horton would catch him. Or worse, Angela. Being ripped to pieces by his once-wife was the worst death Cody could envision, primarily because it would carry with it one final humiliation.

He cast a glance behind him and glimpsed the darkened stage. Wouldn't there be a door back there somewhere? The stage was located at the rear of Marguerite's bar, which meant the backstage area bordered the alley. Surely there was an exit…

When Cody looked back at Dragomir and Adam Price, his breathing faltered and his legs went limp. Price was supporting Dragomir similarly to how Cody had moments ago supported Bittner, only now the two creatures were facing each other, Dragomir bent double, his scythelike talons pawing at his throat, and Price leaning solicitously nearer.

Cody reached the stage. Without taking his eyes off the pair of vampires, he climbed onto it, got gingerly to his feet and began stealing toward the inky blackness at the rear of the stage.

He froze at a flurry of motion. Dragomir had shoved Price away. The twin straightened, his expression of bewilderment easy to discern even in this poor light. He was shaking his ghoulish face, his talons kneading his throat.

Price shouted something in the unfamiliar tongue he'd used

earlier, something that sounded like, "*Neerob too.*" But Dragomir gave no sign of having heard. His Adam's apple bobbed in his throat, his talons now clawing frantically at his flesh.

"*PRESTAN!*" Price commanded, and though Cody didn't understand the actual words, their meaning was clear enough: *Stop that.*

But Dragomir didn't. He continue to rake his throat as if there were something precious buried within that he was intent on exhuming. Ribbons of pale flesh flew from the shovelling claws, the gallons of blood he'd ingested first misting out of the wounds and then, though Price grappled with him, jetting in crimson geysers.

Horton had finally abandoned his kill to witness the bizarre scene. In the foyer of Marguerite's saloon, Cody could see Penders struggling to his feet, though Angela remained slumped over the dead body transfusing her.

Price waded closer and finally grabbed hold of his friend's wrists, but now something was happening to the rest of Dragomir's body that had nothing to do with the lacerations in his throat.

Dragomir's flesh was turning black.

Cody knew he should escape immediately, and indeed he'd made it to the far corner of the stage and was concealed in the shadows. But he had to know if what he'd suspected was true, had to know if he'd claimed a second member of the five original vampires.

In Dragomir's eyes was no longer surprise or confusion. The expression on his darkening face was agony, commingled with a species of horrified sorrow. Dragomir bellowed in anguish. Price loosed Dragomir's wrists and took hold of the vampire's shoulders because no longer was the skin simply changing colour; it was puckering as well, like overripe fruit left desiccating on a windowsill.

Cody watched, elated and appalled, as Dragomir Seneslav withered in Adam Price's freakish hands. The flesh now resembled burned paper. Cody saw it flaking off the vampire's forehead, its cheeks. The eyes remained huge and starey, but the rest of its features had drawn down to a blackened wad, the charred husk of a body sinking gradually into nothingness. Adam Price grasped what was left of Dragomir's shoulders for as long as he could, and then with an inarticulate cry jerked the withered body against him. Price's long, vulpine face contorted in an expression that Cody thought eerily human. Price pressed the flaking remains of his friend against him a few seconds longer; then what was left of Dragomir Seneslav scattered like windblown ashes.

Adam Price watched the black flakes float silently to the floor. Then he turned and stared at Cody.

CHAPTER EIGHTEEN

The moment Cody beheld the fury in those eyes, he understood for the first time exactly how helpless he was, how futile his resistance had been.

But still he ran, plunging into the darkness and rushing blindly along the wall behind the heavy velvet curtain. He had thought there might be rooms back here, corridors, but despite the capaciousness of the stage, the area behind it was little more than a narrow passage. Through the caul of terror that had enshrouded his senses, Cody could dimly make out the sounds of running footsteps, the rasping huff of Price's breathing.

But it wasn't only Adam Price who was pursing him, Cody remembered as he made his fumbling way through the murk. It was also Billy Horton and Steve Penders and maybe even Angela for all he knew. She'd never missed a chance to torture him before; why would she forsake the opportunity now? The heavy velvet tremored against his shoulders, one of the vampires bumping against it at a point not too far away. Whimpering, Cody dragged his hands along the back wall, hoping against hope they would reveal to him an escape route. But his fingers only scraped the unsanded wood, his fingernails cracking and splitting in his frenetic search. The curtain undulated against him, the whole damn thing alive now. The vampires were toying with him, he realised. They'd recovered their sense of purpose and had moved past Dragomir's death. One of them chortled from very close by, the horrid sound amplified by the empty stage.

Cody gritted his teeth, bunched himself against the wall as he sidled nearer to the far side. They knew he was back here, but he needn't aid their search by revealing exactly where. The curtain behind him rippled wildly, and suddenly Cody heard the throaty breathing emanating down the black sliver of walkway he was navigating. It sounded like it was coming from the place from which he'd come, but sound was strange back here. The vampire could be ahead of him for all he knew, lying in wait and ready to add him to the evening's list of victims.

The wall ended and Cody, thinking he'd located a corridor, plunged forward. He slammed into a door, which was inset by only a couple feet. Frantically, he groped for the door handle, found it, but to his horror it wouldn't turn.

He realised there was a lock on the handle. Cody twisted the lock, heard the teeth-rattling shriek of scraping iron. He grasped the handle again and tried to turn it, and though the handle moved freely now, the door didn't budge in the slightest. An anguished humming noise escaped from Cody's throat as he groped up and down the door's length, inspecting it for another lock. His fingers happened on a thick board, a four-by-eight, he estimated, judging by the feel of it. Cody probed higher and encountered another. Both boards were nailed into the door and the surrounding frame.

The vampires had foreseen this, he realised. Of course they had. They'd barred the front door and stationed Angela there to stand sentinel at the windows. Why would they forget to cut off this escape route too? What a damned fool he'd been to think he could simply slip out the back door while they mourned Dragomir.

Cody staggered away from the door, gripping the .38 in mute terror. His bootheel caught on something and pitched him backward. He grunted and almost lost hold of the gun as he landed on some hard surface. He rolled over, disoriented, and fingered the object curiously.

Stairs.

Without pause, Cody clambered up them, realising at once they must lead to the catwalk where the limelight was operated.

And if you make it there, then what? an indignant voice demanded. *You're just cutting off your own escape routes.*

What escape routes? he almost said out loud. The growls and raspy breathing below had intensified, the vampires closing in.

Cody reached a landing, nearly broke his nose bumping against the wall, then turned and scrambled up the next flight of stairs.

Cody gained the top of the staircase and damn near pitched

over the catwalk rail. And wouldn't that have been something? To evade these monstrous creatures only to fall screaming to a clownish death? Or worse, smack the wooden stage just hard enough to incapacitate him but not quite severely enough to kill him? A tidal wave of goose bumps whispered down Cody's arms at the thought of the remaining devils swarming over him and sucking him dry. They'd do it slowly, torturously. Maximising his agony while his useless limbs bled white.

They're coming!

Cody jolted back to himself with a start, threw a terrified glance at the stairs. No one there, not yet. But he could hear them closing in, taking their time about it. He had a chamber full of bullets, but what good were they now? He might get lucky, put one right between Horton's eyes, or maybe in Penders's throat. They bled a lot, he recalled. They bled especially after feeding, and boy, would they be full of blood after the carnage below, like a trio of ticks.

No, he thought, *check that. Not a trio, a quartet.* Angela was one of them now. Vicious, treacherous Angela. Cody backed along the catwalk, one hand gripping the tubular wooden rail, another clutching the .38. The moment Price or Penders or Horton or that slut Angela showed his or her face, he'd blast a hole in it. The .38 was a good gun. It felt solid in his hand, like whoever had owned it had loved it. He took another backward stride, frowning into the dark so he could spot—

"They say you saved my boy," a voice behind him croaked.

With a cry Cody spun around and realised he'd nearly reached the end of the catwalk. There were perhaps four more strides before he would have encountered the squared end of the walkway and the single wooden chair nestled there.

And the woman with the darning needles.

She acted as though it were the most natural thing in the world, meeting like this on a catwalk thirty feet above the stage. Her with a pair of darning needles toiling away at whatever sat in her lap, Cody with a .38 cocked and pointed at her face. There was hardly any illumination up here now that the limelight had been extinguished. And though he hadn't thought about who

Price had gotten to control the lighting up here, the only thing that mattered was the fact that this woman had allied herself to the devils. Why else would she have killed the lights and given the devils a tactical advantage?

You know why, he told himself.

But he refused to believe it. He could not believe that this kindly, handsome woman in her late thirties would willingly become a confederate of these monsters. Why would anyone—

Cody's thoughts broke off as the meaning of her words finally sank in.

They say you saved my boy, she had said.

Cody's eyes were drawn to the faint pearlescent glimmer on her upper lip, the one just above the right corner of her closed mouth. The pale scar tissue resembled a corkscrew.

She's got a pig tail on her lip, Willet had said.

They say you saved my boy.

"Mrs. Black?" Cody ventured.

Someone was climbing the stairs and had almost reached the top, but Cody hardly noticed the heavy thuds of boots on wood.

The woman's mouth broke into a grin, and at that moment all handsomeness disintegrated. He could see why her mouth had been shut before. Her teeth were hanging white pickets, the jaws unhinging twice as far as human jaws should.

And that's because she's no longer human, you fucking ignoramus, he told himself. *Why else would she be helping the devils and how else could she have survived back at Las Cruces?*

The footsteps clumped louder now, the figure having reached the top of the staircase. Cody could feel the catwalk vibrate with each step, whichever devil it was taking his time now because Cody was covered from the front and back, and though he knew he should be shooting, his eyes lowered instead to the thing Willet's mother was darning. He was scarcely surprised when he distinguished the inverted head of the girl Eliza, the one who'd volunteered to be an actress in Price's show and had ended up being defiled and murdered in front of half the town.

Willet's mother – or the monstrous thing that had once been Mrs. Black – took in Cody's appalled stare and nodded conspiratorially. "When Stevie popped that little slut's head off, I knew she was the one. She deserved what she got, by the way. Adam offered her fifty dollars to have sex with Penders on stage, and she was dumb enough to believe she'd get paid. I stole down there during the brawl. No one seemed to notice."

The footsteps behind Cody drew closer, closer.

Mrs. Black nodded, darning needles stitching together the ragged flaps of skin so that the remains of Eliza's gullet resembled the crumpled top of a paper sack. "Those boys don't know when to stop eating, and I'll not go hungry on the journey."

"What journey?" Cody whispered.

"The wagon ride to Escondido," Adam Price said from behind him.

Cody whirled, saw the beast had again become man, though Price's face and clothing were begrimed with blood and viscera. Price was eight feet away.

Cody raised the .38, fixed it on Price's forehead. "I'm not going anywhere with you," Cody said and squeezed the trigger.

But the moment before he did, a fireblast of pain scorched the meat of his right thigh, the darning needle burying itself to the bone. The .38 blast went wide, grazing Price's head above the ear, but the man hardly reacted. Howling with pain, Cody seized the embedded needle, yanked it out and thrust the barrel of the .38 into Mrs. Black's face, which was no longer handsome in any way, which was now a snarling oval of fangs and lurid orange eyes. Cody pulled the trigger again, saw one eye dissolve in a pulpy black cloud. Mrs. Black was driven back against the edge of the rail but did not tumble over.

A hand grabbed Cody's shoulder, squeezed, the fingers so powerful they ripped bloody trenches through his flesh. Gasping, Cody whirled and thrust the darning needle into Adam Price's throat. The slender steel spear punched through the man's neck and out the other side, but Price's grip did not lessen, and the man was not a man any longer, the terrible change accelerating before Cody's bleary eyes. Cody jammed the .38 into Price's belly and squeezed the trigger. The vampire jolted, bent toward him. Cody evaded Price, raced down the catwalk, but Horton appeared, barring his way. Cody did the only thing he could think to do, launched himself sideways, his upper leg smacking the catwalk rail, his body tilting perpendicular to the curtain, which he groped madly for, the plush velvet taunting his seeking fingers, dancing away from his grasp, and then he was plummeting down the curtain. Horton made a desperate grab for his boots, and Cody let go of the .38, dimly aware that the gun no longer mattered. If he struck the stage at full speed, he'd be dead or paralysed, his nightmarish vision from moments before become a self-fulfilling prophecy. Cody's fingers clenched the curtain, his feet swinging violently down. When his legs slapped the curtain, he lost his grip, his upper body twisting away from his only salvation. He had no idea how far he'd fallen or if he'd even helped his cause by grasping the curtain, and desperately he reached out again, groped for the curtain, his body now parallel to the stage, which was flying toward him. His fingers burned down the velvet surface, caught, and he swung into the curtain, the unresisting plushness enveloping him. He lost his grip once more, spinning in the velvety embrace, then it disgorged him, and he landed facedown on the stage.

He lay there a good while, stunned by the impact. Then, slowly, the feeling in his body returned. Amazed, Cody pushed up to his elbows and made to stand, but at that moment something slammed him in the ribs, sent him skidding sideways several feet. On his belly, Cody cast a glance back and saw it was Penders who'd booted him. Cody tried to scramble to his feet, but collided with a pair of hard shins. He didn't need to look up to know it was Billy Horton who'd blocked him. One of Horton's bare feet cocked back, and before Cody could defend himself with a forearm, it caught him in the underjaw, lifted him off his feet in a backward somersault. He crashed down against Penders's legs. Stunned, Cody attempted to rise again, to perhaps locate the .38 wherever it had fallen. But Penders grabbed him with his viselike paws, lifted him above his head and hurled him into the curtain. Cody's flying body tented the curtain inward as far as it would go, then smashed into the unforgiving wall beyond. Cody hit face-first, his nose rupturing against the wall.

Insensate, he sprawled on his back, the curtain half-covering his prone form. Moments later, something got hold of his pant leg and dragged him back onto the stage.

CHAPTER NINETEEN

Cody blinked up at the staring faces. Angela was there, along with Mrs. Black. Penders and Horton stood a little ways off.

Adam Price knelt over Cody. He'd begun to change back again, but somehow the half-vampire appearance of his features was worse than the fully transformed version. He resembled Satan from a drawing Cody had once seen back in Sunday school.

"You've taken more from me than any man ever has," Adam Price said, his silky voice buzzing around the edges. "You'll die for that. But before you do, I'm going to take more from you than you took from me."

Cody's mouth was full of blood and ache, but still he mumbled, "Took my wife."

"That's right," Price said. "We took your wife; we took Willet."

Cody felt something in him squeeze tight. He tried to say no, but no sound escaped.

"You will ride with Willet in our coach. By morning you will have the pleasure of watching us gut and devour your father and anyone else we find on his ranch."

"My dad…" Cody said weakly. "My dad isn't in Escondido anymore. He's moved on—"

"Willet told us everything about you, Cody. You shouldn't have confided in such a young person."

And though he knew he should have only been thinking of Willet at that moment, Cody's thoughts veered in another direction, to Marguerite, to the owner of this place that had become the site of a blood orgy black enough to make Lucifer himself blanch. Where had Marguerite gone? If she had been killed, why hadn't Price taunted him with the fact?

Price nodded, face still caught in that half-vampire state of monstrousness. "Yes," he said, his orange eyes flickering. "The Mexican tramp. I'd ask you if you cheated on your wife" – Price flicked a nod up at Angela, who was leering at him with her hideously altered grin – "but I know from what she's told us that you wouldn't be man enough to seduce such a comely woman."

"What have you done with Marguerite?"

A momentary expression of disdain rippled through Price's features. "We didn't touch her. We couldn't." The disdainful look twisted into a searing hatred. "Judging from what you did to Dragomir, I suspect you know why."

Cody's eyes widened. "The flowers."

Price appraised Cody a long moment, and in that moment a maelstrom of thoughts tumbled through Cody's mind. Price would kill him now. Still seething over the loss of the Seneslav twins, the king vampire would finally take his vengeance. Or Price would take him to where he held Marguerite hostage. Or one of the vampires had found a way to overcome Marguerite and had transformed her into one of the beasts. Nothing would surprise Cody at this point.

At length, Price said, "She is beneath us."

"She's better than you could ever—"

"I mean literally, Mr. Wilson."

Cody frowned up at him. "You buried her under the stage?"

Price seemed faintly amused. "We didn't touch her. She was down in the root cellar when we arrived earlier. Apparently she was selecting a bottle of wine to share with you. When we found her there, we asked her if we could book her saloon for a performance. She declined. She produced a crossbow. Penders wasn't deterred by the weapon. He attempted to persuade her, but he discovered the flowers in her hair just in time. The touch of them is toxic to our flesh." His lips closed, became a thin white line. He said, "And fatal if ingested."

Cody amazed himself by saying, "Guess your buddy over there forgot."

"Dragomir often lost control when gripped by the thrall." Price's face regained its predatory gleam. "But we have plans for a replacement."

"You better not touch Willet."

"You'll see him soon enough. But first we must make certain your dusky maiden is taken care of."

Someone grabbed hold of Cody's shoulders, heaved him up to standing. Cody wobbled a few seconds, nearly fell. Through the leaden fog surrounding him, he said, "You can't go near her. Not with the flowers—"

"We won't need to go near her," Price interrupted, already descending the stage steps. Penders gripped the back of Cody's neck and half-pushed, half-carried him down the steps and through the strewn bodies and entrails that sloshed and squelched underfoot. Cody could hear voices outside, men and women talking in raised voices, several calling out to see if anyone inside Marguerite's would answer.

Go away, Cody thought. *Go away before you die, too.*

Horton ripped the door off its hinges and cast it aside. Price went through, with Penders bearing Cody along in front of him. Behind them Cody could hear Angela, Mrs. Black and Horton, but what drew his attention most of all were three sights: the black coach with its sextet of ebony quarter horses hitched and waiting; another coach, this one a shiny red Concord hitched with four horses, two strong sorrels and a pair of Appaloosas; and a collection of perhaps thirty townspeople watching them with unbelieving gazes.

As the vampires and their hostage ambled out of the saloon, most of the onlookers simply gaped as if uncertain of what they were seeing. A few gasped or muttered incoherent prayers. At least two – a wispy adolescent girl and a man of perhaps forty – turned heels and dashed away into the night. The rest simply stood immobile, or perhaps inched closer to one another for support. Cody couldn't blame them. The procession spilling out of the ravaged façade of Marguerite's saloon must've resembled the refugees from a macabre costume ball. As far as he could tell in the semidarkness of the moonlit street, Horton and Penders had changed most of the way back to their normal selves. Angela and Mrs. Black were still more vampire than woman. Adam Price looked normal, but even when human, Price possessed an undeniably mesmeric quality that made it difficult to look away. As for himself, Cody figured he looked the way he felt – like complete and utter shit.

"Lovely for all of you to join us," Price announced to the crowd.

One man with a bushy brown mustache and a short, plump woman at his side opened his mouth as if to speak, but Price stilled him with an outstretched palm.

"I know this might seem unorthodox to you, but there was a disagreement here this evening, and unfortunately blood was spilled."

The short, plump woman tilted her head suspiciously. "Whose blood?" Cody saw her husband avert his eyes and understood at once how it was in their relationship: the plump woman commanded and Bushy Mustache obeyed. It was disturbingly similar to the dynamic he'd fallen into with Angela, and at thought of his former wife, Cody half turned to see if she'd changed into a person again.

What he saw made his body go limp.

Not only had she not returned to her human form, the transformation had reversed itself, the woman looking like nothing that should draw breath on this earth.

A couple of the gathered townspeople had noticed.

"What's happening to that lady?" one of them, an elderly woman in a white bonnet, asked.

"Our dear Angela has endured many trials of late," Price answered. "She needs a good rest."

Angela drew even with Cody, only six or seven feet away. Her monstrous face was limned by the deep-blue night sky, her orange eyes lambent and hungry.

"That don't look like all she needs," an onlooker remarked.

Price seemed to consider. He'd lost none of his aplomb, but he now regarded the massed citizens of Mesquite with what Cody feared was renewed interest.

A big man with a neat black beard broke through the crowd. Unlike Sheriff Bittner and Boom Catterson, this man was bulky where it mattered, his chest and shoulders stretching the fabric of his pale undershirt like they'd been painted onto him. The big man stepped right up to Adam Price and fixed him with a level stare. "I want to know what happened in there. My brother went to the show tonight."

Price smiled softly. "I think I remember him. Tall fellow, a great bristling mane of black hair?"

Grizzly, Cody thought, thinking of the way the man had died. *Run*, was Cody's next thought. He did his best to push the thought psychically into the big man's mind. *Run now so you don't end up like your brother.*

The big man's eyes narrowed. "That's Teddy all right." The big man's gaze riveted on the front of Marguerite's saloon. "He still inside?"

"Yes," Price said slowly, as if thinking it over. "His corporeal being is still there."

"His what?"

"Take a look for yourself," Price said, his grin becoming sharkish. Had his jaw begun to elongate, or was Cody's overarching fear of the man only making it appear that way?

Invisible fingers of dread caressed Cody's spine. He might be imagining the stretching jaw, but there was no questioning the orange embers that had begun to spark in Price's eyes. *Oh hell*, Cody thought pleadingly at Grizzly's brother. *Please get out of here. Please get yourself and the rest of these poor souls indoors until this black storm blows out of town and leaves you to your mourning.*

But the big man had no intention of leaving. He shouldered past Price, who let him pass with sardonic good cheer.

"I wanna see too," White Bonnet declared. "My Festus came down here tonight to play billiards."

Horton interposed his mostly naked frame – he and Penders had each dragged on pairs of tattered black trousers – between White Bonnet and Grizzly's brother, who'd mounted the front porch and was about to enter a building that hours before had been the town's social epicentre instead of a gore-streaked mausoleum.

Horton said, "While that Eliza got herself pounded in front of God and everybody, your dear old Festus had his hand in his pocket, stroking himself like a teenage boy."

White Bonnet drew back from Horton, aghast. "What are you talking about? And where are your clothes?"

"Don't know," Horton said amiably. "Don't ordinarily wear 'em when I fuck."

"Why you..." The old woman's mouth worked, her lips twisting in affronted disbelief. "Why you disgusting, detestable young man."

Horton brayed laughter, smacked Penders on the chest. "You hear that, Stevie? '*You disgusting, detestable young man,*'" Horton mimicked in a querulous falsetto. "Oh man, lady. If you only knew."

A rustle went through the crowd, several sets of eyes turning toward Marguerite's again. With Penders's hand still perched paternally on his shoulder, Cody turned to see Grizzly's brother walk out of the saloon. But *walk* wasn't the right word for it. *Drifted* was more like it. The big man drifted out, his wraithlike movements a fitting counterpart to his now colourless face. His chin was slicked with either slobber or vomit, it didn't matter which. He'd glimpsed the carnage inside. Perhaps he'd even seen what was left of his dead brother.

"What's happened, Richard?" the short, plump woman asked.

At that moment Cody noticed a face at the rear of the crowd, just behind a blond-haired lady.

Mrs. Black.

He'd forgotten all about Willet's mother, and from the way everyone had their backs to her, the townspeople had too. But Cody saw her all right. Saw her unhinged jaw and her mad orange eyes – one of them injured but already mending itself – and before he could even scream for the blond-haired lady to for God's sakes run away, the creature that had once been Willet Black's mom tilted her head sideways and clamped down on the woman's neck like a bear trap. A breathless little yelp was all the woman mustered before Mrs. Black whipped her back and forth three or four times like a fox snapping a chicken's spine.

The terrible sight of it had the unfortunate effect of diverting everyone's attention from the rest of the vampires, whose opening mouths were only marked by Cody and Grizzly's brother, the one the plump woman had called Richard.

Maybe this explained why Richard died next. In one moment the big man was watching Price loom toward him with a kind of spellbound uncertainty. The next, Price embraced Richard like an old friend.

But the manner in which Price pulled away, jammed his thumbs into the man's eyes and proceeded to peel his face open like a boiled egg was decidedly unfriendly.

Cody bucked to loose himself from Penders's grasp, but the vampire's steely grip only tightened on his shoulder, made Cody wonder how long it would be before the squeezing talons lanced his flesh and attracted the vampire's sanguinary desires.

When Price began to lap at the torrents of blood gushing from Richard's eyes, Angela leaped onto Bushy Mustache and began carving up his face with her razorlike fingernails. With his free hand, Penders punched through a young man's chest, ripped a clump of lung from his lifeless body, and began gnawing on it the way one might a particularly choice morsel of steak. A good deal of blood splattered on Cody, but in his terror, he hardly noticed the crimson dots stippling his cheeks.

Horton took off after White Bonnet, who shrieked, "Stay away from me! You stay away from me, you horrid boy!" But in the next moment he'd dragged her down and ripped her bonnet off her head. She batted frantically at Horton's clawed fingers, but her resistance only brought on a spate of maniacal laughter.

"Aw, come on, Grandma!" Horton chuckled. "Don't tell me you don't want me to show you a good time." He seized a handful of her flowing white hair, began dragging her back toward where Cody stood straining against Penders.

Penders muttered to Price, "Here, your turn to hold this pussy." And with one hand still jammed into Richard's eye, Price took custodianship of Cody by seizing a handful of his collar.

The onlookers were emerging from their horrorstruck fog. A few pelted away into the night. Three or four made futile attempts to save their victimised friends and neighbours. The rest simply stood there in mute disbelief while the vampires finished off the first wave of kills and turned their attentions to their second courses.

The blood from Richard's mutilated face spewed over Cody like a baptismal font, and in avoiding the hot crimson flow of the man's lifeblood, Cody's gaze happened upon the man's belt. There was no holster there, but Cody did spot the handle of what looked like a large hunting knife. It wasn't quite as huge or wicked as the Bowie knife with which he'd stabbed Slim Keeley earlier, but it looked more than capable of dealing some serious damage. Doing his best to ignore the spray of Richard's blood, Cody unsheathed the knife, reared back and swung the wide silver blade at Price's throat.

It almost worked.

At the last possible millisecond, so quickly that Cody hadn't seen the man twitch, Price blocked the knife stroke with an open hand. The mean blade plunged all the way through Price's palm, the tip actually nicking Price's cheek before the vampire jerked the hand and the knife away and raised Cody's face to Price's bloody one. Price hissed, the blood of his most recent victim frothing over his stretched bottom lip, and nose to nose as they were, Cody was assailed by the stench of maggoty death, the ancient carrion cloud of a thousand flyblown corpses.

"I thought you weren't gonna kill me yet," Cody said into the monstrous white face.

"We ain't," a voice said, and Price jolted, ripped for a moment out of his bloodlusting reverie.

They both turned and saw Penders striding toward Marguerite's. From behind Cody a new barrage of screams erupted, Angela and Mrs. Black no doubt riveting onto a new pair of victims.

His vampire's face abruptly donning a strangely human expression of good humour, Penders reached into the pocket of his pants and extracted a pint bottle of some kind of alcohol. "We ain't gonna kill you until we take everything from you. Mr. Price told you that."

"You've already taken everything," Cody said.

Penders chuckled, unscrewed the cap of the glass bottle. "You know that ain't true, Wilson. There's your pa, first of all. We're gonna pay him and his wife a visit." Penders chucked the cap into the street and upended the bottle, splashing alcohol over the weathered boards of the porch and the doorframe. "Shame we can't kill your mama again, Wilson, but I guess the tuberculosis already done that."

Cody clenched his jaw, his lips itching to say something equally hurtful to Penders.

But the big man went on, hurling the empty bottle through the empty doorframe. "We'll just have to settle for what we got though. Course, before we leave town we gotta attend to your girlfriend."

Penders brought out a book of matches.

"Please," Cody said.

"That root cellar of hers is awful handy," Penders said, tearing off a match. "But I doubt it's fireproof."

"You can't do that," the old woman said.

They all turned to regard her. It was the first time she'd spoken since Horton had towed her back into the main group. Without her bonnet, she looked somehow younger, almost girlish. She was on her knees now, her veiny fingers cinched over Horton's hand, which still gripped a goodly skein of her flowing white hair.

"You can't burn that place," she repeated. "Our dry-goods store's been next door going on twenty years now. It abuts the saloon and will go up too if you burn it."

"You old bitch, why the hell do you care?" Horton said, kneeling beside her. "You ain't gonna live long enough to see the sunrise anyhow."

"It's all we have," the old woman persisted. "You can't just destroy it. You burn one building, the whole row will burn. That's a quarter of the town's commerce."

"It ain't enough," Penders said, striking a match. "But it'll have to do."

Cody watched the match flare into life, saw Penders pivot toward the alcohol-soaked doorframe.

"*No!*" Cody screamed.

"Don't worry," Penders said, tipping Cody a wink. "We'll hang around long enough to hear your little senorita burn."

He tossed the lighted match onto the porch. Flames puffed up around the matchstick and spread in a steady blue lick over the porch, up the doorjambs.

The bar began to blaze.

* * *

"You can't!" the old woman screamed.

The plump woman, widow of the now-deceased man with the bushy mustache, lurched over to wrestle with Horton's arm in a vain attempt to disengage his hand from the old woman's white hair.

"*Let...her...go!*" the plump woman demanded, punctuating each word with slaps at Horton's delighted face. Horton crowed, easily dodging the plump woman's attempts. Still cackling, he took hold of the woman's black hair and pushed her down to face the wailing old woman whose dry-goods store was about to go up like dried tinder.

"You care so much about this old hag," Horton said, mashing the women's faces together, "why don't you kiss her? Give 'er a big ole smooch on those wrinkled lips so she knows how sorry you are for her."

"You bastard," Cody muttered.

Horton looked up, his countenance twisted into a hideous parody of defiance. "You got somethin' to say, little sister? You gonna stop me?"

"Tell your boss to let me go," Cody said, throwing a sideways nod at Price, "and you and me will have it out."

Horton's gaze went steely. "I ain't got no boss."

Something began to build inside Cody. "Then why's he order you around like you're some kind of slave?"

Horton's hands, buried as they were in the two women's hair, must've balled into fists, because both the plump woman and White Bonnet let loose with wails of pain. "I ain't no slave."

White Bonnet's scream rose higher, and though Cody exulted in the rage he'd kindled in Horton, he didn't want to cause either lady more pain.

One side of Horton's upper lip curled in a snarl. "You mouthy little shit."

Cody held his tongue. *Store it away for later*, he told himself. *You might be able to use it at some point, but if you don't shut up now, you're going to get these ladies killed.*

"Don't mind him," Penders counselled. "He's just grievin' his senorita." Despite the sensible tone in which he spoke, a moment later Penders pivoted toward a skinny old man and walloped him so hard in the jaw that before the old codger fell, his head lolled on his neck like a flower with a broken stalk.

Horton regarded Cody as if nothing had happened. His orange eyes blazed in the inky night. After a long moment, he turned and began dragging the women toward Marguerite's. The empty windows now flickered with tongues of flame, the heat from the conflagration shimmering the night air.

Cody had thought he'd salvaged the situation by shutting up, but the closer Horton got to the flames, the more he realised the horror was far from ended. Before Cody could say anything, Horton deposited the plump woman on the porch and reached down to grab hold of White Bonnet by one chalky ankle and one liver-spotted wrist.

"I don't want to die!" White Bonnet cried out.

"Shut your damned gob," Horton answered.

Grasping her by the ankle and wrist, he swung her back toward the crowd, then tossed her bodily through the fiery doorway.

Cody was too sickened to scream.

"This isn't happening," a young woman in a pink nightgown moaned. She was on her knees near Cody, weeping. A second or two later, she was sprawled on her back, Willet's mom having pinned her and latched on to her throat like a leech.

The plump woman had scuttled off the porch, but no sooner had she gained her feet than Horton leaped onto her back like a panther. He began dragging her by one leg back toward the bar, which was now spitting white-hot bolts of fire into the night.

Unmindful of the blistering heat, Horton strode up the steps and into the doorway. "Jesus, lady, you ain't been skipping any meals, have you?"

As the smoke surrounded her, the woman's gibbering screams devolved into violent coughs.

"In...ya...go!" Horton shouted, hurling the plump woman into the inferno.

"*No*," Cody whispered. He shook his head, struggling to block out the braying shrieks of the plump woman. Mercifully, she fell silent.

Cody looked up at Horton with bleary eyes. "You're a coward."

"I don't hear nothin'," Horton said, ignoring him. Horton glanced at Penders. "You sure that Mexican bitch is still down there?"

"There'd be lots of smoke," Penders said, moving toward the waiting black wagon. "She breathes just a little of it, it'd be just about impossible for her to do aught but choke."

Horton nodded, but he didn't seem convinced. Cody had an image of Marguerite coughing on smoke down there in that lightless cellar and did his best to shove it away. Perhaps the smoke would all rise, and she'd remain safe from it. But the heat would be unbearable. Marguerite would be broiled alive by the inferno raging over her.

Cody gritted his teeth. He had to do something, but what could he realistically do? He supposed he could try to break away from the devils, but what would that prove? They'd stop him before he got to the door, and if he did make it to the bar, he'd die before saving Marguerite. And say he did reach her in the cellar — what then? They'd perish down there like rats, or they'd miraculously elude the flames and the smoke only to be slaughtered out here on the street like the rest of Mesquite's people.

No. The only thing to do now was to go with them. He doubted he could save his father or Willet, but these pursuits were where he had to focus his thinking.

"Time we push on," Penders said, looking at Price. Price wore a bemused expression, his slowly transforming face halfway between vampire and human. Penders caught the indecision in Price's orange eyes. "We have to go now, Adam."

Cody had never heard anyone speak to Price in such an authoritative way, yet rather than bellowing at Penders in rage, Price surrendered his grip on Cody and moved toward the waiting red coach. Penders gripped Cody roughly by the scruff of the neck and shoved him toward the black coach. Cody stumbled, regained his balance and for a fleeting second debated fleeing down one of the nearby side streets.

Then he thought of Willet and made his way toward the coach.

"Back door, right side," Penders commanded.

Cody moved in that direction. Someone bumped into him from the left, nearly pitching him headlong into the street. It was Horton, of course. Horton who'd just cast two innocent women into the flames of a burning building the same way a smoker would flick a spent cigarette butt into a campfire.

"Howdy, princess," Horton said. "You remember how your little buddy shot me in the face?"

"I remember seeing you bleed," Cody said.

"You do, huh? Get your ass in the coach." Horton shoved Cody hard in the back. Cody was just able to catch himself before smashing face-first into the coach. He opened the black door and hoisted himself inside. Mrs. Black climbed into the coach with him, the front of her powder-blue dress now scrimmed with the congealing blood of half a dozen of Mesquite's citizens.

Mrs. Black pulled the door closed and regarded him in the near darkness. The shade covering the window to his left, Cody noticed, hadn't been drawn all the way down, so that a bar of light washed through. He couldn't see Mrs. Black too clearly, but what he could see was more than enough. Her face was changing back into a woman's again, but even when the hellish orange glow had left her eyes and the distorted jaws and teeth had ceased their resemblance to a bear trap, there would still be the blood smeared all over her dress, the beard of viscera caked around her mouth. In her lap she held the head of Eliza, the one she'd been sewing up earlier.

Upside down, Eliza's lifeless eyes stared at him.

Cody had to look away.

"You weren't to see him yet," Mrs. Black said.

Cody blocked her out. From his left came the roar and crackle of the still-growing blaze. The flames consuming Marguerite's saloon sent lemon-coloured flickers through the slit beneath the blind. Cody wanted to draw it all the way down so he wouldn't have to be reminded of Marguerite's death, but that would leave him alone in the dark with Willet's mother.

He glanced bleakly around the coach, noted the finery, the black velvet lining the ceiling. The bench on which Cody sat was cushioned and reminded him very much of a bed. Chances were good that he was sitting on the very spot where Horton or one of the other devils had taken Angela. An unmistakable undercurrent of old blood tinged his nostrils. Like a slaughterhouse that had never been properly cleaned.

"You weren't supposed to see him until later," Mrs. Black persisted.

Cody frowned. Next to Willet's mother there was a shapeless bundle wadded in the corner.

His throat went dry. "Who am I not supposed to see, Mrs. Black?"

Willet's mother smiled, a gruesome, inhuman smile. She reached out, massaged the sable lump beside her.

The lump stirred. Something in Cody died. He knew what he would see even before the amorphous hump rose and gained definition. A small, scrawny figure sat up, the black blanket that had covered it slithering to the floor.

Willet looked at Cody without recognition. The boy's eyes were orange and ravenous.

Willet's mouth unhinged, a deep growl trembling in his throat. Slaver dripped from his icepick teeth.

Cody screamed.

PART THREE
LAST STAND AT ESCONDIDO
CHAPTER TWENTY

Willet stared at Cody as though he wanted to rip his throat out. Even after all Cody had seen, after watching his wife murder and eat innocent townsfolk, after witnessing two shrieking women heaved thoughtlessly into a burning building, after all the fathomless horrors of the past few days, he was still too stunned to do anything but gape when he saw how Willet had been changed.

"Here," Martha Black said to her son, offering him Eliza's severed head. "I want you to snack on this while we ride."

The boy reached for the head, but Cody shouted, "Don't do that!"

Mother and son stared at Cody in annoyed surprise.

"I want you to hear something," Cody said to Willet.

"Don't talk to my boy," Mrs. Black said stiffly.

"He ceased to be your boy when you gave him up to these monsters."

"Lies," Mrs. Black said. "You only dabble in lies."

Cody ignored her. Fixing Willet with his firmest stare, he said, "You need to know something about the man these creatures are planning to kill."

"He's heard enough from you," Mrs. Black said. "Making your father out to be some kind of—"

"Shut up," Cody said.

Mrs. Black's eyes glinted with wrath, but she said nothing.

"When my mama died," Cody went on, "my dad was forced into being both parents to me."

Cody saw no comprehension in Willet's eyes. Granted, they were looking at him, but they were vapid, emotionless. The boy's hair was askew, his skin filthy. All of the former vitality was gone, all the ornery good humour. Were Willet not sitting up, Cody would've mistaken him for a corpse. Still, Cody thought, he had to try.

"I must've been about seven years old at the time. Dad always made sure I was presentable for school. My clothes weren't fancy, but they were clean. Anyway, he'd ride me to town on his big red mare every morning. One day – this would've been near the beginning of the school year because I remember not knowing anybody – I was climbing up into the saddle with him when my pants split in the crotch."

Cody waited for the boy to laugh, to smile even, but Willet only gazed blankly back at him and evinced no discernible human emotion.

Cody said, "We had time for the rip to be mended, but Dad hadn't sewn anything in years. That was always Mama's department. He didn't even know where the needles and thread were kept."

Cody nodded, remembering the frantic expression Jack Wilson had worn that morning. "We hustled inside, but by the time he located the sewing kit, we were already late. He could've kept me home, but he hated the thought of me missing school when I wasn't sick. He pulled off my pants and started to sew them up. He'd stitched up men a few times on the battlefield, but mending pants is different than stitching up a wound. As you might imagine, he made a mess of the job and had to rip out the stitches he'd made. He found a safety pin and cinched the hole shut as best he could. When I got to school, several of my classmates noticed my underpants were showing and ribbed me something fierce. The teacher sent a note home informing Dad that he was not to send me to school looking so indecent again."

Cody fell silent, remembering the shame of that day. The derision of his peers. But worst of all was the crestfallen look on his dad's face when he saw the teacher's note. Cody had shared with him a few of his classmates' comments, but when he'd seen how guilty his father felt, he'd cut short his account.

Mrs. Black's lips were pursed in disapproval. "I fail to see the point of your diatribe, Mr. Wilson."

Cody patted the plush bench of the coach. "That's because you're no more a woman anymore than this seat right here. Your heart is gone. Also, I haven't gotten to the end of my story yet.

"As I was saying, Dad felt awful, like he'd failed me or something, and at the time I suppose I thought he *had* failed me. I wasn't vicious toward him, but I certainly didn't go out of my way to make him feel better about his parenting.

"We had supper that night like always, and like always we read together and went through our Bible verses. I went to bed and was a long time in falling asleep, which was why I noticed the lights were on in the main room despite the fact that it was going on midnight."

As Cody spoke, it was like being a rider in his seven-year-old body again. He felt the blanket slip off his body, felt the frigid floorboards beneath his feet. The door to his bedroom creaked a little as he opened it, but the noise didn't bother him. He wasn't scared. Just curious.

"When I rounded the corner, can you guess what I saw?" He leaned forward and stared meaningfully into Willet's vacant eyes. "There was Jack Wilson, as tough a rancher as I've ever encountered, putting all his concentration into sewing up an old dress shirt I'd long since outgrown."

In the silence that followed, Mrs. Black shook her head and made a priggish tutting sound. "A pointless fable."

"You see what it means, don't you, Willet? Dad wasn't mending that shirt for me to wear – the only thing it was good for was tearing into strips to use for kitchen rags. He was practicing his sewing skills. Making sure that if another situation like that arose, he'd be better prepared."

"It sounds to me," Martha Black said, a nasty grin on her face, "that he didn't like that teacher getting uppity with him. It was simple male pride, Mr. Wilson, and that's hardly something to glorify your father over."

Cody nodded. "That was part of it, sure. But only a small part of it. Jack Wilson didn't want his son to feel embarrassed. He didn't want his son to want for a mother. And since he couldn't provide one in the flesh for me – at least not for another seven years – he was determined to fill that role as best he could."

Martha Black rolled her eyes. "Empty sentiment."

"My dad bathed me, Willet. He learned to cut my hair from a woman in town." Cody chuckled. "Paid her extra to keep quiet about it. He sang me bedtime songs and taught me how to fry an egg. He did everything for me he could...or rather, he made sure I learned how to take care of myself, which was even better. And now Adam Price – who took your life from you just to spite me – plans to kill my father. Does that sound right to you?"

Willet only watched Cody with that same unseeing expression. If there was anything in Willet's orange-flecked eyes, it was barely suppressed hunger. For several seconds Cody listened to the primal growls rumbling in the back of Willet's throat. Finally, Mrs. Black was able to distract her son by offering him Eliza's severed head.

Cody watched dismally as Willet ripped open the threaded flaps of flesh and plunged his fanged maw into the glistening meat of Eliza's neck.

"Now you make do on that until we get to Escondido," Mrs. Black said. "Mr. Wilson here won't be any less full of blood when we reach his father's ranch." She regarded Cody good-humouredly. "Unless of course Horton decides to ride with us."

Cody became aware of the heat emanating from the blaze. The coaches were parked two buildings down from Marguerite's, but the fire had either grown so intense that the heat was affecting the coaches, or the flames had spread to the adjacent buildings. At any rate, the black quarter horses to which the coach was hitched had begun to stamp and whinny. Moments later, Cody heard a creaking overhead and knew someone had sat in the driver's box. This was confirmed by the curt snapping of reins and a subsequent lurch forward. Ahead, Cody heard the red coach begin to roll too.

In the corner of the black coach, Willet's face bobbed ravenously in the underside of Eliza's head. The smacking sounds the boy was making turned Cody's stomach.

"Who's driving us?" Cody asked.

Mrs. Black smiled companionably. "Mr. Horton, I expect. He's usually the reinsman. At least he's been since I took up with them."

Cody grunted. "Took up with them. You make it sound like you had a choice."

"At first I was very afraid of them. When Adam carried me toward this coach, I screamed until my voice gave out. I'd seen them murder my husband and my daughters. I thought they would kill me next."

"Then you resisted?"

Mrs. Black looked at him as though he'd lost his mind. "Of course I resisted, darling. I'm not a harlot."

"You mean you weren't one."

She folded her hands primly in her lap. "I meant what I said."

"You're telling me you haven't slept with Horton? With any of them?"

"My relationship with the players is none of your concern."

Cody shook his head. "You talk about them like they're real actors, like they're anything more than animals."

Mrs. Black drew herself up. "I'll have you know that Adam hails from Europe. He's been alive for centuries. He's more cultured than you could ever hope to be."

"I find it hard to talk to you with that black shit all over your mouth."

"It's blood, my dear."

"I know what it is. How can you live with it?"

"I don't notice it," Mrs. Black said. "I'll wash up when we stop to water the horses."

"That's not what I meant," Cody said hotly. "I mean how can you live with what you've become? Killing innocent folks. Doing to families what Price and his bastard friends did to yours. Doesn't it make you sick? Doesn't it make you want to kill yourself?"

Willet had ceased his smacking sounds and was looking up at Cody, his freckled face smeared with blood and contorted with anger.

Mrs. Black placed a mollifying hand on Willet's forearm. "It's all right, my dear. Mr. Wilson can't be expected to understand. He's still smarting from the horns he was made to wear."

"You're a damned bitch," Cody said.

"I'm going to live forever," Mrs. Black said.

"Not if I have something to say about it."

"You won't, dear. Adam plans to kill you after he kills your father."

"He'll find Jack Wilson a lot harder to kill than the average man."

Mrs. Black reached up, stroked her son's greasy hair. "I doubt it, Mr. Wilson. If he was anything more than average, he would have brought his son up better."

★　★　★

Willet fed for the better part of an hour. Cody's stomach roiled and clenched with the noises, but he was determined not to show it. But though he couldn't stand the sight of the feasting young vampire, the smarminess of Mrs. Black's smile was somehow even worse. So Cody raised the blind, leaned on an elbow and peered out the side glass.

He gazed out over the prairie scrub. It was still full dark out, but Cody knew within an hour or two they'd be able to see the Organ Mountains, before which lay Escondido. His father's ranch would be five miles south of town, at the foot of Mount Alexandra. Cody closed his eyes and wished there was some way to warn his dad of what was coming. With any luck, Jack and Gladys Wilson had taken a trip somewhere and would be spared.

You know they'll be at the ranch, a voice declared. *Everyone you meet comes to ruin. Haven't you realised that by now? Angela, Willet, Marguerite...soon your father and stepmother. Probably by sunrise...*

Cody tensed, a sudden idea arresting his attention. He looked up at Mrs. Black, who was caressing her son's forehead. Willet was drifting into a sated doze, which was just as well. He still hadn't looked at Cody as if Cody was anything but an especially appetising entrée.

Mrs. Black regarded him with twinkling gaiety. *Get her talking*, his dad's voice whispered. *You might learn something useful.*

"Something on your mind, Mr. Wilson?"

He returned Mrs. Black's cheerful grin. "As a matter of fact, there is. I'm wondering if you're afraid of crosses."

"Why would I be afraid of crosses, Mr. Wilson? A Christian woman has nothing to fear from the Lord."

"I doubt the Lord appreciated your exhibition back there in Mesquite."

Her grin slipped a little, a cloud darkening her eyes. "I cannot help what I've become, Mr. Wilson. I can only provide the sustenance necessary for me and my son."

Cody leaned back, spread his arms on the top of the velvet couch-back. "It didn't look to me like you were worried about providing sustenance for you two. Looked to me like you were ripping and tearing anything that moved. It looked to me like you enjoyed it."

A little shudder coursed through her. She sniffed, peered down at her son. Stroking Willet's brow, she said, "Our appetites are prodigious, Mr. Wilson. We need blood to sustain us."

Cody nodded. "I see. So the reason you opened that little girl's belly was because you needed to be sustained."

Mrs. Black's voice was sullen. "I don't think that's fair, Mr. Wilson."

"How old you reckon she was?" Cody asked. "Ten? No more than eleven, I'd wager."

Mrs. Black shuddered again. Her voice quivered. "She was a vessel carrying the needed—"

"She was an innocent child who had her whole life ahead of her—"

"—fluid, so I partook of her—"

"—just like Willet was before you let them turn him into a beast."

Mrs. Black's mouth and eyes shuttered wide. "I did *not* let them—"

"You gave them your little boy, and you didn't even bat an

eyelash. You cared more about having him back with you than you did about his soul."

Mrs. Black's upper lip curled. "How *dare* you?"

"Or maybe you just care more about appeasing your new idol than you do about your own child."

"Will you stop saying that?" Orange flames guttered in Mrs. Black's eyes.

Easy, his dad reminded him. *You got the confirmation you were after. They experience the change when they get mad, and when they get mad, they get wild and reckless. That's why you were able to trick Dragomir. That's why he didn't heed Price's warnings. Now don't push your luck.*

Cody forced his expression to remain neutral. He realised that on some level, this was what he'd been after. If he kept Willet's mom talking, he might learn more.

"Beg your pardon, Mrs. Black. I am sorry for saying those things to you."

Her eyes narrowed, but the snarl remained fixed in place.

He said, "You still believe in God then?"

She uttered a mirthless little laugh. "Why wouldn't I? He has given me eternal life."

"Wait a minute. We talkin' about the Almighty or Adam Price here?"

"Your blasphemy is duly noted, Mr. Wilson. Don't you realise that Billy Horton can hear everything you say?"

Cody glanced up at the ceiling. "He can?"

"Our hearing is very acute."

"So if I called him a brainless whoreson, he'd hear me?"

The coach gave a hard lurch. Cody heard the reins snapping and the black horses neighing their protests.

"I guess you're right," Cody agreed.

Mrs. Black gazed at him balefully but said nothing.

They rode in silence for several minutes. The coach began to fill with the sound of Willet's tranquil snoring. At length Cody said, "You know, my dad's not a wealthy man, but he's amassed quite a private library over the course of his fifty years."

"He knows nothing," Mrs. Black said.

Cody chuckled. "That's not very generous of you. You don't seem the type to dismiss learning as unimportant."

"Don't put words in my mouth."

"I didn't think I did."

"Angela was right about you. You're nothing but a fool."

"I notice you dropped the 'Mr. Wilson.'"

"You've read nothing but tawdry novels. How could you be expected to understand the majesty of what we are?"

"You changed allegiances awfully fast."

Mrs. Black leaned forward, eyes bright. "Because I've *learned*, Mr. Wilson. I've learned more in the past twenty-four hours than I had in the thirty-six years prior."

Cody shrugged. "You *are* good at killing little girls."

She nodded sagely. "You mock me, Mr. Wilson, because you don't know what power flows through my veins." She paused, considering. "We are virtually invulnerable, but I'm not an idiot. Do you really think I'd tell you how to kill us?"

"There must be ways, else you wouldn't say that."

"Anything can die, Mr. Wilson. It's the nature of life."

"That's right," Cody said. "Anything can die, especially when there's no one there to protect it. Tell me something, Mrs. Black."

She gazed down at her son, stroking his forehead and waiting.

"I'm just wondering if you were there when they bit your boy."

The hand froze over Willet's grimy forehead. In a controlled voice, Mrs. Black said, "I was not present at the time."

"Couldn't bear to see it."

"I didn't say that."

"You didn't have to."

"Mr. Wil—"

"How did you rationalise it? Turning your only living child into a monster?"

She glared up at him, eyes suddenly iridescent in the gloom of the coach. "He is *not* a monster," she hissed.

"I don't know how you'd define it, but I just watched a twelve-year-old kid digging into a woman's severed head like it was a porterhouse steak. That seems pretty monstrous to me."

"Shut your mouth."

"I don't think I will."

The eyes flickered orange. "Then I'll silence it for you."

"If this vampire thing is so wonderful," Cody went on, grinning savagely, "then why the hell wouldn't you stick around to see your boy become one? I'd have thought that'd be a real proud moment for a mother."

All semblance of propriety had fallen away from Mrs. Black. Her hinged jaw opened wider with each raspy respiration. Slaver dripped from her deadly white fangs. In a voice that scarcely resembled a woman's, she said, "I'll not warn you again, Mr. Wilson. Stop talking about my son's..."

Her monstrous face clouded, an eerily human emotion seeping into it. Cody saw it inscribed on her vulpine features but didn't immediately cotton to its meaning.

Then it hit him.

"You *were* there, weren't you? You were the one who told Willet it was okay to let Price bite him."

With a squalling scream, Mrs. Black leaped at Cody.

CHAPTER TWENTY-ONE

Horton must have been aware of what was about to happen, for in the moments before Mrs. Black attacked him, Cody sensed the quarter horses slowing. The woman's body slammed into his with the force of a steam engine and drove him backward into the deep velvet cushion. The vampire woman was a flurry of claws and teeth, Cody's forearms instantly striped with gashes. Cody heard someone shout; then Mrs. Black was being dragged off him. She slashed him one more time just above the knee for good measure, her claw slicing deep into the meat of his leg.

It was Willet, Cody now realised, who had saved him, Willet who had dragged his spitting mother off Cody. Despite the size difference, Willet managed his mother easily, grasping her around the waist and holding on to her until she calmed down. But she was only calm for a moment.

Then she noticed Cody's blood.

Her orange eyes suddenly slitted with yearning. She lunged for him again, but this time Cody anticipated her. Sprawled on his back as he was, it was easy for him to kick her ghastly face when she darted at him. But though his bootheel caught her square in the nose, the blow didn't seem to faze her. She clawed at his legs again, snarling, but again Willet restrained her. The boy looked the same as he had that morning – that was the painful part – yet his strength surpassed even the stoutest of men.

It was Adam Price who changed Willet, Cody reflected. *That's why he's already so powerful. He was bitten by the king vampire.*

Cody had no idea if this was so, but it made sense to him. Now the boy was muttering something to his mother about the master's plans, about holding off a trifle longer.

Cody said, "Don't worry, Willet. She's good at following

the master's directions. She's just like Horton up there — a mindless slave."

A dark shape sprang into the coach and filled Cody's vision. It was Horton, the young vampire's cockiness buried under red strata of wrath. "You're gonna die the worst death imaginable, Wilson. You realise that? I'm gonna stick it in your wife while the others peel your flesh from your body. You're gonna watch your daddy scream like a little girl while Penders eats him alive."

"Two of you are dead," Cody reminded him. "And I'm still here."

Horton's hand flashed and a scalding heat sizzled in Cody's right ear. As Cody fingered the bloody area, Horton dangled something small and pink in front of Cody's face. "Here," Horton said, "taste for yourself." And before Cody could react, Horton had shoved the severed earlobe into Cody's open mouth. For one awful moment, he gagged on it and was certain it would choke him. Then he dislodged it and spat it onto the floor. The bloody chunk of meat landed with a sick plopping sound. The moment it hit, Willet's mom dove for it, stuffed it into her maw and gobbled it down. Cody glanced up at Willet, who was looking on miserably.

"That what you want to be, Willet?"

Willet stared back at Cody with what might have been sorrow. "It's what I am."

"What if there's still a choice?"

Willet's voice was inflectionless, defeated. "There ain't no choice."

"The boy's smarter'n you," Horton cut in. "Course, that ain't sayin' much. I been alive more'n fifty years, and you're the dumbest sonofabitch I met yet."

Cody looked at him, amazed. "You've been the same age for that long?"

"Eternal youth," Horton said and tipped him a wink. "Live forever and get all the pussy you can handle."

"You'll never have a family though," Cody said, and as he said it, he realised it was the truth.

Horton scowled. "These folks are my family."

"They're not family," Cody said. "They're parasites squabbling over fresh meat. You and Penders and the rest."

Horton leaned forward, the tendons in his neck taut and straining. "Don't test me, boy."

"You're maggots," Cody persisted. "Only that's too generous. Maggots become something else. They can beget life. You'll never make anything but death."

"I helped turn your wife into one of us. I'd call that bein' a daddy."

"That's just infection," Cody said. "You'll never be a father. Your seed dies with you, Horton. You can only bring death to others." Cody inhaled Horton's sickly sweet breath. It smelled like rot, like decay. "You're lower than the worms."

Horton roared and grasped Cody by the shoulders. Cody was propelled upward, his head cracking against the ceiling. His vision swam; his hearing turned muzzy. He was jerked forward to find himself touching noses with Horton, who'd changed almost instantly into his bestial form. The vampire shook him violently. He heard Horton's huge jaws yawn open, smelled the reek of putrescence closing over him.

A voice thundered, "ENOUGH!"

Cody realised he'd shut his eyes. He opened them now and saw how close he'd been to death. Horton's dripping jaws were poised an inch from his throat.

"Put him down, Billy," Price said in a quieter voice that was no less stern.

Horton obeyed, dropping Cody roughly onto the seat. Horton receded across the coach until his legs abutted the opposite bench, but he did not sit. Price climbed into the coach and stood between Cody and Horton.

Price smiled cordially. "I see you're making friends, Mr. Wilson." Price glanced first at Horton, then at Mrs. Black. Both vampires were glaring at Cody with unbridled hatred. "You do have a talent for incurring the wrath of my brethren," Price said. "If we don't alter the travelling arrangements, you'll not make it to your father's ranch alive."

"You won't make it there by sunup," Cody said.

"We'll arrive in Escondido with time to spare," Price said and turned to Horton. "Billy, you take Martha and her son to the Concord. You'll relieve Penders of his duties and allow him to rest inside."

Horton's voice was deep, more the rumble of a wolf than the voice of a human being. "Who'll drive you?"

"I will," Price said.

"Sir—" Horton began.

But Price cut him off. "Go, Billy. And tell Angela that she'll ride the rest of the way with her husband."

Some new emotion rippled over Horton's vampiric features, and after a moment, Cody realised what it was: jealousy.

"Sir," Horton said. "I don't think—"

"She'll be quite all right, Billy. Your amorous activities will not be affected."

"But she'll kill him, sir."

For the first time, Price glanced over at Horton. He pursed his lips, thinking. Then, he gave a little nod. "Tell her to come to the black coach, Billy. If she kills him, I will be disappointed, but at least there will be closure."

Horton shook his head, licked his lips with a serpentlike tongue. "I don't think she should—"

"Bring her, Billy."

Horton glowered at Price a long time. Then he dropped his gaze and went out. Willet and his mother followed, and for the first time since the jail cell, Cody found himself alone with Adam Price.

★   ★   ★

"Anything you'd like to ask me, Mr. Wilson?"

Cody experienced a delirious mixture of revulsion, fear, and loathing as he looked up into Price's dark eyes. "I've got plenty of questions, but I doubt you want to answer them."

"On the contrary, Mr. Wilson. This might be our last opportunity for discourse." Price's eyes danced with impish humour. "I suspect we'll find ourselves quite busy when we arrive at your father's ranch."

"Why didn't you show what you were back at the valley?"

Price smiled. "That was before you killed Dmitri. We hadn't shown our true forms for many months and had no reason to do so. Until you claimed one of our own, that is. At that point I told the others that they were free to let their true natures come forth."

"What's the difference? You still killed people."

"The difference," Price said, sitting on the bench and interlacing his fingers, "is the risk we take when we become. You don't think we'd last very long if we went around changing in front of everyone, do you?"

"You roasted the old man," Cody said. "Willet's grandfather. Why'd you do that if you live off the blood?"

Price frowned. "Whatever gave you that idea?"

Cody grunted. "In the bar, you guys drank like—"

"Blood is a restorative, Mr. Wilson, but we also crave the taste. As far as Willet's grandfather is concerned, we still need to eat, don't we? So why should we have allowed perfectly good meat to go to waste?"

Remembering the gamey odour of the old man's roasting flesh, Cody suppressed a wave of revulsion.

"Now, Mr. Wilson," Price said, leaning forward and placing his hands on his knees, "are these the answers you truly seek? Quizzing me about our eating habits and our reasons for changing? Think of the opportunity you have! How many men get the chance to learn about my kind?"

Cody drew in a deep breath, blew it out slowly. "Why'd you turn Willet?"

"You care about the boy."

Cody bared his teeth. "Not in the way you told that bastard Bittner."

"A means to an end, Mr. Wilson. I used the man's twisted psyche to achieve my desired effect. And as you saw, it worked well." A shadow crept into Price's face. "Up to a point."

"You mean the point where I used Bittner to kill your friend?"

Price favoured Cody with a soft, patient smile, the look of a veteran schoolteacher dealing with an impudent but tractable child. "You'll not bait me again, Mr. Wilson. Though I do have to give you credit for doing to me what no man has done for quite some time. I rarely lose control."

"But you see the beauty in it, don't you?" Cody said. "Bittner and Dragomir were filled with poison, so both of them got what they deserved."

Price nodded. "There was a certain symmetry in the moment. That I won't deny. Nor can you deny the irony of bringing death to the man who gave you life."

Cody felt some of his confidence fade. "Or it's just you being sadistic."

"You idolise your father, Mr. Wilson. Even when you despised him, you idolised him. Like Ahab, you sought to strike at the face of God. Or in your case, your earthly father. That's why you hurt him by marrying a tart."

"That's a mean way to talk about your new concubine."

"I know what Angela is," Price said.

"If you did, you wouldn't have taken her with you."

"But you did," Price said, eyebrows rising. "You struck at your father in the cruellest manner possible. Not only did you marry a woman certain to bring you to ruin, but in doing so you deprived him of his only child."

Cody looked away. "I made a mistake."

"Indeed," Price agreed. "As for Angela, she will serve her purpose for a time, whether that's luring prey to our group or satisfying our carnal urges. But she is just one of many. There have been harlots before her, and there will be harlots in the centuries to come. It is the nature of women."

"Horseshit."

Price drew back, surprised. "You disagree? I'd have thought you, above all men, would hold the fairer sex in contempt."

"I was hurt and ashamed and more embarrassed than any living thing has a right to be. So I suppose over the past several days I've harboured some mean notions. But that's changed now."

"Let me posit a guess. It was your lovely barmaid who disabused you of this prejudice."

"Part of it was Marguerite," Cody allowed. "But most of it

was Dad. He didn't raise me up to demean women. He taught me to honour them. To respect them. Which I guess is why I was so nice to Angela. Why I didn't see what she was."

A voice spoke up from the open door of the coach. "Cody loves and hates his daddy more than any boy ever did."

Angela climbed into the coach, her pallid flesh bulging sensuously over the bodice of her white dress. "Cody talked about Daddy all the time. Some of it was good, some of it wasn't. But if *I* ever said anything against the old bastard—" Angela rolled her eyes and made a whistling sound. "Jesus, you'd've thought I'd burned the Bible by the way he hollered at me."

"I never raised my hand to you," Cody said.

"Of course you didn't," Angela said, sitting across from him. "You were too much of a coward to do that."

Price regarded his shoes in embarrassment. "I can see you two want to spend these last few moments discussing your differences." He hopped agilely out of the coach and addressed Angela. "We should be there within the hour. Say what you want to him before he dies. But don't let him goad you into violence."

Price grasped the door, appeared about to close it, but paused, a thoughtful expression on his face. "He's smarter than I at first thought. Much smarter, it seems. Had events transpired differently, he might have been very useful to me. He might have even made a powerful ally. But we've long since passed that point. He must die, and he must die in agony. We will make his father's ranch a place of horror, a warning to all who seek to oppose us in the future." He stared intently at Angela. "Please keep your head. Please allow me the pleasure of his screams."

With that, Price closed the door.

Angela looked at Cody and arched an eyebrow. "Would you like to make love to me one last time?"

CHAPTER TWENTY-TWO

Cody stared at her across the coach, her pale cleavage trembling with each bump on the trail. "Would I like to *what?*"

"Make love to me. Surely you remember how?"

Cody laughed. "You are a piece of work, Angela. You think I'd touch you after all you've done?"

Angela leaned forward, her breasts bunching against the décolletage. "I could make you."

"You'd have to kill me first."

There was smoke in her gaze, her voice a low purr. "You know you want to."

Cody clenched his jaw. "You let that bastard Horton screw you right on the stage. You probably let all of 'em have a turn on you. Penders, Price, even the twins."

Angela's gaze was unwavering. "They're not here now."

Cody noticed how her legs were crossed, the left one positioned over the right so the slit in her white dress opened all the way up to the cleft between her legs. Against his will, Cody's eyes went there, took in the white satin triangle of underwear covering her cleft.

His voice husky, he said, "You're the worst kind of animal. You take what you've been given..." His eyes flicked to her crotch, then roamed over her bulging breasts. "...and I don't deny you've been given a lot. But you take what could be a special thing, a beautiful thing, and turn it into something unnatural."

Without a word, she reached up, unlaced the bodice of her dress.

"The hell are you doing?" he asked in a tight voice.

"*You* know," she said. The laces loosened, the ample breasts pushing free of their strictures. They sagged as the dress opened up, but they didn't sag much.

Jesus, Cody thought. *Price says it's women who're animals, but they're nothing compared to men. For me to even consider what this monster is proposing…good God, I'm no better than a dog in heat.*

Angela appeared to catch the drift of his thoughts. Her lusty grin grew triumphant, a wanton glaze seeming to envelope her. She shook loose of the shoulder straps – she wore no brassiere – and was suddenly, horribly, naked to the waist. Her tummy was a trifle plump, the smooth flesh there adorned with a soft, colourless sheen of down. Cody remembered the way she used to let him play around down there. When he begged her to let him. He remembered the colour of her pubic hair, dark blond and seeming to prickle to attention when he'd run his tongue through it.

"That's right, baby," Angela coaxed. "Imagine how it'll be. Imagine how I'll taste."

Cody did. God help him, he did. He remembered those rare times when Angela let him act like a man and have his run of her body, permitted him to give her pleasure without complicating it with her insults and her games. He wanted to spread her legs, he wanted to prime her, prepare her. And dammit if he didn't want to impale her and rut like an animal, go wild with this woman, slap bellies with her until his basest desires were quenched.

Once again, she seemed to hear his thoughts. She stood, wiggled a little as she pushed the dress over her hips. He caught a glimpse of her dark blond thatch, but it was the sight of her belly that gave him pause. Her tummy was distended a little, but that wasn't what bothered him. What bothered him was what was *in* her belly, the reason why her stomach was so round.

The dress slithering down her legs, Angela said, "It doesn't matter, baby. Come over here and give me what I need."

But it did matter. Dear God, it did. For in that belly were the digesting remains of at least five people, and that only counted the ones Cody witnessed Angela killing and eating. Who knew how many lives she'd taken that night, how many gobbets of flesh she'd torn from screaming victims and chewed up like some unfeeling lioness?

There was no tenderness in her voice now. Only steel. "Get over here," she commanded.

Cody wetted his lips, felt icy sweat bead on his forehead. "Uh-uh. I've seen all I need to."

"I won't tell you again," she said, her voice deepening. "Get over here and lick my cunt."

Cody looked up at her. "Lick your own cunt. That new tongue of yours ought to be long enough."

The change started. "You little sissy."

The coach began to slow. Cody shot a glance out the window, spotted the mountains rising in the distance. Had they reached the ranch, or was Price stopping to delay Cody's death one last time?

Whatever the case, it better happen quickly, Cody thought. Angela's eyes had begun their weird colour change, orange sparks beginning to flicker in her irises. Their shape altered too, the eyes transforming into vertical and faintly crocodilian lozenges.

Angela's speech was impacted by the pallid spears now sprouting out of her gums, but Cody made out the words well enough. "You were never a man," she said, stepping toward him and out of her dress, which lay pooled on the floor. "You expected me to be a proper lady, but you never set me up like one."

Cody knew he should stall, should somehow put off her change by making nice, but the words were out before he knew he was going to utter them. "Your nature is corrupt, Angela. Always was. I was beguiled by your looks, but I never took the measure of your heart."

The satanic glow of her eyes lit up the coach now, the lower jaw stretching down to render her words nearly incomprehensible. "You never knew my heart."

Shut up! a voice in his mind cried out. *Shut up before she kills you!*

But the words kept coming, everything he'd wanted to say but had never known how. "Your heart's cold, Angela. It's shot through with selfishness. No marriage can work when one doesn't care a whit about the other."

The coach shuddered to a halt. Angela stood over him now, her sex less than a foot from his face. But any thoughts of copulating with his once-wife had scattered like windblown dust. Her body remained largely unchanged, but from the shoulders up she had become something abhorrent, the stuff of nightmares. Cody could scarcely meet her gaze, but that was apparently what she was waiting for.

She said something else, but he couldn't make it out. Voices sounded from outside the coach. Price and perhaps Horton.

Open the door, Cody thought. *Let me out of this black cage of death so I can at least see my father before we both die.*

"*Look at me!*" Angela snarled, though the *L* and the *M* were rendered indistinguishable by her gruesome serrated teeth.

Reluctantly, Cody glanced up at her.

She was a freak show, her transformation more hideous even than before. In Mesquite she'd looked like a monster, but there had yet lingered a strong reminder of her other, human self in her features.

What faced him now was an abomination.

The mandibles were elongated, but they had widened too. The result of this widening was a fixed, monstrous grin that chilled him to the core. The icepick teeth moved slightly with her heavy breathing. Cody watched, fascinated, as the tapered tips first met, then punctured her gums. Blood trickled down her jaw, swirling with the noxious slaver that ran in runnels down her throat. Cody wanted to scream, but he would not provide her that one final triumph.

She tensed as if to attack, but the coach door swung open. They both looked and saw Adam Price peering up at them. "Have we reached a stalemate?" Price asked.

"She was about to kill me, if you call that a stalemate," Cody answered.

"Then I'm afraid she'll have to wait. We've reached the ranch."

Angela climbed down and stood blinking, looking very much dazed by the intrusion of her master and the interruption of her feeding. Cody saw with a sinking feeling that they had indeed reached his father's ranch. His dad had bought the place only six years before Cody had met Angela, so Cody never really considered it home. But still, he felt a sharp pang of regret as he regarded the modest but well-kept adobe house, the stables and barns that spread on either side of the homestead.

Penders had parked the Concord coach about thirty yards from the front gate, which was a simple, swinging wooden door constructed of three horizontal slats and their supports. The black quarter horses had halted only a few feet from the red coach, so that Cody could clearly see the faces of Martha Black and her boy as they climbed down. Horton followed them, looking far too eager for more carnage.

Cody turned away before Horton caught him staring. It was bad enough what the son of a bitch was about to do; Cody didn't need to endure any more gloating about it. He peered at the hulking rock formation that lay just in front of the gate and to the left. Above that and in the distance, the tops of the Organ Mountains had begun to catch the first ghostly rays of the new sun, but it would be an hour or more before it could be considered daylight.

That was plenty of time for the devils to do whatever they planned.

Cody followed Price toward the others, who had massed to the left of the Concord. Angela trudged alongside him, looking surly and just as awful as she had in the coach.

When they stopped next to the others, Cody said, "You're not going to have much time to kill us."

"We got all the time in the world," Penders said without turning. "That house'll be nice and cool in the heat. Dark enough, too. We'll have our fun in there."

Cody's insides shrivelled. He tried but was unable to keep the panic out of his voice. "My dad won't go down without a fight."

Horton gave him a withering look. "There are six of us, dumbass. There's only you, your daddy, and his squaw. And you don't even count."

"You don't know my dad," Cody said.

Horton grinned. "I'll know him soon enough, won't I? Him and his bitch?"

"I get to kill Cody's father," Angela croaked. "I get to rip out—"

But she never finished. Because at that moment they heard a thwacking sound followed by an abbreviated whoosh.

The arrow pierced Angela's forehead dead centre, its tip splitting through the back of her blond hair and glistening with what looked like a chunk of her brain. Her expression never changed. She sank to her knees and teetered there for a full three seconds. Then, as they all stared at her in stunned silence, she thumped forward face-first and lay without moving. Cody looked up.

A figure stepped out from behind the rock formation, a crossbow dangling at its side.

"She deserved to die first," Marguerite said. She raised the crossbow. "Who wants it next?"

CHAPTER TWENTY-THREE

"You died," Martha Black said, gaping at Marguerite. "You were in the cellar when the building burned."

Cody grinned. "Looks like she found a way out."

Bringing the crossbow to rest on Martha Black, Marguerite said, "I almost died. I thought I *was* dead. When the place started to go up, I smelled the smoke. I knew these monsters wouldn't burn the place and stay inside it. I chanced it and made it out the kitchen window before it came down on top of me."

Price's tone was admiring. "And you saddled your horse and raced to this ranch."

"It wasn't my horse," Marguerite said. "It belonged to one of my customers. I assume he's dead now and won't mind."

Horton stepped forward. "You're one saucy woman, Miss Marguerita. I bet you know how to *ride*."

She shifted the crossbow until it was fixed on Horton's face. "My father taught me about horses."

"What else he teach you, sweetie? He teach you how to satisfy a man?"

"Careful, Billy," Price said. "She will have roused the others."

"What others?" Horton asked, chuckling. "The old man and his wife? Hell, he won't be much. Can't be if the only kind of son he could produce is Wilson here."

The side of Horton's head exploded.

After that everything happened very fast. Horton flopped down in the dust, his limbs flailing wildly in what Cody hoped were death spasms. He didn't want to count his chickens too quickly, however. He'd seen Horton get shot in the head once before.

Price took cover behind the red coach, as did Willet and Mrs. Black. Penders took off in a lumbering sprint that nonetheless covered the space between where he'd stood and the clump of sage from which the shot had come with alarming speed.

Look out, Dad, Cody thought.

Marguerite stalked forward, tracking Penders with the crossbow as she moved.

In the head, Cody thought and broke toward the front of the red coach. *Just like the last one, Marguerite. Get Penders in the head the same way you got Angela.* He cast one last glance at Angela before he climbed up onto the Concord's bench. She hadn't stirred. Not yet at least.

Cody seized the reins, gave them a vicious snap, and the already bucking team leaped into action. At the same moment the rifle from the sage cracked again and spun Penders sideways.

But the shooter's timing couldn't have been worse. At that moment, the second crossbow arrow punctured Pender's throat.

Damn it, Cody thought. *If he hadn't been shot first, Marguerite would've gotten him in the brain.* No matter though. Cody drove the team toward Penders's spinning form, meaning to both trample the huge man and to expose the three vampires who'd taken refuge behind the coach.

The frightened sorrels and Appaloosas were pounding straight toward the bleeding man, who was simultaneously pawing at the arrow in his throat and transforming into a vampire. Just before the team rode over him, Penders wrested the arrow from his neck, turned and slammed the arrow's tip into the exposed breast of the right lead horse. The sorrel shrieked, buckling in agony, and the whole rig bounced over Penders's big body. Cody was ejected forward out of the box, the rig overturning behind him. Cody landed on his shoulder and tumbled end over end toward the fence. He came to rest on his belly, and in a half daze he saw a figure rise out of the sage and point a rifle at him.

Don't shoot me, Dad! he thought.

But the figure didn't shoot him.

And it wasn't his father.

Gladys Wilson, Cody's stepmother, reached into a California-style holster and drew out a pistol. Tossing it to Cody, she said, "Your daddy warned you about Angela, didn't he?"

Cody caught the gun, a Colt .38, and uttered a breathless laugh. "If you're the one doing the shooting, where the hell's Dad?"

A cry to their left drew their attention. Adam Price, Willet and Willet's mother had started toward them, but now they stopped, Mrs. Black letting loose with a surprised yelp.

Cody's father strode out of the dark chaparral beside the black coach, a bone saw resting on his shoulder. Cody thought he'd wade right into the trio of vampires and take down as many as he could, but Jack Wilson instead marched over to where Horton lay. Though Horton's body was still wracked with spasms, he didn't look like he'd be standing up any time soon.

But Jack Wilson made sure of that.

"Don't touch him!" Price called, his voice raw with fear.

Without answering, Cody's father reached down, grasped the gunshot Horton by his bloody hair, and placed a knee on the man's chest.

"*I said don't do—*"

But before Price could finish, Jack Wilson began to saw through Horton's throat.

Price hustled toward the pair, but Jack Wilson's saw was too sharp, the jerking motion of his arm much too savage. Price was ten paces away when the head came off.

Jack Wilson stood. "Here you go," he said and tossed Horton's head toward Price.

The severed head rolled to a stop between Price's black leather boots.

Price looked up slowly and stared at Jack Wilson. "You will suffer for this."

Cody approached them, the Colt cocked and poised at his side. "It's me you want, Price. Leave my dad out of this."

"You're all gonna pay," a voice to Cody's left said. He turned and looked at the one who'd spoken.

Willet leered at him, his white fangs gleaming in the faint morning light.

★　　★　　★

Cody's first thought was *I can't do this*. His second thought was that he better save his father from Adam Price, who wouldn't be distracted for long. Ignoring the child who, less than twenty-four hours ago, had been his only friend in the world and was now a cold-blooded killing machine, Cody took aim at Price's head.

"You had better shoot true," Price said without turning. "If you don't, I'll have that measly little noisemaker out of your hands within seconds, and then you and your father will join the women inside for a day of agony."

Marguerite moved up next to Cody. He could smell the sweat on her, wondered how much smoke she'd inhaled and how hard she'd had to ride to beat them here.

She looked ethereal.

"You've not yet noticed then," Marguerite said to Price. "Your vulgar henchman has been beheaded, and that whore who took up with you has an arrow through her head."

"It appears we're at an impasse," Mrs. Black said, her lips pursed.

"It's four to three," Gladys said. The rifle was pointed skyward as she sidled around the wrecked coach and approached them, but her face showed plainly that she meant business. Cody had never noticed it before, but his stepmother was a rather pretty woman. Not as beautiful as the two photographs he still had of his birth mother, but at least he could now see why his father had been attracted to Gladys. Her skin was tawny like Marguerite's, but her Apache heritage was also clearly writ in her cheekbones and her hair. Gladys had nearly made it around the mangled coach when the horses that were still alive began to buck and whinny.

Mrs. Black eyed Gladys with resentment. "You don't know Angela's dead. For that matter, you don't know that Mr. Penders is dead. We're very resilient, you know."

Jack Wilson was looking at the unmoving form of Cody's once-wife. "Her? You telling me she might still come back to life?"

Mrs. Black gave a complacent little shrug. "If Adam wills it."

"Well hell then," Jack Wilson said and turned on his heels to walk over to Angela.

"What are you doing?" Price asked, the alarm back in his voice.

"What do you think I'm doing?" Jack Wilson said. He reached down, took hold of Angela's blood-matted hair, and lifted her to a sitting position. The arrow jutting out of her forehead with the gaudy yellow fletching made her look like a sinister unicorn.

Cody's dad examined her slack face. "She doesn't look too spry to me."

"Dad," Cody began.

Angela's eyes swung open.

Jack Wilson gasped, shrank away from the hissing vampire. Angela climbed drunkenly to her feet, arms extended toward Cody's backpedalling father.

"Jack, look out!" Gladys yelled.

The horses still attached to the crashed rig neighed in terror.

"What's wrong with them?" Marguerite asked.

Willet and Mrs. Black were both edging closer to Cody and Marguerite.

Angela sprung at Jack Wilson.

Faster than Cody would have thought possible, his dad came up with the Schofield and blasted another hole in Angela's face, this one right in her teeth. Her head snapped back, the arrow momentarily pointing heavenward. Then she fell face-first on a bed of scree, the arrow point pushed farther out the back of her head.

Everyone froze for a pregnant moment. Then Jack Wilson bent over Angela with the bone saw. "I held my tongue when you were within earshot, little missy, but I don't mind telling you now – I never liked you. Not one bit." He rolled her over. Her glazed eyes peered sightlessly at the dimming stars. "You shouldn't have hurt my boy," he added and began to saw.

"*No!*" Adam Price bellowed and made for the pair.

Cody was after him instantly, gun raised. Beyond Price he could make out his father's violent sawing motions, could hear the slushy tearing of Angela's gullet as the saw teeth decapitated her by degrees.

Price was too fast for Cody, was almost upon Jack and Angela. Cody stopped, took aim. He knew if he fired wild his father might get hit, and wouldn't that be something?

Don't shoot wild then, he told himself.

Okay, Cody thought and squeezed the trigger.

The slug hit Price in the lower back, but it didn't fell him. He spun sideways but staggered toward Jack Wilson.

Cody fired again, saw a splash of red between Price's shoulder blades. Price went down a few feet from where Jack Wilson knelt over Angela. Then Cody's father was up and grasping her severed head like Perseus after slaying Medusa. Price wormed toward Cody's father, then pushed up to his knees.

"Here," Jack Wilson said and flung the head at Price, who batted it aside. "Let's have our next customer."

And before Cody could stop him, his father was striding toward Adam Price. Jack Wilson brought up the bone saw and grasped Price by the collar.

"Dad!" Cody screamed.

His dad's eyes widened, and at the last moment he tried to jerk his hand away. But by that time Adam Price had already sunk his fangs into Jack Wilson's forearm.

CHAPTER TWENTY-FOUR

Cody bolted toward the struggling pair. His father swung the bone saw and embedded it in the meat of Price's shoulder, but the vampire's mouth was riveted to Jack Wilson's forearm, the slurping sounds telling Cody far more than he wanted to know. Price rose as Jack Wilson began to sink to his knees.

From his periphery Cody saw Willet go for Gladys. At the same instant, Mrs. Black attacked Marguerite. For an endless moment Cody stood frozen, plagued by an excruciating fit of indecision. Then his father's howls broke through the uncertainty, and Cody made up his mind.

Cody tackled Adam Price on a dead sprint. There was a sick ripping sound as Price's teeth came free of Jack Wilson's arm. Price hit the ground with Cody atop him. Cody tumbled over, had the presence of mind to jerk the gun up, and as Price leaped at him, Cody opened up, the first slug vaporising two of Price's fingers, another slamming him in the ribs. But the vampire pounced on him anyway, Adam Price's strength in no way diminished by the .38's assault.

The struggle was brief. Cody threw an arm up, but Price caught his wrist, jerked the arm down hard enough to cause a dull pop in Cody's shoulder. Price darted at Cody's exposed neck, and though Price was impossibly fast, Cody was able to jerk his chin down in time to block Price's lethal jaws. Price's head came up, a goodly portion of Cody's collar caught in the vampire's scimitar teeth. Price spat the fabric aside, dove in again, but this time Cody anticipated him. With a desperate cry he interposed the barrel of the Colt sideways between his throat and the closing teeth. Price's fangs snapped down on the unyielding steel. There came a horrid splintering noise as several of Price's teeth shattered on the barrel. But rather than letting go of the gun, Price glared at Cody over the Colt, and Cody saw plainly that Price meant to wrest the gun from his hand with his teeth. Cody did the only thing he could think to do. He pulled the trigger.

The shot was deafening, Cody's ears instantly filled with a high-pitched ringing. He let go of the gun and clapped his hands over his ears.

Price's reaction, however, was even more dramatic. He pushed back on his knees, and an ungodly squeal fractured the early dawn air. Price's taloned fingers battered his temples in rage and agony.

Jack Wilson stepped close to Price, placed the Schofield against his forehead, and squeezed the trigger. The back of Price's head exploded in a brilliant vermilion splash. Price teetered a moment, then thumped down sideways in the rocky scree.

His father went for the bone saw, but Cody grabbed hold of his pant leg.

"What?" his dad yelled.

Cody nodded at the crashed coach, said, "Look."

The large figure rose among the unmoving forms of the horses. Cody's stomach gave a lurch when he realised why the horses had been bucking and neighing so wildly.

Penders had been feeding.

The huge man turned and leered at them, the entire front of his massive body slicked with horse blood.

"Come on," Cody said, rising and dragging his father toward the gate.

Jack Wilson gestured toward Price. "We've gotta kill this son of a bitch while we've got the chance."

"What about the women?"

Jack Wilson froze. He twitched his head from side to side, scanning the shadowy ranch for signs of Gladys and Marguerite, but neither woman was visible. Neither were Willet or his mother.

"Where the hell—" his dad began to say.

An answering scream told them more than they wanted to know.

It came from the largest barn, the one to the left of the house.

It came from Gladys.

*   *   *

Cody knew he'd talked his dad into forsaking Adam Price in order to save the women, but even as they burst through the open gate he began to question his own argument. Penders was already recovering from whatever wounds he'd sustained in his violent collision with the four now-dead horses and the Concord coach. The man's ursine form trailed after them as they made for the barn, Penders moving with an unsettling species of foggy agility. True, he kept yawing left and right as he ran, but those glaring orange eyes never seemed to blink, the toothy grin festooning the bearded face as fixed as some evil constellation. Cody felt a pressing desire to glance over his shoulder to make sure that Price was still down, but he worried that if he did, Penders would overtake them.

"This was a mistake, son," Jack Wilson said, panting. "You shoulda let me at least put another couple in him with this Schofield."

They were nearing the barn.

"Bullets wouldn't have hurt him, Dad. I saw Penders—"

"Who's Penders?"

"The one behind us," Cody said and jerked a thumb. "You know, the one looks like a mountain? I saw him and Angela get shot more times than I could count and still get back up again."

They'd reached the open barn doors.

Jack Wilson made to push inside, but Cody barred him with an outstretched arm. "Careful, Dad. They might be waiting for us."

"Murdering bastards," his dad said, his light blue eyes darting about the murky barn. Since the weather had been clear for a good while, all the cattle were grazing in the pasture, which at least meant it was quiet enough to hear. That was, if Cody *could* hear. The ringing in his ears sounded like New Year's Eve.

His dad waded deeper into the darkness. Cody aimed the gun at the doorway behind them, ready to put one in Penders's forehead the moment the big son of a bitch stumbled through.

Turning, Cody gasped and grabbed hold of his father's shoulder. "Watch where you're walking," he said.

Jack Wilson looked down at the harrow he'd almost stumbled on top of.

"Thanks," his dad said.

They walked a couple more paces, but saw no movement save a plover that had been sheltering on a rafter. With a surly chirp and a flutter of wings, the plover disappeared the way they'd come in. Cody threw a glance back at the doorway, but Penders had either faltered or decided to attack them from a different direction.

"Wait a minute," his dad said, stopping. "You hear that?"

Cody shook his head, was about to explain that he couldn't hear any sound unless it was made by a cannon. But then it came to him, something that reminded him of hogs at slop time.

Oh shit, he thought.

Cody followed his father's gaze to the hay mount. The noises were coming from up there.

"You sons of bitches!" his father shouted. Jack Wilson started up the ladder. Nervelessly, Cody climbed after him. When his dad reached the top, Jack Wilson stopped climbing. Cody hung onto the wooden rungs, waiting, terrified that Penders would come barreling through the door. Then the huge vampire would leap up and snatch him off the ladder as easily as a well-trained dog snags a thrown stick from the air. And then it would be over.

And what about Marguerite, a voice asked him. *You remember her, Mr. Self-Absorbed? The gal who rode fifty miles just to save your sorry hide?*

The panic in Jack Wilson's voice froze Cody's blood. "*Get away from her!*"

Illuminated by the scant glow filtering through the single upper window, his dad climbed into the hayloft. Cody hustled after him, and when he'd gone a few paces, he realised why his father's voice had sounded so tortured.

Willet and Mrs. Black had Gladys splayed out in the hay, each of them supping from one of her slit wrists.

Cody's stomach sank, but he reached for the Colt anyway. Faintly, he wondered where Marguerite had gone, but he didn't have time to consider the thought for long. His dad was rushing at Willet Black, who was nearest to them. Jack Wilson aimed his Schofield, fired. The top of Willet's head disappeared, though one big flap of hair pirouetted in the air a moment before landing on a bale of hay. Willet himself went somersaulting backward before coming to rest in a tangle of scrawny limbs.

Cody noted with mounting dread that Gladys did not look up or even twitch at the sound of her husband's gun.

But Mrs. Black did. Hissing, she hurtled at Jack Wilson, her claws flashing in the faint morning light. Cody's dad fired at her just before she hit him, and her head jerked backward as the slug rammed home. She landed in a convulsing heap at Jack Wilson's feet. He immediately went to Gladys's prone form and began speaking to her in harsh, imploring whispers.

But Cody could've told him it was too late. What blood the vampires hadn't imbibed had soaked into the loose hay and the wood dust. Gladys would never move again.

Unless it was as a vampire.

"Goddamn them," Jack Wilson growled, body shaking. "*Goddamn them!*"

His father began to weep.

From outside came a sound Cody couldn't at first place. But when he did, he doubted the veracity of what the sound suggested. He rushed to the window and peered out.

The black coach had wheeled around and was moving away down the trail. Cody couldn't quite make out who sat the box. The shape was oddly slumped. Was it Price? Marguerite?

He returned to stand over his father. The man's sobs were horrible to hear. Cody longed to soothe his dad, to place a comforting hand on the back of the man's sunburned neck, but he knew it would be a feeble gesture.

Cody bit his lip. He fidgeted with the knots on his head, unable to keep still. He kept glancing over at the top of the ladder, expecting at any moment for Penders's big, shaggy head to appear. And then the eyes glowing like hellfire...the gleaming razor teeth...

"Let's get inside, Dad."

"We're not going anywhere," Jack Wilson answered thickly. "Go down and get my scythe off the wall."

"We don't have time."

"We will if you hurry."

"But you didn't do it to Price," Cody argued. "Why do it to them?"

His dad whirled and glared at him with fierce, wet eyes. "Price didn't murder my wife, now did he?"

Cody's muscles were knots of tension, his body seeming to calcify with his fear. "Dad, if we can get inside, the sunlight might—"

"Get my scythe *now*, boy. I'm not going to ask again."

Cody did as he was told, knowing as he angled toward the ladder he was reverting back to his childhood self, before he'd begun to rebel, before he'd started finding ways to hurt his father without realising that's what he was striving to do or how wrong it was to do it.

He reached the ladder, bent to put his foot on a rung.

His foot came down on Penders's hand.

Cody shot a horrified look down at the huge vampire.

Penders leered up at him.

Grasped him by the butt of his pants and yanked him backward off the ladder.

CHAPTER TWENTY-FIVE

Cody twisted as he fell, the compacted barn floor racing up to meet him. He landed well enough not to break anything, but the wind was still pounded from his lungs. Unable to breathe, his sternum, balls, and knees on fire from landing face down, Cody's terror was nonetheless powerful enough to compel him to his feet just before Penders landed on top of him. As it was, Cody was shuffling forward with a blundering, pained gait when Penders hit the barn floor. A shot sounded from somewhere in the barn, and for a wild second Cody was sure Penders had decided chasing him was too much trouble and had opted to simply shoot him in the back to save himself the trouble. But the gunshot had come from somewhere above Cody, and as he advanced into the darkness toward the opposite barn wall, he realised it had probably been his father's Schofield, his dad putting one of the vampires in the loft down while he waited for Cody to return with the scythe.

But to accomplish that, Cody'd not only have to make it to the other side of the barn, he'd have to locate the scythe among the numerous hanging tools, lift it from the wall, then either fight off Penders or make it past him without dying.

The odds weren't good.

A moan sounded up ahead, but Cody couldn't immediately place where he'd heard the voice before.

Then he remembered Marguerite.

A barrage of thoughts assailed him. If Marguerite was here, that meant Price had taken the black coach away. That would have filled Cody with joy, but he knew Penders would be upon him within moments. He could hear the big vampire back there, huffing closer. But Marguerite's moaning swept away all other thought, even his desire to find the scythe.

When Cody reached the opposite barn wall and the array of tools hung on either side of the door, he understood why Marguerite was moaning.

And he found the scythe, too.

Mrs. Black and Willet had somehow lifted Marguerite ten feet in the air and used the scythe to fasten her to the wall. How the hell they'd managed it, he couldn't begin to guess. There was a stepladder nearby, but…Jesus, Cody thought. They must've been desperate to save her for later. The handle of the five-foot-long implement had been hammered horizontally into the wood with a long nail, the tip of the blade slammed into the wall to hold it there.

Marguerite's throat was pinned to the wall by the curved blade, which was embedded deeply enough to brook no escape. The aperture between wall and blade was scarcely large enough to accommodate her neck, much less her head should she try to slip it through the gap. But as he reached her, Cody saw with a leap of hope that her bootheels were scrabbling against the wall to push her higher and thus spare her throat the bite of the gleaming scythe blade. She *was* bleeding a little, but her hands were gripping the scythe, pulling desperately against it to keep her throat from being savaged by the blade.

Marguerite was gazing mournfully down at Cody, but then her eyes shifted to something right behind him. Cody whirled, the Colt out and firing.

He only had two bullets left, but they were enough to bring down Penders. He fell a mere six feet away, his hands pawing at the holes Cody had opened in his gut.

Cody hustled over, grabbed the stepladder, positioned it below Marguerite, and climbed up. Halfway up, he spotted a short box saw and on a whim lifted it off the wall, thinking he could perhaps use it as a pry. When he reached the top, his father's gun went off three more times. *Must have reloaded*, Cody thought, then tried not to linger on the fact that he himself was no longer armed.

Now that he was closer to Marguerite he could see how the blade had sunk into the soft flesh under her jaw, how the blood had begun to leak down her throat and stain her bosom. He got his arms around her midsection, began to lift her, but she made a strangled, protesting noise, clearly wanting him to rip the scythe out of the wall instead.

"But you'll fall," he said.

Rather than answering, she stared back at him fixedly. Absent of a nod, of which he knew she wasn't capable, it was the clearest confirmation she could provide.

Grimacing, Cody tossed the box saw to the floor and got hold of the scythe handle with both hands just before the wood became steel. He looked at her. "When this thing comes loose, you're gonna fall. Try to land on the top of the stepladder, all right?"

She watched him steadily.

Cody heaved a sigh, put one boot against the wall, and yanked. At first, there was no give. Whoever had slammed the blade tip into the wall must have done so with incredible force. But as Cody strained, putting his whole body into it, the blade gave a little jerk. He heard Penders's breathing on the floor behind him, knew the huge vampire wouldn't stay down much longer.

Knowing he couldn't possibly land with any kind of grace or safety, Cody planted both his feet against the wall and heaved backward. The blade snicked free. Cody plummeted into the dark and landed on something that grunted.

Penders.

He heard Marguerite clatter against the stepladder, saw the whole thing canting sideways, then watched her leap off it with catlike agility. Penders was stirring. For all Cody knew, his falling on the vampire might have been what roused Penders. Before Cody could gain his feet, he saw Marguerite cross to the downhanging scythe blade. She adjusted the stepladder, climbed up, grabbed hold of the wooden handle with both hands, then stepped off the ladder so her whole weight would exert itself on the scythe.

It worked. The scythe handle popped free of its nail.

"Cody!" his father's voice called from the loft.

"Come on," Cody said to Marguerite. "Give me the scythe."

But rather than obeying him, Marguerite stepped around Penders's immense body, braced her feet far apart, and swung the scythe in a swooshing arc.

The vampire's hand shot up, caught the top of the handle.

The blade stopped mere inches from Penders's throat.

Penders laughed up at them, his mouth congealed in a menacing grin. Penders ripped the scythe out of Marguerite's grip. He chopped down at her with the scythe, but she dodged it at the last moment. The force of the swing buried the blade tip deep into the wood of the barn wall. Furious, Penders strained to yank it free. Cody took a step toward Marguerite, his toe bumping something on the floor. He glanced down frantically and saw what it was.

The box saw.

Cody retrieved the saw, stepped behind Penders. The vampire ripped the scythe free, but just as he did, Cody grasped a handful of Penders's shaggy hair and dragged the saw's rusty teeth over the big vampire's eyes.

Penders roared. He let go of the scythe and rolled away from Cody and Marguerite. He clamped his great paws over his eyes, but twin gouts of bloody sclera oozed from between his fingers. Marguerite was on Penders in an instant, the scythe whistling down at him like grim death. The blade embedded itself in his shoulder, then wrenched free when Marguerite held on and Penders continued to roll. The big vampire stumbled to his feet and began shambling in the direction of the barn opening, moving, Cody was certain, almost entirely by memory. If Penders wasn't totally blind with his mutilated eyes, he was close to it. Marguerite pelted after him, looking like some artist's depiction of female vengeance. Her flowing black hair swished behind her, her white dress torn in several places but still hauntingly beautiful on her strong body. She aimed another stroke at Penders, this time parting the shirt and the flesh between the vampire's broad shoulders. The blood he'd drunk from the horses poured from the gash in swollen rills.

Cody realised he'd been standing and watching after them, gaping at Marguerite like a slack-jawed suitor. He took off in their direction just as his father's voice sounded from above. "I'm almost outta ammo, Cody! Where the hell's my scythe?"

Penders was slowing now, Marguerite's blows taking their toll. Something just ahead of Penders glistened in the growing dawn light.

From above, his father was screaming for them to *Hurry, goddammit, hurry!*

Cody shouted to Marguerite, "Take the scythe up to my dad. He's got two vampires in the loft."

She glanced back at him, a pained expression knitting her pretty brow. "But we have to finish this one."

"We will," Cody said, shoving her past Penders, who was staggering forward like a soldier dazed by a too-near blast.

Marguerite bared her teeth a moment, clearly anxious to finish off Penders, but she did as Cody had requested, hustling over to the ladder and beginning the climb toward the loft.

Cody circled around Penders. "Come on, Stevie," he said. "Follow my voice. I'm gonna whup your sorry ass."

Penders roared, perhaps forgetting for a moment his tremendous pain, and shambled toward Cody.

"That's right," Cody said, guiding him. "Come on, big guy."

Penders's boot caught on the front of the harrow, and before he could catch himself, he crashed down on top of it, the multitudinous steel spikes skewering his huge body like knives sliding into an enormous block of cheese. His chest, his gut, his meaty thighs, even his arms were punctured. One hard iron spike crunched through his teeth, pierced the back of his mouth, and split through the hair at the base of his skull. Penders wriggled on the harrow like a baited minnow, the horse blood flooding the barn floor beneath him as though someone had thumbed on a hundred spigots.

From above came shouts, the sounds of a struggle.

Blocking it out as well as he could, Cody fitted the box saw between two harrow spikes so that its teeth met Penders's flesh just below the hairline. Cody began to saw feverishly, the blood splattering his knuckles, his forearm, his face. But he kept at it, listening for his father or for Marguerite, and by the time he'd made it through, he'd begun to hope they'd had the same good luck up in the loft.

The box saw ripped through the last tendrils of flesh joining the vampire's head and his body. For good measure, Cody gripped Penders's hair, peeled his head off the spike with an unwholesome squelching noise, and tossed it aside. He could just imagine Penders's head rejoining his body were Cody to leave them both where they'd been.

"*Help us!*" Marguerite screamed.

With a start, Cody crossed toward the ladder, but before

he reached it, he glimpsed two figures grappling at the edge of the hayloft.

His father and Mrs. Black.

A second later Marguerite was climbing down the ladder with the scythe, shouting for Cody to run for the house. He met her at the base of the ladder, shouldered past her and began to climb.

"You can't!" she yelled.

He heard a grunt from above and looked up just in time to see his dad windmilling his arms.

"Dad!"

But Jack Wilson fell just the same. Cody experienced a soul-destroying sureness that his father would land next to Penders on the spiked harrow, but his dad landed wide of the bed of spikes by a good three or four feet. The sound of crunching bone, however, was unmistakable, as was the way his dad bellowed and grabbed his ankle. Cody rushed over to him, saw the way his dad's foot flopped at the end of his leg like a flower with a wind-bent stalk.

"It's the boy," Marguerite said and joined Cody in getting an arm under Jack Wilson's thrashing body. "He's stronger than the rest of them."

They began to drag Jack Wilson backward out the barn door, the older man's face a mask of pain and obstinacy. *You stubborn old fool*, Cody thought admiringly. *You'd still stay and fight, wouldn't you? With one good leg and no rounds left for the Schofield, you'd still stay and take them both on.*

A dark shape flew from the hayloft and landed on its feet before them.

Willet Black.

The boy was bleeding from numerous gunshot wounds, but he seemed to be returning to his human state. His mother thumped down on the barn floor behind him, though not nearly so nimbly. She looked worse off than her boy, a nasty scythe slash bisecting her torso, her face more vampire than human.

Cody and Marguerite continued to backpedal, their burden no longer so eager to do battle. Jack Wilson said, "Watch him, Cody. You won't believe the things he can do."

Cody doubted that was true.

They had about thirty yards to go before they reached the front door of the house. Willet kept the distance between them at about ten yards, his mother moving apace.

"You don't want to kill us," Cody said to Willet, and as he said it, he realised he believed it. Though the boy did look frightening – no one with glowing orange eyes and blood slathered over the front of his body looked particularly friendly – there was enough of the former Willet to give Cody hope. "I know you don't like doing this to people, Willet. You're not that kind."

Willet slowed, his forehead furrowing.

Mrs. Black brushed past him, her face a rictus of loathing. "He's *my* child. I know better than you what he likes."

Marguerite said, "You feel guilty. You know what you're doing to your son, and it makes you want to kill yourself."

Martha Black's eyes flared. "You stinking Mexican whore."

Twenty yards now, the house tantalisingly near.

"Marguerite's right," Cody said. "You wouldn't be so angry if you weren't conflicted."

Martha Black turned her dreadful gaze on him. "Is that so, Mr. Wilson? Suppose my Willet knew the truth about you?"

Something in Cody's belly did a sick, nauseating roll, but he kept moving.

Mrs. Black turned to her boy, who stood just outside in the yard, the bewilderment etched on his face. "Mr. Wilson never told you he was there the night they came to our ranch, did he?"

Hell, Cody thought. He threw a look over his shoulder, realised he and Marguerite had misjudged and were heading too far to the left. He corrected their course, his father gasping as Cody jarred his shattered ankle.

"What's she talkin' about, Cody?" Willet asked. His voice was nearly returned to its normal high drawl. It made Cody's heart ache, but the fear of what would happen soon rode roughshod over the sadness.

"He didn't tell you before, so why would he admit it now?" Martha Black said. A vicious sneer had spread on her revolting face. "He saw the whole thing, Willet. Mr. Wilson hid among the pines on the eastern ridge while they dragged your sisters screaming from the house. He watched them butcher Ellen and Clara like a pair of hogs. He didn't lift a finger when they raped Clara." She turned to Cody. "Nor when they broke your brother's neck."

Willet's face had begun to pinch, his bottom lip trembling. "This true, Cody? Were you really there?"

Though it was the hardest thing he'd ever had to do, Cody met Willet's gaze, hoping against hope he could put off the change by begging the child's forgiveness.

But as comprehension seeped into Willet's face, Cody realised there would be no forgiveness.

Fifteen yards to go.

"Of *course* he was there, darling," Mrs. Black cooed in her buzzing vampire voice. "He saw them slay your poor grandfather. Watched them dismember your father while he screamed and screamed for someone to come to his rescue."

Willet took a step toward them. "Is it *true*?" he demanded. His voice had dropped an octave, his jaw elongating.

"I won't deny anything," Cody said. "I hid the same way you did, up in your hayloft. I thought they'd killed Angela, but I'd never seen them...never seen them in action. It shocked me. I was afraid, Willet, and for that I'll be forever sorry."

Ten yards.

"I should've intervened," Cody continued, "though we both know how little good it would have done."

Willet's fists were balled at his sides, his steps quickening.

"*Cody*..." Marguerite said.

"Run," Cody whispered.

Their arms still around Cody's father, Cody and Marguerite began an awkward shuffle toward the covered porch, Jack Wilson hopping as briskly as he could to keep pace.

Willet moved with impossible swiftness. One moment Cody was sure they would reach the sanctuary of the house in plenty of time; the next a small, snarling body was leaping at him, the sprouting fingernails already ripping and tearing, shredding his bicep into strips of bloody bacon. The force of Willet's body knocked him over, drove him sideways into the wood of the covered porch. It knocked the air out of him, the pain in his ribs sending starbursts twirling through his vision. Willet skidded on the porch, bumped the house under a windowsill, then pounced again. Distantly, Cody realised his father had disappeared – dragged away by Mrs. Black? – but Marguerite was still beside him. Marguerite met Willet just before the boy fell on Cody. With a savage cry she reared back and delivered a mighty kick to Willet's underjaw. The boy's lower jaw was driven upward, the serrated, stalagmite teeth perforating the soft flesh at the roof of his mouth. Squalling, Willet slapped at his gored mouth, flopped over on his belly, his wounds drizzling brackish blood all over the porch. A shadow loomed over Cody, and just as he glanced up and saw Martha Black, her orange eyes aflame with maternal outrage, Marguerite aimed a fist at the woman's face.

The blow had little effect. Martha's head merely moved imperceptibly before the glowing eyes came to rest on Marguerite. Cody grabbed the hem of Martha Black's powder-blue dress, hoping he could divert her attention long enough to spare Marguerite the mother's wrath.

But Martha Black was not to be deterred. Rather than swinging at the younger woman, Mrs. Black spun Marguerite around, and before Marguerite could react or mount any sort of defence, Mrs. Black caught the back of Marguerite's head and slammed her face-first into the unforgiving adobe façade. There was a dull crunching sound – Cody prayed it wasn't Marguerite's skull. Then Marguerite slumped sideways.

And landed at the feet of Jack Wilson, who'd appeared in the open doorway.

Mrs. Black went for him, but before she got halfway across the porch, he opened up with his Schofield, which he'd apparently gone inside to reload.

Tough old bastard, Cody thought.

Martha Black's forehead dissolved into red pulp, her body folding over and slouching in a motionless mound on the edge of the porch. Still dizzy, Cody grabbed at the scythe, which lay discarded next to him. Rising, he took a step toward Mrs. Black, but his dad hissed something unintelligible at him.

Cody blinked at him uncomprehendingly. Jack Wilson, broken ankle and all, had hopped over to Marguerite, whose lovely body lay twisted at a horrible angle near the door. "Help me get her inside," his father commanded.

"But," Cody started and nodded at Mrs. Black.

"We don't have *time*, boy. That thing's gonna come back and we're in no condition to hold him off."

The thing to which his dad was referring, Cody saw, was Willet Black, who cut a grotesque picture in the yard just north of the house. Willet was stumbling about, uttering garbled curses. His long, taloned fingers were worming their way between his bloodied lips, which were nailed together by the swordlike teeth that Marguerite had driven into the roof of his mouth.

Finally prying his jaws apart, Willet rounded on them and began to approach.

Cody moved up beside his father and told him to get inside. For once, Jack Wilson took his advice, keeping the Schofield trained on Willet as Cody carried Marguerite through the doorway and over to the couch. Cody glanced up and saw his dad fetch the scythe, which he tossed through the doorway to land clattering on the floor.

Cody situated Marguerite on the dark brown sofa, the same one his father had furnished the place with a decade ago. He heard the door slam shut, the bolt shot. His dad hopped over to the windows and shuttered them fast. Cody glanced about, took in the window on the north side of the main room, the window beyond the dining area adjacent to the kitchen. Behind the kitchen, he knew there was another door leading to the backyard. And behind Cody there were two bedrooms, both of them with windows. Thinking of all those windows and doors, his throat dried up. He had little hope they could defend all of them, especially with Marguerite either unconscious or dying and his father with one good leg.

Jack Wilson cinched tight the shutters, then fastened the other window lock in the main room. He hobbled up beside Cody and peered down at Marguerite.

"She gonna live?" his father asked.

"How the hell should I know? You're the medic."

"Medic's assistant," his dad corrected. "And that was only when I wasn't carrying a musket." He shook his head. "I saw some things in the war, but I never saw anything like tonight."

Cody grabbed a white cotton arm cover from a nearby chair and held it to the gash in Marguerite's forehead.

"That's not sanitised," his dad said.

"I think an infection's the least of her worries."

Jack Wilson sighed. "You may be right."

Cody fought to smother his terror. "What do we do, Dad?"

His dad stood up, hopped around the couch toward the dining area. Making his way toward the window there, his dad said, "We prepare for an attack. They might try a siege, but I doubt it. That woman won't stay on the porch long, and that boy sure as hell doesn't look very patient."

Cody said, "You stay with Marguerite. I'll get the back door."

On his way through the kitchen, he heard his father ask, "What happened to your ear?"

Cody fingered the moist place where his earlobe had been. "Horton."

"Your shoulder?"

"Penders."

"It's a good thing you got here when you did," his dad said. "There wouldn't have been anything left of you."

"I'll need bullets for my Colt."

His father nodded. "In the cupboard."

Cody went to lock the back door.

CHAPTER TWENTY-SIX

Jack Wilson stood by the window, the side of the Schofield's barrel pressed to his cheek. "Marguerite was right about the boy being stronger than the others. I never saw such a thing."

"He was a good boy," Cody said. "It's my fault they got him."

"Don't look back," his dad said without taking his eyes off the window. "You ever gonna take that advice? I've been giving it to you since you were little."

Cody wrung out the washcloth over the bowl and gently mopped the fresh blood from Marguerite's forehead. "Forgetting isn't my specialty."

"Never was mine either."

Wincing, Jack Wilson hopped over to where Marguerite lay on the sofa. His father's kind eyes surveyed her face. "She's a beauty, ain't she?"

"What I want to know," Cody said, "is how she convinced you the vampires were real."

But his dad was gazing down at Marguerite, a curiously avid expression on his face.

"Dad?"

Jack Wilson blinked up at him like he had no idea where he was.

Cody grasped his father's arm around the elbow, just above where the gore of Price's bite wound glistened like two dozen diamonds. "Do I need to keep you away from her?"

His father stared back at him a long time before finally looking away. Jack Wilson made his way over to the kitchen table, his dishevelled, silvering hair and the worry lines on his forehead making him look like an infirm old man.

"I'm sorry, Dad. I didn't mean—"

"Don't apologise," his father interrupted. "I do feel different.

In time, we might have to worry." He glanced up at Cody. "But for now I'm all right. I'm with you until the end. I'd put a gun in my mouth before I ever laid a hand on you or this girl."

"Dad, I want to say something—"

"You don't have to say a word, boy. I already know."

"You deserved a better son."

His dad eyed him for a long moment. Then he pushed away from the table and put his hands on Cody's shoulders. Cody had always thought of his father as being a good deal taller than him, but now Cody realised he had his dad by an inch at least. The revelation stunned him.

His dad said, "You came home, Cody. That's what matters. I probably tried too hard to be both of your parents. Then, when I married Gladys..." Jack Wilson's voice faltered. He cleared his throat. "I held it against you for not taking a shine to Gladys right away, and that wasn't fair either. I thought you were mad at me for dishonouring the memory of your mother, but what you were really worried about..." His father averted his eyes.

"Dad, you don't have to say it."

His father inhaled a shuddering breath. "What you were really afraid of was losing me."

Cody beheld his father's moist eyes and understood for the first time that what he'd said was right. Cody *had* been jealous of Gladys, plain and simple. So he broke from his father before his father could break from him. Marrying Angela had made that abandonment permanent, or at least semipermanent.

He opened his mouth to say all this, but when his dad gazed up at him with that heartbroken smile, Cody realised he didn't have to. His father knew it already.

Cody said, "I never knew a finer man than you."

His dad's lips trembled, but instead of turning away, he drew Cody's cheek to his lips and gave him a long kiss. Then, he rested his forehead against Cody's for a long moment. Cody realised he was weeping too and felt a trifle foolish, but more powerful than this emotion was an aching desire for the embrace to never end.

Jack Wilson tensed and suddenly reached for his Schofield.

Cody whirled, but there was no one in the window. "Are you sure—"

"It was her," Jack Wilson said, the Schofield drawn and covering the window. "It was the kid's mother."

*   *   *

Cody carried Marguerite to the bedroom and fastened the shutters and window locks tight. Jack Wilson limped to the window and double-checked it. Then, gesturing toward the big armoire Gladys had used for her clothes, he said, "Help me get this in front of the window."

The armoire weighed a ton. Cody did most of the work, his dad cursing under his breath about not being able to help more. Panting, Cody crossed to where Marguerite lay, drew up the covers far enough to cover her torn dress.

When Cody straightened, he found his father's old Civil War Colt musket with its bayonet attachment displayed on the wall. "That thing still fire?"

"I suppose it would," his dad said. "If I still had musket balls and powder for it."

Cody arched an eyebrow at him. "If you don't use it, why's it—"

His dad fluttered an impatient hand. "Gladys insisted on keeping it there. Said it reminded her that I'd fought for a noble cause. That men weren't supposed to own other men. I guess she was proud of me for helping put a stop to all that."

Cody imagined his father fighting for Ferrero's first division at Blue Springs, the Union soldiers overrunning the Confederates. "I don't blame her for displaying it," he said.

His dad hobbled to the door. "You take the other bedroom. I'll guard the rest."

Cody followed his dad into the hall. "That doesn't make any sense. You can't watch all those directions at once. Besides, if they sneak up on you, how are you gonna get away on one leg?"

"That's the point," his dad said. "You can cover more ground. I'm gonna sit in the central part of the house, where it'll take longer to get to me."

"But that won't work."

"I've got a voice, don't I? I hear anything, I'll call for you, and we'll face them together."

"I still don't know why we have to split up. They're the ones who're sensitive to the light. They're the ones who need to feed. Let's hole up here with Marguerite and make them come to us. We've got the advantage."

"*Listen*," his dad said, a strong hand clutching Cody's shoulder. "It might seem like that, but we don't. Marguerite said they move in daylight. They don't like the sun, but it doesn't hurt them. Remember how early they got to Mesquite?"

Cody tensed, recalling the massacre at the bar. "You have any blue flowers nearby?"

But his dad was already shaking his head. "It's called wolfsbane, son. Up until tonight I figured it was just another superstition."

"It's true, Dad. When they get near it—"

His father waved him off. "We went through all that. Marguerite told us how the big vampire reacted in the cellar when he looked at the flowers in her hair. She wasn't certain, but she thought they might be allergic to them. So Gladys and I talked it over, and we both agreed the nearest wolfsbane we know of is up in the mountains."

Cody said wonderingly, "Marguerite told you everything, didn't she?"

"She had to," his dad agreed. "You think I would've believed a crazy story like that otherwise?"

Cody frowned. "I still don't—"

"They like to feed, but they don't have to drink from *people*," his dad went on. "You saw that big one bleeding those horses, didn't you?"

Cody nodded.

"Well this is a *ranch*, son. There're cattle, horses...hell, Gladys even keeps..." His voice cut off a moment. He cleared his throat. "Gladys even kept a few chickens in a coop just off the tack room. You think they'll have any trouble finding food if we stay in here like a couple of cornered rats?"

"So we try to draw them out? We make ourselves the bait?"

Jack Wilson sighed. "Cody, I don't like to say this, but I might not have much time." He gritted his teeth, his nostrils flaring. "Every time I look at the girl now...even at you...I have this burning in my mind."

"You'd never hurt us."

"*I'd* never hurt you," he said fiercely. "But the thing crawling around in my head *isn't me.* Don't you get that? I believe that monster out there was a sweet little boy before they got hold of him, but now look at him. You saw the way he guzzled at Gladys's wrists. *That's gonna be me in a few hours.*"

Cody blew out weary breath. "Okay, we split up for now. But if you hear anything, you holler. We get them inside the house, there'll be nowhere for them to go."

Jack Wilson nodded, following Cody into the hallway. "I've got enough rounds for the Schofield to hold off a whole cavalry, and I've seen you reload that Colt. There's no way two of them will be able to beat the two of us as long as we're ready." His dad reached out, grabbed the scythe, which they'd propped against the wall. "You take this. I've got enough to think about without running around like the Grim Reaper."

Cody took the scythe, eyed the congealed blood on the blade.

His dad hopped into the kitchen. Cody called after him, "You sure all the windows in there are locked?"

"Windows, doors, every way in or out. There's nothing they can do I won't know about."

Cody headed for the spare bedroom, the one in which he'd slept before he moved away. He turned in the doorway, regarded his dad, who sat at the kitchen table, laying out rounds for the Schofield.

Cody said, "Why can't I shake the feeling you're still trying to protect me?"

Jack Wilson looked up at him with a wry smile. "Of course I'm trying to protect you. You're my son."

CHAPTER TWENTY-SEVEN

With an overpowering sense of misgiving, Cody closed the door and faced the room in which he'd spent four tempestuous years. It looked much as he remembered, though perhaps a bit smaller and not nearly so depressing. By the window there was a plain table with a leather-bound Bible on it. The window faced south, where his father's land stretched for only a mile or so. Beyond that, another rancher's spread began, though a barbed wire fence marked the boundary. Cody leaned the scythe against the wall to the right of the window and peered out.

The morning light had grown brighter but was suffused with a peculiar bluish cast. It reminded Cody of the time, just after his father had married Gladys, that the three of them had journeyed all the way through southern Texas, spending a couple days in San Antonio, before ultimately reaching Corpus Christi and the Gulf of Mexico. The sky outside now was much the same pale blue as it had been over the ocean. Cody had been short with Gladys most of the trip, but whenever they'd ventured down to the Gulf, which was every day for the better part of a week, a deep calm had breathed over him, and their little family had been uncharacteristically happy.

Thinking of Gladys, the woman whom he'd never really given a chance and who now was dead – or, God help them all, worse – Cody walked over to his old bed and inspected the fluted bedposts. When Jack Wilson remarried, he'd refused to use the same bed in which he and Cody's mother had slept. But the ornately carved mahogany frame had been a gift from Cody's maternal grandparents, so instead of getting rid of it, the whole thing had gone to Cody, who'd always found the notion comforting, like his mother's spirit was somehow closer to him when he slept.

Thinking of his mother, Cody turned and saw Willet staring at him through the window.

Though his pulse quickened, his right hand going immediately to the Colt's frigid handle, he could see right away that something was different about the boy. *No*, Cody amended, *not different. The same as before, before the vampires had gotten him.* It wasn't just the boy's features, which were wan and runneled with dirt and dried blood; it was something more, something fundamental, and for a long, breathless moment, Cody permitted himself to hope Willet might return to the way he'd been.

Then Cody remembered the way Willet had helped drain Gladys Wilson, and what hope he had vanished.

Cody scanned the window for signs of Martha Black, but nothing but Willet and the brightening southern sky presented itself. "You alone?" Cody asked in a low voice. Despite the panes of glass between them, he knew how keen Willet's hearing was. In fact, he suspected the boy might be able to read his thoughts. Cody had several times thought that of Adam Price.

"It's just me," Willet said. Cody barely made out the words, so weak was the boy's voice. He didn't want to venture any nearer – he'd seen what the vampires could do, how suddenly they could attack – but he had to get closer so he could ask Willet something.

"When you're like this," Cody said, the hand tight on the butt of his Colt. If Willet so much as scratched his nose, Cody would have the .38 out and blazing before the boy's hand fell. "When you're like this, are you partly human?"

Willet regarded him through the window, the same mournful cast to his face.

"What I mean is," Cody went on, "do you think the same way? Feel the same as you used to? Inside, I mean?"

Willet said, "I don't want to kill you."

Cody was stunned to see the boy's eyes fill with tears.

Watch it, he told himself. *They're actors, remember. Even if this creature was a boy not twenty-four hours ago, he's one of them now. He's a bloodsucker. And he'll not scruple to bleed you the same way he bled Gladys.*

Cody's fingers stroked the Colt's handle. He could sound the alarm, bring his dad in here to help him cut down Willet, but that would send things toward a rapid, ineffable conclusion, and Cody had no idea whether the outcome would be sweet or dire. What if he died and Marguerite became one of them? What if his dad, in the thrall of his new master, turned on his own son?

No! his mind screamed at the thought. *Stop thinking like that.*

"You don't believe me," Willet said. It wasn't a question.

Cody fought off the wave of self-condemnation that threatened to scatter his concentration. "I can't afford to believe you, Willet. Not after what I've seen."

Willet nodded. "I like it when I'm drinking," he said. "When I'm drinking, it feels like a hearth fire in my veins. I'm with Mama again. I'm like a baby at the teat."

"That's somebody's life you're taking."

"Don't you think I *know* that?" Willet said, his voice breaking. "I like it on the surface, but deep down I'm burying myself as far below as I can so I won't think about it...I'm hidin'...but no matter where I try to go, I still know it's murder." His eyes riveted on Cody. Tears were streaming down his freckled cheeks. "I can't do it anymore, Cody. You've gotta kill me."

"Willet..."

"You've gotta kill me and my momma. I can't take what we are. We're doin' what those bastards did the night they torched our ranch. They never even changed, Cody. Don't you see that? Those monsters...Penders, Horton, the twins..." He looked at Cody pleadingly. "Even Mr. Price. They don't need to have the change to do what they do. You see what that means, don't you?"

Cody shook his head. "Willet, I—"

"It means they *enjoy* it! Enjoy slaughtering children and rippin' the throats out of horses and taking down good men like my pa—" He broke off, a sob racking his body and stealing his voice.

Cody ran a shaking hand over his lips, forced himself to speak. "It's my fault they got you, Willet. I'm so sorry. I shoulda—"

"It's the danger of readin' too many books." Willet gave him a brief, poignant smile. "They tell you pretty lies and you get to believin' 'em. Get to thinkin' things are gonna work out like they should. Get to thinkin' there's justice. I could tell that about you right away, that you were still seein' yourself in a book. That's why you were holdin' back. You kept tellin' yourself something would happen to make you act like a hero, but that's not how it is in real life. In real life you just gotta do somethin' and hope it's right. Things happen faster in real life."

Cody's voice was little more than a croak. "What do you want me to do?"

"If there ain't no cure for what I'm becomin'—"

"There might—"

"*There ain't.* Don't think about that happenin', Cody. The change is part of me now. I can feel it takin' hold." Willet's voice got husky again, the boy pushing through his tears. "Even now I have a hard time lookin' at you. I can smell you right now. I can smell the meat of your legs and the life bubblin' in your throat. I...I..." Willet's face twisted angrily, his eyes fierce and perhaps flecked with orange. "No," he moaned. "I won't do it anymore. I won't hurt anyone else. Least of all you."

Willet looked up at him with more sorrow than Cody would have thought it possible for one face to contain. "Cody, I..."

"Willet," Cody said. "Willet, I wish to God there was a way..."

Willet smiled sadly. "You was my friend."

The tears came then and there was nothing Cody could do to stop them. He shot a glance back at the interior door, not out of fear of the vampires, but because he didn't want his father or Marguerite to see him this way. But Willet's next words stopped his crying faster than anything else could have.

"Open the window, Cody."

Cody stared unbelievingly at the boy. He waited for the rest of it, for the supplicating voice, the soft cajoling. But Willet only stared at him, his grimy face a pathetic mingling of doom and desperation.

"You know I can't do that," Cody said slowly.

"You don't understand," Willet said. "I'll put my head over the sill so you can take care of things for me."

Willet's words echoed through Cody's mind, but he couldn't

catch a sense of their meaning. *So you can take care of things for me. So you can take care of things.* Now what the hell...

Cody began to shake his head. "Come on now, Willet."

"It's the only way," Willet pleaded. "I don't wanna kill anymore, but if things go on like this, you know I'll have to."

Cody licked his lips. "You don't have to kill, Willet. Why not go out in that barn there—"

"*You don't understand,*" Willet said loudly enough to worry Cody that Mrs. Black might hear, wherever she was.

Cody motioned toward the barn. "Just go up there and pull some hay over you so the—"

"There ain't no time!" Willet said, voice rising. "I'm holdin' it off the best I can, but in a little while that won't matter anymore. It's comin', Cody, I can feel it. Now please do this one thing for me so I can still go to heaven."

Cody stared at the boy, incapable of speech.

"Please," Willet urged. "Then you can do the same for my mama. I don't know if her soul's still right with...she's done more killin' than I have...but if there's a chance..."

Cody slumped against the sill, deflating. Without meeting Willet's gaze, he flicked open the lock and pushed up the window. It slid easily; his father always kept things well-oiled. When the outside air kissed Cody's hands, he was sure the boy would dive at him through the window and fill his last moments with screaming and self-reproach.

But the boy did not attack. He merely waited for Cody to get the window up and then prop it ajar with the nearest thing he could find, which turned out to be the Bible. Cody wasn't sure if this was ironic or apt, so he pushed it from his mind and strode over to the scythe that leaned against the wall. Coming back with it, he had another moment of uncertainty. It would be so easy for Willet, who was suddenly so fearsome and agile, to spring through the open window and attack. He remembered the way Willet had leaped out of the hayloft like some kind of mountain lion and later taken Cody down like he was nothing.

But Willet's words scattered the images. "I don't blame you, you know. Not for this, not for anything."

Cody reached out, lifted the scythe. Its handle was very cold, very hard.

Cody stood over Willet. "I'm sorry I was too scared to help you the night they burned your ranch."

Without looking up, Willet said, "Bein' scared is what makes you different from them. You're only scared because it matters to you what happens to people. They ain't scared because they only care about themselves. About feeding themselves."

"You're letting me off too easy."

"No, I ain't. There's nothin' wrong with bein' scared, Cody. Please do this before I lose that."

You can't do it, a voice declared in Cody's head. *You can't kill a child.*

I have to, he answered. *I can't fail him again.*

He's just a boy.

He won't stay a boy for long, Cody thought and fingered the scythe handle. His palms had begun to sweat. *Look at Horton. He'd been with Price for a long time, but he'd never aged. Is that what you want for Willet? For him to stay a child in body but a beast in mind and behaviour?*

No, he thought. *It's not what I want.*

He was raising the scythe when Mrs. Black appeared in the left corner of the window.

*   *   *

"NO!" Mrs. Black roared, her eyes huge with panic.

"Please, Cody," Willet breathed.

"*YOU CAN'T HURT HIM!*" Martha Black raged, lurching toward Willet.

Cody brought the scythe down as hard as he could, sure the stroke wouldn't be powerful enough to decapitate the boy. But the blade had been kept sharp, and Cody's aim was true. The curved blade cleaved through Willet's neck cleanly and stuck in the floor. The head tumbled into the bedroom, the suddenly boneless body sliding backward out the window and pumping freshets of blood over the sill, the Bible, over Cody's quivering hands.

Martha Black gaped at her son's severed head. It lay facing her, so that Cody couldn't see Willet's final expression. But whatever it was that Martha Black saw on her son's dead face robbed her of speech and held her immobile for an endless moment.

Slowly, her eyes rose. They riveted on Cody's. Her expression darkened.

Then, she amazed him by stalking away.

Jack Wilson's voice nearly made Cody jump out of his boots. "Where do you reckon she's going?"

"Jesus, Dad," Cody said in a hoarse voice. He'd clapped a hand over his slamming heart, his other hand bracing himself against the wall.

His father went on as though speaking to himself. "She's not giving up, that much is sure."

"Course she isn't," Cody said, his breathing slowing enough so that it now approximated normalcy.

His dad was gazing at the floor, but Cody could see he was thinking hard. It was the way his father looked whenever he was concentrating his considerable intellect on a particularly irksome problem.

But before Jack Wilson said anything, they both heard the plangent screech of shattering glass. It had come through the wall. It had come from the other bedroom.

Cody looked at his dad, who stared back at him with huge eyes.

"Dad," he started to say, but before the word was out, Jack Wilson was lurching toward the bedroom door.

Cody hustled after him, the .38 up and cocked. He made it into the bedroom on his father's heels and saw what he'd feared.

Martha Black was scuttling over the top of the armoire.

Martha Black was going after Marguerite.

The Schofield exploded in the dim bedroom, the bullet slamming the woman in the top of the head. Without pause, Jack Wilson limped over to Martha Black's slumped figure, reached up, and began to drag her off the armoire.

His dad said, "Hand me the—" But when he saw Cody, he bared his teeth. "Dammit, boy, get me that scythe!"

Cody jolted, realising his mistake. He whirled and bolted

through the door, damn near slipping on the hardwood floor in the hallway, and then he was in the room where Willet's head lay gaping at the window in eternal surprise.

Cody averted his eyes and bent to retrieve the scythe. He froze, his fingers curled around the handle.

From the other room, his father was screaming.

"*Dammit*," Cody muttered as he reeled toward the door. The scythe handle was slick in his grip, Willet's blood having doused it after its wicked blade did its business. The noises from the other bedroom had ceased, which Cody took for a very bad sign. He made it down the hallway in three long strides and lunged through the doorway, expecting to see Martha Black guzzling his father's blood the way she and her son had Gladys's. But Jack Wilson was still very much alive.

He was simply in a dire situation.

Martha Black had cinched the crook of her elbow around Jack Wilson's throat, so that he was facing Cody as the vampire woman's hostage. But rather than a gun poised against his temple, Martha Black's long, serrated fangs hovered only inches from Jack Wilson's neck. She was peering up at Cody through filthy strands of blond hair that were matted with gore. How the gunshot to the head hadn't slowed her down more, Cody had no idea. Perhaps the more often they regenerated, the more powerful they grew.

Whatever the case, it mattered little now. What mattered was that his father was about to be bitten again, but Cody had a feeling this time the damage would be bad enough that Jack Wilson wouldn't walk away.

"Put the scythe down!" Martha Black growled.

Cody let it clatter to the floor.

"Now drop that gun," Martha Black commanded in a deep, buzzing voice.

Cody nodded, began to lower the Colt.

"No," his father grunted. "She won't kill me."

Martha Black increased the pressure on his dad's throat, the scimitar teeth drawing nearer to his flesh.

Cody frowned. "She sure looks ready to me."

"I'll be one of them soon," his father rasped. "She – she needs a tribe. She won't kill the only one left who's like her."

"You don't think I'll bite him?" Martha Black asked. She snaked her forked tongue out and licked a glistening streak along Jack Wilson's jawbone.

"Dad..." Cody began.

"Shoot her now, son. You're good enough to do it."

Whether his dad meant Cody was a good enough person to save them or that Cody was a good enough shot to hit Martha without killing his dad, Cody had no idea. He readied himself for the shot, keenly aware of Marguerite's unmoving form on the bed to his left. If Cody missed and things did go awry, Cody would have to interpose his body between her and Martha Black before the vampire woman could hurt Marguerite.

A quarter-inch from the side of his father's neck, Martha Black's mouth opened wider, her lips stretching in a hideously mocking grin.

Cody swung the Colt up and fired.

The slug tore a flap of skin from the woman's scalp, the point farthest from his dad's face. The sound was deafening in the bedroom, and perhaps this was why Martha Black let go of his dad to clamp her hands over her ears. Jack Wilson stumbled toward Cody. Sidestepping his dad, Cody fired again, but the vampire woman had raised her arms to shield her face. The bullet splintered her right forearm and sent twin fountains of blood pumping from the entrance and exit wounds. But Martha Black staggered toward Cody, a look of ruthless determination in her lambent eyes.

Cody began to squeeze the trigger again but caught himself just in time. His father straightened in front of him, the scythe gripped in both hands.

Martha made a grab for it. Cody almost risked another shot over his father's shoulder, but at the last second he held off. His dad whipped the scythe handle straight over the vampire woman's head, and before she could fend it off, he chopped down. The curved blade furrowed the middle of the woman's face, cleaving her from the top of the head to the roof of her mouth. The blade chunked free with a pulpy, squirting sound. The force of yanking out the scythe blade knocked his dad off balance. Before his father could stand erect again, Cody took aim with the .38.

He put one in her left eye.

Her face a horror of gushing wounds, Martha Black reeled toward the wall. Before she got there, his father swung the scythe sideways in a whistling line. The curved blade slashed Martha Black's neck cleanly this time, the head tumbling at her feet before her body hit the floor. A second later, Martha's body did fall, the spurting stump of her neck showering the armoire in a cheerful red gush.

Jack Wilson let the scythe clatter to the floor. Cody holstered the Colt.

Cody's dad leaned against the foot of the bedstead, his face weary but smiling. "We got 'em, didn't we, boy?"

"You got 'em, dad."

Jack Wilson shook his head and opened his mouth to say something, but at that moment the doors of the armoire behind him were flung open and a pair of powerful arms enfolded him.

Adam Price sank his teeth into the side of Jack Wilson's neck.

CHAPTER TWENTY-EIGHT

Speechless, Cody fumbled for the Colt in his holster, but the sight of his father writhing against the vampire, the noise of Jack Wilson's screams, robbed Cody of what composure he still had. Price burrowed deeper into his father's neck, gobbling like a starved wolf, and just before Cody got the .38 out and brought the business end to rest on Price's face, the vampire had already wrenched Jack Wilson's head violently around, snapping the man's neck.

Bellowing in heartbreak, Cody squeezed the trigger once, twice, three times, but after the first two reports the Colt only clicked emptily, the sounds of the dry fires like the percussion of a funeral dirge. Cody advanced on the vampire, knowing as he did so how fruitless it was. The first bullet had burrowed a trench through the side of Price's neck; the second had gone wild. Cody paused six feet from the vampire, the gun suddenly like a kid's toy in his hand. Smirking in triumph, Price hurled Jack Wilson's broken body at Cody, driving him backward into the doorway. His father's head lolled pitifully, and without thought of Adam Price or Marguerite, who still lay unconscious on the bed, Cody scrambled to support Jack Wilson and somehow spare him further indignity.

Cody was holding his father's head and upper body in his lap when the tears took hold of him. He pressed his forehead against his father's and begged the dead man for forgiveness. He knew how ignoble it was to sit there clutching his father while Marguerite needed his protection, but he couldn't help it. He told Jack Wilson again and again how sorry he was. He kissed his father's cheeks, his brow.

After a time, he became aware of Adam Price's pitiless gaze.

"So weak," Price murmured. "After all that has occurred, you're still so weak."

Cody glowered up at Price, his eyes brimming with salty

tears. "Why didn't you go for us earlier? Why'd you wait in that damned cabinet while we killed Willet and his mom?"

"I don't measure time the way you do," Price said unconcernedly. "An epoch for you is a mere instant for me. Every age brings different choices and different opportunities."

"You heartless...*gutless* bastard."

Price continued as though Cody hadn't spoken. "I've grown weary of America. A century is a long time for any creature to remain in the same place. The past few decades, I've been yearning for Europe. I've grown slovenly in my habits. Sloppy. Perhaps this is why you and your father were able to achieve a modicum of success against my servants."

Cody cradled his father's head and bared his teeth at Price. "Killed every goddamn one of them is what we did."

"It was time for me to reinvent myself," Price said, staring down at Marguerite. "Penders, the Seneslavs, Horton...they were useful for a time. Loyal. Very strong. Yet I cannot make a new life if I'm chained to an entourage." His gaze crawled over Marguerite's softly susurrating chest. "At most I can take one faithful servant."

Cody eased his father's head to the floor and stood up. He moved around the foot of the bed and stood face to face with Price.

"You can't have her," Cody said.

Price looked amused. "She's already mine."

"I won't let you take her."

Price laughed softly. "Is this one last ploy to put me off? Do you think you can persuade me you're not really a coward?"

If you're going to die, Cody thought, *do it by honouring the man who's lying back there in the doorway. Die honouring Jack Wilson's memory.*

Cody stepped closer, only a foot away from Price's grinning face, and as he did, his boot knocked against something hard. He glanced down and saw, lying among the things that had fallen out of the armoire when Price had popped out of it, a wooden object that Cody hadn't seen in over a decade.

"What is that?" Price asked, looking at it too.

Cody reached down, picked up the wooden toy by the peg

and its thick block of wood. "It's a grogger," Cody said. "I got rid of it when I was fourteen, but my stepmom must've rescued it from the garbage."

"Absurd-looking thing," Price remarked.

Cody gazed down at it fondly. "It's a noisemaker. See?" And he rotated the peg around the cogged wheel to demonstrate.

The reaction was immediate. Price recoiled and scowled at the grogger. "Stop that horrid noise."

"Why?" Cody asked, swinging the grogger now, the wooden slat clacking frantically over the tensioned cog. "Does it bother you?"

Price cupped his palms over his ears, his lips become a thin, bloodless line. "I told you to *stop* that."

Cody rotated it faster, a gleeful smile on his face. "I don't think I will."

Price made a grab for it, but Cody stepped nimbly backward. The racket from the noisemaker was frightful, painful even to Cody's ears in the small bedroom. But the outrage on Price's face made it worth it.

"You stupid, puling, *brainless* boy," Price said, stepping toward him. The man's face had begun to alter, the eyes to glow an eerie orange. "Do you truly believe this matters? Does this petty gesture of defiance change anything?"

"Don't get too riled," Cody said, nearing the head of the bed. "You wouldn't want to lose control, would you?"

"*Miserable wretch*," Price spat. His teeth grew longer, began to taper into wicked points. The lower jaw began to judder, the bones there describing their unnatural metamorphosis. "I will revel in your slow death and then transform your woman into a slavering beast. She will bow to me, she will drink with me, she will—"

"Will I be allowed to make love to you?" a sultry voice asked.

Cody and Price both gaped down at Marguerite, who had awakened, who, despite her wounds and ragged appearance, had never looked more voluptuous or more seductive.

The grogger hung silent in Cody's hand. He was as transfixed by Marguerite as Price was. She pushed up to lean on her elbows, her supple brown breasts bulging over the bodice of her torn dress. Cody felt a molten wave of desire, but if anything the vampire seemed even more stimulated by the sight of Marguerite's sumptuous body. Price was absolutely mesmerised.

Cody began to edge toward the musket. *Got him dead centre at the jail...*

Price stepped over to the bedside, an unholy brew of bloodlust and carnal desire glittering in his huge eyes. Cody watched in disbelief as Marguerite untied the bodice of her dress, then drew open the white flaps. Her glorious, naked breasts reflected the hellfire from Price's eyes. Her nipples were large and dark, their tips taut and firm.

Cody's fingers closed over the musket. He lifted it as quietly as he could off its pegs. *Aim for the heart now...*

Price reached down, the tip of one hooked talon whispering over the flesh between Marguerite's breasts. The vampire's long black tongue slithered out, slicked a wet, glimmering trail over his upper lip.

"She's not your slave," Cody said.

Growling, Price turned. Cody plunged the bayonet into Price's chest, straight into the vampire's heart. At the same moment Price lunged for him, and the combined force of the vampire's momentum and the bayonet's thrust drove the still-sharp blade through the back of Price's overcoat. Beyond the spray of blood from the vampire's back, Cody glimpsed a flurry of movement, Marguerite scrambling off the other side of the bed. A tide of blood sluiced over Cody's arms. The vampire howled, but the demented orange eyes scarcely glanced at the musket. Price reached out, scrabbling for Cody's shoulders. Gritting his teeth, Cody shoved harder, the barrel now buried in Price's gushing chest. Oblivious to whatever pain he might have felt or whatever damage the musket might be doing to his chest, Price seized hold of Cody's shoulders and tugged him closer. The barrel continued to sink deeper into the vampire's chest, impaling him as they came together. But Price's wrath was boundless. The vampire's face loomed closer, rivers of blood now issuing from his chest and dousing the front of Cody's body.

The black tongue flicked toward Cody's face, the fulsome stench rotting out of Price enveloping Cody like a death shroud.

But astonishingly, Cody found that he no longer feared death, no longer feared Price. The vampire might kill him, but at least he'd given Marguerite a chance at survival.

The vampire's mouth yawned wider, a measureless hatred in its hellish gaze. Cody thrust the musket deeper, all the way to the hammer, the edge of the trigger guard entering the monster's chest.

Price turned to Cody's right, the vampire's eyes shuttering wide with horror.

The scythe blade swept toward Price's throat, the vampire throwing up a hand — too late — to ward off the blow. The curved blade buried itself deep in Price's neck, the scythe slicing it most of the way through. Price clawed at the blade, but it was embedded too deeply. Cody let go of the musket, stepped behind the convulsing vampire, and grasped Price's long brown hair with both hands. Cody yanked down with his full weight. The head tilted sideways, blood pumping upward in a dark, raging fountain. With a vicious tug, Marguerite jerked the scythe free of the vampire's flesh and raised it again.

Cody yanked down on Price's head, which now hung from a single tendril of flesh like an open box lid. Amid the jetting blood and the ugly flaps of mangled flesh, Cody caught a glimpse of Price's severed windpipe, the pallid stub of cleaved spine.

"Stand back," Marguerite commanded.

Cody stood back.

With a savage grunt, Marguerite brought down the scythe like an axe. The blade chopped through the remaining connective tissue easily, the lopped-off head thumping to the floor with dull finality.

Rather than hugging Cody or covering her bare breasts, Marguerite tossed the scythe aside and bent down. She came up holding Price's head. Before Cody knew what was happening, she marched out of the bedroom and into the main room. Cody followed her, too bewildered to speak. She crossed straight to the hearth, cast the monstrous head onto the logs. Blessedly, the orange eyes and snarl of teeth landed facedown. As Marguerite reached up to the mantle for the stick matches, Cody noted with a shiver how Price's black tongue had dangled down through the logs so that its tip brushed the floor of the hearth.

Marguerite lit a match and tossed it in, but it winked out right away. Grimacing, she lit another one, but her hand trembled so violently that it extinguished before she could lower it to the logs.

Price's black tongue coiled around her wrist. Marguerite shrieked, yanked her hand away, but the head came with it, tumbling onto the stone of the hearth and sliding nearer to her wrist.

Cody stomped on Price's severed head. Marguerite struggled for a moment, whimpering. Then, with a fierce tug, she disengaged her wrist from the snakelike tongue and scrambled against the sofa.

Careful to grip it by the hair in back, Cody lugged the severed head over to the hearth again and mashed it facedown in the logs.

When he was certain the head was fixed in place, he padded over to the bookcase, selected a volume at random and began to rip out pages. He bent, and taking care not to let his fingers venture too near the vampire's mouth, arranged the pages for kindling.

"Matches," he said, crouching before the hearth.

He accepted them from Marguerite, struck one and held it to one of the pages. Immediately, the dry paper curled and blackened, a small but brilliant orange flame licking the wood around it. Cody shifted the match to another page. It was about to burn his fingertips, but he didn't want to be this close to the vampire's head any longer than he had to be. While he held the match to the crumpled page, he kept throwing nervous glances at the forest of sharp white teeth, the long, gaping jaw. He waited for the black tongue to slip around his wrist and drag him screaming toward the vampire's maw, but this time the tongue remained motionless. When the flame singed Cody's fingertips, he finally dropped the match in the hearth and stood back.

He and Marguerite watched the fire spread. The flames began

to catch in Price's brown hair, and soon the entire head was consumed. Cody's gaze happened on the book he'd used for kindling. He was unsurprised to see it was *Moby-Dick*.

"Is this the end of it?" Marguerite asked, her bleak gaze still riveted to the blazing head.

"I expect we should burn the rest of them. The heads and the bodies."

She nodded. Then her breath caught and she looked at him with startled eyes. "What about the coach?"

Cody looked at her, frowning.

"The black coach," she said, her voice curiously hushed. "We saw someone drive it away. I thought it was Price, but it wasn't. So who drove it?"

"Horton," Cody said.

Marguerite shook her head, a pained look on her face. "He couldn't have. Your father cut off—"

"The figure driving the coach didn't have a head," Cody said. "I knew it didn't look right, but with the distance and the darkness, I couldn't figure why. Price must've put Horton's body on the bench and then started the team down the trail."

"Would the team go without a driver?"

"Horton had driven that team for years. The horses wouldn't care if he was headless." Cody chuckled softly. "I expect we'll find the coach stranded somewhere a couple miles down the road."

Marguerite searched his face. "We're going to burn Horton's body too?"

"You're damn right we are," Cody said. "Just as soon as we burn the others."

Marguerite nodded slowly. Then she too began to smile.

CHAPTER TWENTY-NINE

It took them the better part of the day to take care of all the bodies. A good deal of that time was spent in locating and corralling the black coach with its headless driver. They took one of his dad's horses out to search for it and found, unsurprisingly, the black quarter horses had veered off the trail. The search from there had been considerably more challenging, though in the end, the vultures helped lead them to the gulch where the coach had ended up.

Horton himself didn't present much of a problem – the lack of a head made him far more tractable than he'd been in life. But the six quarter horses were another matter entirely. They avoided Cody like he'd been set aflame, and though he was ordinarily a trig hand with horses, he found that none of his usual methods would calm them. Marguerite fared little better. At first Cody held a scant hope of her being able to cow them by virtue of her stunning beauty, but apparently the sight of Marguerite's voluptuous body and soulful eyes did less for the animals than it did for Cody. Or maybe, he reasoned, he was the animal and the horses were the more logical of the two species.

In the end it was a matter of thirst and fatigue for the quarter horses. Though one of them – a large mare that bucked and whinnied like her ass was on fire no matter how composedly the other horses behaved – never was much help in towing the deathwagon back to the ranch, the other five were insistent enough on being watered that Cody and Marguerite were able to manage. Cody untied Horton from the bench and dragged him over to the small bonfire they'd built up, while Marguerite unhitched the horses and led them to the watering trough. Cody went into the house, dragged Price's body out, and heaped it onto Horton's corpse, which had begun to smoulder. Soon both vampires' bodies had shrivelled to black husks. Cody and Marguerite looked on until the humanoid shapes collapsed into ash piles that were indistinguishable from the burned wood.

Then they burned the coach too.

It wouldn't do, they realised, to give the appearance of incinerating evidence – not when they'd surely have several deaths for which to answer, including those of Jack and Gladys Wilson – but the thought of leaving that accursed black coach parked outside the house any longer than they had to was impossible to stomach. So they burned it, along with Horton's head, which they'd found lying by the roadside.

They cremated Angela next. Both pieces of her. After much debate they cremated Martha Black and Willet simultaneously, deciding that by the time Cody had met the woman, Martha Black had become someone else. Willet had claimed she'd been a good mother, and that was sufficient testimony for Cody. They laid the bodies and their heads side by side – a good twenty feet away from the other vampires – covered them with kerosene-soaked shrouds, and said a few words. Cody didn't make it far before he began to choke up, and though he hated blubbering in front of Marguerite, he managed to complete his eulogy, such as it was.

The acrid tang of smoke still fresh in his nostrils, he and Marguerite moved on to the barn. It was hell peeling Penders off the harrow, but in the end they were able to. After they grappled with his giant carcass for the better part of an hour and set its stinking hulk to blaze, they lounged in the yard for several minutes to catch their breath. Marguerite removed her shoes to let her feet breathe, and when Cody caught sight of her right foot, his breath clotted in his throat.

Marguerite noticed him staring. She lifted the foot and held it closer so he could see. The long toe next to her big toe was missing, in its place a pale mass of scar tissue that reminded him of a spider egg sac. "That's the toe Slim took," she said. "It bled a lot, but I've managed without it."

Cody tried to imagine Slim Keeley chopping off Marguerite's toe with an adze, but could not. "I'm sorry you had to be married to such a ruthless son of a bitch."

"I didn't have to be, but I was." She regarded Cody timidly. "I'd say we both chose badly with our first spouses. Maybe we'll do better the second time around."

Cody stared out at the light blue horizon. It was early afternoon, and the heat was growing severe. But even though he'd begun to sweat, his hands were cold and unsteady. "You've seen me at my worst," he said to her. "You know I've been weak before. You know how many times I've failed. So I figure since you know all those things, I might as well come out and ask you straight."

Her eyes were large. "Ask me."

"Is this the second time around?"

One corner of her mouth rose. "That's up to you."

"Then it is," he said.

She leaned toward him, and they kissed. He let himself enjoy it for a long, glorious moment. Then he broke the kiss and pushed to his feet.

She visored her eyes and gazed up at him. "Don't you like to kiss me?"

"It isn't that," he said and offered her a hand. Helping her up, he explained, "We still have two to burn."

She sobered immediately.

They went for Gladys first. On the way up the ladder, Cody told himself there was no way his stepmother could've turned into a vampire. First of all, he'd seen Willet and Martha Black bleed Gladys dry, and to live, the vampires needed blood. Secondly, he thought as he reached the hayloft, it surely took longer than a few hours for a person to transform into a different species of creature, didn't it?

But it was still a relief to find Gladys in the same position in which they'd last seen her. Her eyes gazed sightlessly at the barn rafters, the hue of her skin a dingy grey. She certainly looked dead.

Cody waited for Marguerite to pull up alongside him before bending closer to Gladys's prone form. He was about to draw her eyelids down when Marguerite grabbed his shoulder. "Wait," she said.

He felt his scrotum tighten. "What is it?"

"What if she's…"

"What if she is?"

He glanced up at Marguerite, who was shaking her head in superstitious terror. "She might attack you. Move back, Cody."

"We've got to do something about her body," he said, doing his best to keep the anxiety out of his voice. "Waiting's only gonna make what we're scared of more likely to happen."

"Let's get the scythe," she said.

Cody winced. He tried to imagine beheading his stepmother's corpse but couldn't. "Let's just get her to the yard so we can pay our respects and do it right."

"Cremate her?"

Cody nodded.

Marguerite said, "What if she wakes up while we're burning her?"

Cody's breath caught in his throat. He caught a vision of Gladys, transformed into a vampire and very much alive, thrashing in agony as the flames consumed her.

He exhaled wearily. "Go get the scythe. I'll stay here with her."

*　　*　　*

After it was done, Marguerite carried the head out of the hayloft and waited for Cody at the base of the ladder. It wasn't easy hauling Gladys's body down the groaning rungs after all he'd been through, but he managed. Side by side with Marguerite, he bore Gladys's headless form to the opposite side of the yard, where she'd once tended a small herb garden. They soaked her head and her body with kerosene, said some words, then stood with bowed heads while she burned. Cody tried to think about the woman and her life, but he was too preoccupied. Gladys's body was unrecognisable within minutes, but still Cody stood with his head down, knowing he was avoiding the next job, the last thing that needed to be done.

Marguerite placed a hand on his shoulder and spoke in a voice that was gentle and loving. "We have to do it soon. We don't know when the change happens."

Cody kept his head down, his breathing harsh and ragged.

"Cody," Marguerite persisted.

He clenched his jaw, took a steadying breath. "All right. Let's go."

The feeling in him on the way to bedroom was nothing like it had been during their approach toward Gladys's body. With Gladys he had been apprehensive, a part of him convinced she'd gone through the change. He'd felt reasonably confident about their odds against one vampire, especially one who'd just turned and hadn't killed anything yet, but despite this confidence there had also been the fear.

But now, as Marguerite led him through the main room toward the back hall, what Cody felt was a different sort of dread that was infinitely worse than any terror could have been. An insane part of him wanted his dad's body to be gone. Not that thinking of Jack Wilson as a vampire made the grief any less suffocating, but at least it would save him from burying his father, and in one grotesque sense his father would go on existing.

They passed through the hallway and found Jack Wilson on the bedroom floor.

Wordlessly, Marguerite hunkered low and got her arms around Jack Wilson's back. She hoisted him to a sitting position, but the way his head hung sideways made Cody's heart ache.

"Let's get him onto the bed," he said in a voice that was little more than a whisper.

Soon they had his father in much the same position as Marguerite had been earlier. But with Margeurite the bloom of life had been clearly indicated by the rise and fall of her chest and the healthy, if untidy, appearance of her skin.

Jack Wilson already looked embalmed.

To Cody's anguished mind it was worse than seeing his dad displayed in some church, because this version of his father looked sad and defeated. The raw gore of his neck wound and the place where Price had bitten his forearm were further desecrations to what should have been an unblemished body that had earned its eternal slumber. *Senseless*, was what Cody's mind kept repeating. *Senseless*. His mind uttered the word again and again like a doleful litany.

Something cold and hard was fitted into Cody's hand. He stared dumbly down at the scythe Marguerite had handed him. He met her big brown eyes and understood what she intended him to do, but the idea of it seemed absurd, unthinkable. How could he be expected to decapitate his own dad? He dropped his gaze to the scythe blade and began shaking his head.

"Marguerite, I..."

"Would you like me to do it?"

Cody glanced up at her, knowing his eyes were red and full of tears. She stared back at him, waiting for him to speak. He hated her in that moment, hated her cold implacability. What if it were her dad on the bed here? What if the master carpenter was the one about to have his head chopped off?

Cody looked away first, unable to bear the hardness in those penetrating brown eyes.

The moment drew out.

"You must do it now," Marguerite said.

Cody gestured feebly with the scythe. "We don't even know he'd turn into one."

"You told me he was," Marguerite said. "Earlier, you told me your father had begun to change. He was worried he'd become like Willet."

Cody had a vague recollection of telling Marguerite about what had happened when she'd been unconscious, but he couldn't recall telling her about Jack Wilson's growing interest in drinking blood. The day had been a blur of hauling bodies around, of eulogies for the lost, and of burning. Most of all the burning.

Cody glanced at his father's corpse again. The pillow and bedclothes were soft enough to conform to Jack Wilson's recumbent body. The neck wound wasn't entirely concealed, but enough of it was hidden from view to make the sight of it less startling. As for the forearm, Marguerite had turned it inward so that had Cody not known the wound was there, he'd have never guessed of its existence.

Cody fetched a sigh, brought the scythe to rest on his shoulder. He supposed they should have positioned his dad's body so that the head hung over the edge of the bed and thus made it a cleaner stroke. But that thought, of course, brought back memories of Willet's beheading. He couldn't imagine performing the same act on his father.

His fingers clenched, unclenched on the wooden scythe handle. He realised he was bouncing softly on his heels.

"Cody?"

"I know," he said. "Just...give me a minute, okay?"

Marguerite said nothing.

Another minute went by, though it seemed much longer than that. Cody raised the scythe. After several gravid moments, he lowered it. "Can't we at least do it in the yard?"

"I don't think we should wait."

Cody glanced at Marguerite in mute appeal, but though not uncaring, the woman's dark face contained a grimness that advertised plainly that if Cody wouldn't do what needed to be done, she would.

Cody hung his head. He stood there irresolute and wished it were done already. He glanced at his father's still form and all of a sudden knew he had to kiss Jack Wilson one more time before decapitating him. Cody leaned over, heart throbbing in his chest, and brought his face close to his dad's.

And now, as Cody bent over his father's unmoving form, the notion that Jack Wilson had transformed into a vampire and would at any moment seize Cody and kill him descended with a grisly certitude. Cody clenched his jaw, felt the weight of Marguerite's stare on his back, and willed himself to focus on his father.

Staring at the man's closed lids is what did it. What steadied him. Cody put his lips to his dad's grizzled cheek and kissed him. He whispered something in Jack Wilson's ear. Then, without pause – he knew he could no longer hesitate, for if he did, this would never get done – he straightened, raised the scythe, and hammered at his father's neck with all his might. The blade snicked through Jack Wilson's throat with hardly a sound. What blood there was poured out of the wound and was instantly absorbed by the ivory bedclothes. A slow, burgundy stain spread from Jack Wilson's cleaved neck, but soon the trickle of blood began to abate, and the broadening stain ceased to grow. Cody became aware that Marguerite was grasping his shoulder and that she was weeping.

And through it all, his father never moved.

CHAPTER THIRTY

The eulogy and cremation didn't take long. When they'd shovelled his father's ashes into a hole Cody had dug, it wasn't yet twilight, though he felt as though he hadn't slept in months. Marguerite helped him through the burial, taking her turn shovelling the sandy soil into the hole so Cody could rest his hands, which had first blistered and proceeded to split open in angry pink blossoms.

They were sitting together on the front porch, sipping water Marguerite had pumped from the well, when a remote cloud formed where the lane met the horizon. The cloud, Cody soon realised, was a pair of riders, moving fast and purposefully toward the ranch.

"More of them?" Marguerite asked.

Squinting against the reddish early evening sun, Cody shook his head and took another sip of water.

"Friends of your father's then?" she asked, her voice raw not only with exhaustion but trepidation as well.

"I'm guessing it'll be the law," Cody said.

The light brown cloud scudded nearer, the shapes of the riders crystalising. The sound of thundering hooves drifted to them on the porch.

"What should we tell them?" Marguerite said.

"There's only one thing."

Peripherally, he could sense Marguerite's frown, the disbelieving shake of her head. "They won't believe us, Cody. They can't. I wouldn't believe such a story if I heard it."

The riders were very close now. In seconds they would reach the remains of the wrecked Concord coach, the dead horses that hadn't been touched since Penders had drained them.

Very deliberately, Cody took a last swig of cool water and placed the wooden cup on the porch. He picked up his father's leather hat, which had once been dark brown but was now a faded noncolour from so many days spent in the sun, and placed it on his head. Surprisingly, it fit rather well. With Marguerite watching him fretfully, he started toward the ranch gate. There was a diamondback rattlesnake as big around as a stout man's arm stationed a short distance from the overturned red coach. Cody tried not to take it as an omen.

When Marguerite caught up to him, she said, "What if they blame us? Burning the bodies looks suspicious. They won't listen to—"

"They'll have come from Mesquite," Cody said. "You saw how many townspeople they left alive. The ones that got away, Price and the rest never even went after."

Twenty feet from the gate now, the riders slackened their pace, both men drawing out their revolvers.

Cody said, "They won't believe us at first, but we'll be able to trace it all back to Tonuco, where they'll find the woman's bones that I mistook for Angela's. Then they'll go on and figure out whose bones they were."

"How do you know that?"

The riders stopped short of the wrecked red coach, dismounted. One of them, a man wearing a black, flat-brimmed hat, trained his revolver on Cody while the other moved toward the Concord, the man taking care to give the diamondback a wide berth. Cody paused at the gate, watching the man examine the exsanguinated horses.

Cody turned to Marguerite. "I don't know that. But I know we had to do what we did. Then we could've either ridden away like we were the ones who did something wrong, or wait here for these guys to ask us questions."

Both lawmen were approaching them now, one of them short, thin and clean-shaven, the other tall and angular. A brown handlebar mustache perched on his upper lip.

"They might not believe us," Marguerite said under her breath.

"My conscience is clean," Cody muttered back.

Marguerite appeared about to respond to him, but by then

the lawmen were too close. They both had their guns trained on Cody, a hard look in their eyes.

But for the first time in several days, Cody felt completely at ease. He favoured the lawmen with a small grin. "How about you two come sit on the porch with us. Marguerite just pumped us a nice pitcher of water."

★   ★   ★

It was nearly nine o'clock when the lawmen agreed to come inside. One of them, Tod Clark, the tall sheriff of Las Cruces, seemed dubious of their story. Allison had been one of the first to arrive at the Black ranch and had seen what was left of Willet's home reduced to ashes. He'd had no reason to suspect anything other than an unfortunate and highly fatal house fire until one of his men, the one who'd been charged with combing through the ashes for human remains, informed him that at least three individuals – Willet, Martha Black and Willet's grandfather – were unaccounted for. The same day, Tim Slauter, a small but formidable federal marshal, had arrived in Las Cruces with a whopper of a tale about a travelling quintet of actors who had a habit of stealing men's wives and, even more disquietingly, leaving dead bodies in their wake.

It was Tim Slauter who believed every word of their story. Because it was Tim Slauter who'd traced Adam Price all the way back to the East Coast and who was preparing to arrest Price and his men on suspicion of mass murder. They'd been working their way from state to state, usually preying on individuals who wouldn't be missed – the homeless, the hermits who were rarely seen by others. Prostitutes. Only infrequently did they attack entire families, as they had Willet's.

By the time the two lawmen arrived in Mesquite, the town had already begun to mourn its losses. The eyewitness accounts of what had happened on the street in front of Marguerite's saloon were only further confirmation of what Tim Slauter already knew. But despite the uncanny uniformity of the witnesses' stories, Tod Clark still couldn't swallow a story about vampires.

The four of them were sitting at the kitchen table when

Marguerite turned to Tod Clark and said, "If we showed you proof, would you then leave us alone?"

Allison reddened, his fingers stroking the brim of the black hat he'd placed on the table. "It isn't that I don't believe you, miss. But you've gotta understand what you're asking of me."

Tim Slauter was staring at Marguerite steadily, his small eyes earnest. "You have proof for us?"

Marguerite's gaze fixed on Cody for a moment. Cody merely watched her, as curious now as the two lawmen were. Receiving no protest from Cody, Marguerite said, "Follow me."

She stood and moved past them. Tod Clark got up immediately and followed her through the main room. Cody and Tim Slauter exchanged a look and then trailed after them. Marguerite paused only long enough to lift a small kerosene lamp off the table and light its cloth wick.

They passed through the yard and into the barn, and it wasn't until Tod Clark pulled up short and gasped that Cody realised what it was that Marguerite had brought them out here to see. Cody had thought that they'd burned everything to do with the devils, save the red Concord coach. But the amber glow of the lantern revealed one thing they'd missed, an object lying in the dust outside one of the cattle pens.

The decapitated head of Steve Penders.

It lay on its side, facing away from them, but even from this angle Cody could tell Penders's face was still frozen in its vampiric form. Tod Clark's face had drained of colour, the man's handlebar mustache aquiver with what might have been horror. Marguerite led them around the head to afford them a better view of the face, and despite a muttered oath from Tod Clark, she brought the kerosene lamp down to rest beside the severed head.

"Good God Almighty," Tim Slauter whispered. Beneath the flat brim of his hat, his eyes were wide with fright. Cody couldn't blame him. The sight of Steve Penders's face still imbued him with an icy dread.

The teeth were as long and nasty as Cody remembered. The upper lip was drawn back in a perpetual snarl, the eyes no longer glowing but every bit as orange as they'd been the night before.

But it was the look of measureless hatred, Tod Clark said a few minutes later – after he'd finally regained the power of speech – that had ultimately convinced him of their story. Leaning on the porch with a stiff drink in his hand, his forehead beaded with huge drops of perspiration, Tod Clark had shaken his head and proclaimed he'd never seen such unmitigated evil in all his life.

He took a swig of whiskey and dragged a forearm over his trembling lips. "I won't be advertising what I saw tonight, you understand. I did that, I wouldn't have a hope in hell of staying sheriff. Not in Las Cruces, not in any town." He glanced at Cody, then Marguerite. "But I believe you now. God as my witness, I do. And I gotta believe He's not a bit sad you got rid of those devils the way you did. I know I'm sure as hell not."

It was Tim Slauter who'd taken Cody aside before leaving and assured him that he'd personally see to it that no legal entanglements would befall Cody and Marguerite. Furthermore, Slauter informed Cody, he'd make sure the insurance company compensated Marguerite handsomely for her lost saloon and that they'd have plenty of money to keep his father's ranch afloat for as long as they desired.

Cody thanked him, thinking he desired very much to live on his father's ranch with Marguerite.

*　　*　　*

Their lovemaking that first night was tender and almost shy. They slept in the following day till well past noon and made love again, this time with all the vigor of newlyweds, despite the soreness plaguing their bodies.

It was that night, twenty-four hours after the lawmen had departed, twenty-eight hours after he had buried his father's remains, that he'd taken a knee and asked Marguerite to marry him.

"Do you think it's too soon?" she asked him.

"I can't see the point in waiting."

They were on the porch again, but this time they'd brought out the rocking chairs from the main room. As they rocked together quietly, Marguerite put her hand on Cody's.

It was all the answer he needed.

Sometime later, when full night was upon them and the sky around the homestead was alive with the tenebrous flutter of bats, Marguerite had asked him what they'd do about his ranch in Tonuco.

"I reckon I'll sell it to Bailey Griggs," Cody said. "He's the one who's been looking after the stock for me."

"What about your cattle?"

"Next week we can make the trip to Tonuco. The Griggses are good people. I'll give them a discount on the ranch, and they'll help me with the cattle drive." Cody shook his head, peered up at the darting bats. "Course, I'll only need a couple men to help since my herd is so small."

"Will it be enough for us to survive on?"

"Combined with my dad's stock, it'll be more than enough. The days of the big ranches are coming to an end. My dad saw that way back in 1870, even before they came up with barbed wire. Before the drought a couple years ago. He only owned as many as he could manage himself, and I figure I'll do just fine too."

Lying in bed that night, sated and beaded with salty droplets of sweat, Marguerite had asked him in a hesitant voice, "When we have children?"

Cody turned, gazed into her lovely dark eyes. "Yeah?"

"If it's a boy...if any of them are boys..."

Cody smiled. "Yeah?"

She bit her lip. "You won't want to call them Willet, will you?"

He chuckled at that, though he winced at the throb in his shoulder. "I figure we'll get a nice marker for Willet instead. Put it in the ground where he's buried."

She seemed to crumple with relief.

A bit later, after he was sure she'd fallen asleep, she said, "What about Jack?"

Cody turned to her, took in her closed lids, and thought for a moment she was talking in her sleep.

Then it dawned on him what she meant.

He gazed up at the ceiling, the same ceiling he used to stare at on sleepless nights in his teens. He supposed they'd move this bed into the larger bedroom eventually, but that could wait for a while. He thought of his dad sewing on that small blue dress shirt back when Cody was seven, the way the tip of his father's tongue had jutted out between his lips in concentration as he taught himself how to mend.

"I think Jack would be a good name for our son," Cody said. He turned and regarded Marguerite in the near darkness of the bedroom.

But Marguerite was asleep, her chin resting against his shoulder.